Advance Praise for *Death Comes*

"They're back! If you loved *On the Rocks*, you'll be thrilled to have this new adventure of Willa and Edith. This time they're in New Mexico tracking down the unsolved murders of too many women. Sue Hallgarth has done it again: the combination of deep knowledge of the geographic terrain, its history, Cather's literary preoccupations, and Hallgarth's feminist sensibility have brought us another suspenseful, terrific read." —Joan W. Scott, author of *Gender and the Politics of History* and *The Fantasy of Feminist History*

"My new favorite book is *Death Comes!* It made distant memories real and simpatico. What a delight to see them. And the beautiful Taos you let me walk through. I especially want to thank you for including Spud. He was always there, so it's nice to have him recognized. I only knew him as an old man who always stopped to listen to a child. You showed me a young man who would become the one I knew and loved." —Claudia Smith Miller, great-granddaughter of Mabel Dodge Luhan

"*Death Comes* is a clever play on the novel that Willa Cather worked on in Taos, New Mexico, in the summers of 1925 and 1926, *Death Comes for the Archbishop*. Hallgarth has done serious historical and cultural research, cleverly highlighting Willa Cather's virtues as a strong-willed sleuth.... This is a very good read: as a story of 1920s Taos—including race and class relations, as a portrait of the Mabel Dodge Luhan circle, and, last but not least, as a murder mystery." —Lois Rudnick, author of *Mabel Dodge Luhan: New Woman, New Worlds*

"Willa Cather is traveling in northern New Mexico while polishing her manuscript *Death Comes for the Archbishop* when she and her companion Edith Lewis are caught up in the mystery surrounding the deaths of three women near D.H. Lawrence's ranch. An intriguing story for those of us who always wished we had been there when Mabel Dodge Luhan held court in Taos for luminaries of art and literature." —Judith Ryan Hendricks, author of *Isabel's Daughter* and *The Laws of Harmony*

"The second book in Hallgarth's Willa Cather and Edith Lewis mystery series captures the vivid and compelling landscape of the Taos, NM territorial west. A historical mystery with real people—think Mabel Dodge and Tony Luhan, Long John Dunn, Arthur Manby—and everyday life in the settling west. Compelling and richly imagined by a masterful storyteller. I didn't want it to end." —Betty Palmer, Events Coordinator, *op.cit.books,* Taos NM

"Our favorite literary sleuths are back! And this time Willa Cather and Edith Lewis are summering in Taos, New Mexico. Guests of Mabel Dodge Luhan, the amiable pair are planning for nothing more taxing than a month's worth of writing and painting. Then an unsettling excursion to the D. H. Lawrence Ranch changes everything. Entertaining and edifying, *Death Comes* is a compelling mystery set in New Mexico, that place Cather described as a 'landscape one longed for when one was away'." —Sharon Oard Warner, co-director D.H. Lawrence Ranch and author of *Sophie's House of Cards*

Praise for *On the Rocks*

" One of 'Ten Titles to Pick Up Now'.... A fictionalized glimpse into the partnership between the novelist and her artist companion, who team up to solve a murder on an island in the Bay of Fundy." —*O, The Oprah Magazine*

"Cather fans will enjoy the atmosphere, and Hallgarth captures the local color well, providing a look at the eccentric island residents, the small-town politics, and the life of the [two] women's communities." —American Library Association *Booklist*

"This historic, literary mystery is the first of what could be a terrific new series. The setting—on the Canadian island of Grand Manan in 1929—is captivating and the story engaging. *On the Rocks* is a real treat!" —*Rose City Reader*

"I enjoyed the fun and energy of *On the Rocks!*" —Lucia Woods Lindley, member of Board of Governors, The Willa Cather Foundation

"*On The Rocks* is a riveting addition to historical fiction collections and those with a love for the artistic life." —*The Midwest Book Review*

"Utterly absorbing, compulsively readable. Hallgarth spins her tale with an artistry that allows us to imagine a time and place as compelling as a dream." —Kathleen Hill, author of *Who Occupies This House* and *Still Waters in Niger*

"Sue Hallgarth incorporates the spectacular setting of Grand Manan into a mystery set among summer colonies of feminist artists, colorful island types, and suspicious visitors. Cather readers will detect her pronouncements on writing and life, and the island rock itself, a Cather symbol of survival, becomes here a solid contrast to the human foibles that play out on its surface." —John Murphy, member of Board of Governors, The Willa Cather Foundation

"*On the Rocks* is sophisticated and yet has a wonderful innocence. It conveys a convincing sense of the period. The characters are rounded, real. It is funny. It is compelling. It is a good tale." —Jake Page, author of the Mo Bowdre mystery series

"Cather aficionados will be especially interested in the author's new take on Willa Cather's personal history. The amiable cottage colony on Grand Manan island in the Bay of Fundy, where Edith and Willa built their summer retreat in the 1920s, is lovingly captured in this first book in a sparkling new literary mystery series." —Nancy Rutland, founder of *Bookworks,* Albuquerque, NM

"Love, love, love.... Highly recommended to those who enjoy this historical genre, and to fans of great women authors! I'll be curious to see if Ms. Hallgarth has this as the start of a series or not. She is an expert on Cather and clearly 'knows' her well." —*Beth's Book-Nook Blog*

"...the strength of the book is in Hallgarth's ability to paint a scene. Her research about Grand Manan, Cather and Lewis, and the time period are obviously top notch." —*WildmooBooks*

"Nice read with a beautiful portrait of a Canadian island in the 1920s, a strong feminist portrait of Willa Cather and her partner Edith, and a murder mystery to boot! Well-written with some beautifully 'painted' scenes and an intriguing insight to the way we all tend to think, wandering from one association to another before we catch ourselves! I've never seen that in a book before and thoroughly enjoyed it." —David Roberts, M.D., author of *Practice Makes Perfect: How One Doctor Found the Meaning of Lives*

Death Comes

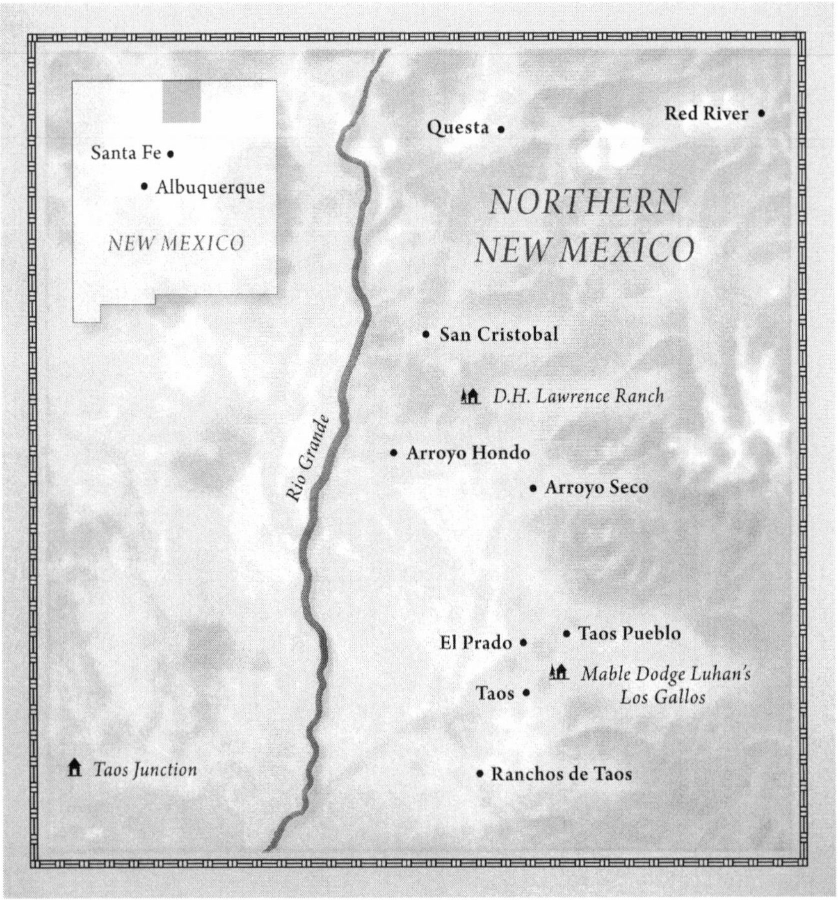

Questa

Red River

Santa Fe

Albuquerque

NEW MEXICO

NORTHERN NEW MEXICO

San Cristobal

D.H. Lawrence Ranch

Rio Grande

Arroyo Hondo

Arroyo Seco

El Prado

Taos Pueblo

Mable Dodge Luhan's Los Gallos

Taos

Taos Junction

Ranchos de Taos

Death Comes

A Willa Cather and Edith Lewis Mystery

Sue Hallgarth

Sue Hallgarth

ARBOR FARM PRESS
Albuquerque

afp

ARBOR FARM PRESS
P.O. Box 56783, Albuquerque, New Mexico 87187
arborfarmpress.com

Printed by BookMobile, Minneapolis, Minnesota USA bookmobile.com
Distributed by Itasca Books, Minneapolis, Minnesota USA itascabooks.com
Cover design by Ann Weinstock
Interior design, illustration, and typesetting by Sara DeHaan
p. 103, Nicolai Fechin, Portrait of Willa Cather, c. 1923-1927, (AC1997.28.1).
Courtesy of Museum Associates / LACMA. Licensed by Art Resource, NY

Publisher's Cataloging-in-Publication

Hallgarth, Susan A., author.
Death comes / Sue Hallgarth.
pages cm—(A Willa Cather and Edith Lewis mystery)
LCCN 2017933595
ISBN 978-0-9855200-4-5 (paper)
ISBN 978-0-9855200-5-2 (ebook)

1. Cather, Willa, 1873-1947—Fiction. 2. Lewis, Edith—Fiction. 3. Luhan, Mabel Dodge, 1879-1962—Fiction. 4. Taos Indians—New Mexico—Fiction. 5. Taos County (N.M.)—Fiction. 6. Detective and mystery fiction. 7. Historical fiction. I. Title. II. Series: Hallgarth, Susan A. Willa Cather and Edith Lewis mystery.

PS3608.A54834D43 2017 813'.6
QBI17-900036

For Hilda Raz
poet, friend, editor extraordinaire

Death Comes

A Willa Cather and
Edith Lewis Mystery

Sue Hallgarth

Sue Hallgarth

ARBOR FARM PRESS
Albuquerque

afp

ARBOR FARM PRESS
P.O. Box 56783, Albuquerque, New Mexico 87187
arborfarmpress.com

Printed by BookMobile, Minneapolis, Minnesota USA bookmobile.com
Distributed by Itasca Books, Minneapolis, Minnesota USA itascabooks.com
Cover design by Ann Weinstock
Interior design, illustration, and typesetting by Sara DeHaan
p. 103, Nicolai Fechin, Portrait of Willa Cather, c. 1923-1927, (AC1997.28.1). Courtesy of Museum Associates / LACMA. Licensed by Art Resource, NY

Publisher's Cataloging-in-Publication

Hallgarth, Susan A., author.
Death comes / Sue Hallgarth.
pages cm—(A Willa Cather and Edith Lewis mystery)
LCCN 2017933595
ISBN 978-0-9855200-4-5 (paper)
ISBN 978-0-9855200-5-2 (ebook)

1. Cather, Willa, 1873-1947—Fiction. 2. Lewis, Edith—Fiction. 3. Luhan, Mabel Dodge, 1879-1962—Fiction. 4. Taos Indians—New Mexico—Fiction. 5. Taos County (N.M.)—Fiction. 6. Detective and mystery fiction. 7. Historical fiction. I. Title. II. Series: Hallgarth, Susan A. Willa Cather and Edith Lewis mystery.

PS3608.A54834D43 2017 813'.6
QBI17-900036

I

TAOS JUNCTION, NEW MEXICO, the sign said. WELCOME.

Nowhere could air clear her senses so quickly. Edith breathed again deeply. The pale blue sky poured into her. And silence. Sun-baked silence. So much silence. It filled her ears and pressed against her skin. And space, forever space. And light and hue.

No. Hues, Edith corrected herself. Multifarious hues. Glorious hues. Blues, purples, greens, browns. She let her gaze pass beyond the nearby juniper and piñon and the few clapboard buildings clustered near the railroad tracks to cross the high desert plains and come to rest on distant mountains. Taos Mountain, the words sang through her mind, then repeated.

"Well, here we are," Willa announced. Edith heard the edge in her voice. "And no one's here to greet us."

Edith turned. The train had long since disappeared, its familiar bell and whistle gone with the chug and hiss of its engine. They were alone on the platform, their baggage stacked nearby.

Willa was shaking her skirts to free them of soot. Then she squared her shoulders and followed Edith's example, taking a deep breath. "Well," she finally pronounced, the air sighing from her lungs, "what does it matter? We're here, that's what matters." A grin flickered. She looked more herself. Willa often smiled with her eyes, blue and teasing, before dimples creased her cheeks.

That was happening now. Edith placed her hand on Willa's arm. "Let's try the waiting room."

Taos Junction, New Mexico

—||—

"Well, now, you'll be Miss Cather and Miss Lewis?" The high-pitched drawl came from a long face peering around the door and into the station's waiting room. The face was tanned and deeply creased, with steel-blue eyes and a bushy grey mustache that almost entirely obscured the stub of an unlit cigar. A long, thin body quickly followed and the face broke into a grin.

"Long John Dunn." Willa rose and strode across the waiting area to shake his hand. "Delighted to see you again."

"Yep," John Dunn nodded. The way he said it, *yep* contained at least three syllables. "Drove the two of you up from Alcalde and after your visit put you on the train right here bound for Denver and parts east."

"How good of you to remember," Edith found her hand swallowed in John Dunn's grip.

"Couldn't forget. It was just a year ago July, same time as now. Anyway, remember the two of you from ten years back. You stayed at the Columbian and rode my horses." Long John reached for their luggage.

"You have a very good memory, Mr. Dunn."

"Yep. Where you going this time, the Columbian or the Luhans?"

"Luhans, the pink adobe," Edith's grin grew as broad as Willa's. "We loved it there last year."

"Nice little house, quiet place, much better than a hotel."

John Dunn continued to make conversation while Edith gathered up their few small items from the waiting-room bench, sure that John Dunn had already loaded their trunks from the platform. "Been out here long this summer?"

"Since the end of May," Edith answered, "just drifting around from Lamy to Gallup."

"What a hell of place that is," Willa interjected with a sputter. "Why on earth anyone ever decided to sell liquor to the Navajos, I'll never understand. They're such nice people without it."

"We had a wonderful day trip to Zuni," Edith interrupted, "and a thrilling ride into Canyon de Chelly."

John Dunn whistled in admiration, "Long, hard pack trip from Gallup to Chelly."

"But it was well worth it. The wranglers were good and the canyon . . . well, the cliff dwellings, the river . . . there's just so much beauty. And history. And the Navajo. Still so much life happening among those ancient places."

"Edith, you're positively gushing." Willa's humor restored, she turned to John Dunn with a change of subject. "You being a gambling man, I'll bet we made better time getting there than you did getting here this morning, it took you so long."

"Yep, somewhat like that," John Dunn grinned around his cigar. "Sand bogs slowed me down. The road is bad today."

With a small bag under each arm and another in each hand, John Dunn propped the station door open with a well-worn boot heel.

"After you, ladies."

—||—

The grind of changing gears drew Willa's attention first. She pointed to the edge of an arroyo a few miles ahead. Then Edith saw it, too, a pencil-thin line jutting vertically down the sky.

"Is that a man?" Willa shaded her eyes.

"Looks like," John Dunn replied.

"How can that be," Edith heard the wonder in her own voice. The pencil-thin line, stark against its pale blue surround, dangled from a barren cottonwood. The line and the limb that held it were black. Neither looked quite like what it was. Shadow, Edith thought. It must be all a matter of shadow.

"What happened?" Willa demanded of Long John.

"Hanged, I guess."

"But who would hang him," Edith caught her breath, "and then leave him?'

John Dunn turned his head to look at the two of them, no longer so comfortably settled in the back seat. "Vigilantes," he grinned and turned his eyes back to the sandy tracks ahead. "Devil of a road," he growled between sentences. "Bothered some folks, I guess. Maybe stole some cattle or a horse or something."

No, Edith thought, that sort of thing only happens in Zane Grey. Whoever did that should have taken the body down. Should at least have attempted some sort of burial. Like the shallow grave they stumbled on last summer, really just a hollowed trough that monsoon rains had revealed a few feet below the trail. No vigilante justice for that death, but at least an attempt at burial. An unsuccessful attempt. Edith felt herself wince and saw again the woman's body in her shallow grave, limbs askew, brown skin ripped open at the neck and just below the ribcage on her left side, clothes and hair matted with dirt and a red so dark it looked black.

"No," Edith interrupted her own thoughts. "People," she began, "people wouldn't," but John Dunn was still talking.

"Just need a stout rope to correct a wrong out here. Done it myself any number of times."

"But this is 1926." Willa's protest came as if from a long distance.

"Yes, ma'am, it is." John Dunn stared straight ahead. "And this is Northern New Mexico."

Within seconds John Dunn's shoulders begin to jerk up and down. A muffled guffaw followed and he turned again to look at them. "And, yes, ma'am, I am pulling your legs. All four of them," his laugh grew. "We fill bags with straw and hang them out here like that just to scare the tourists."

"What tourists?" Willa wanted to know. "Koshare Tours don't come all the way up here, do they?"

John Dunn shook his head, his laughter spent. "No, no," he agreed. "But that Erna Fergusson and Ethel Hickey, they sold their Koshare Tours to Fred Harvey at La Fonda. He's calling it Indian Detours for the de-tourists. Ha."

Neither Willa nor Edith smiled. John Dunn turned his attention back to the road and worked the gearshift to pull them through a patch of soft sand. Then he said, "De-tourists could be coming this way any time now. Heard someone say they saw a De-tour car heading for Red River, of all places. No stopping progress, they say." He glanced again at his passengers and rolled his cigar from one side of his mustache to the other before adding, "Anyway, can't scare you, I know."

"No. Can't scare us," Willa repeated and settled back firmly into her side of the seat.

No, we aren't to be frightened by the false image of a hanging corpse, Edith found herself thinking, her eyes again seeking the distant mountains. That's not what they felt. Not now and not when they discovered the body last summer. Outrage. Shock. Disgust.

And finally sadness, an overwhelming sadness and sense of helplessness in the face of such brutality, at the woman's body splayed half-naked in sand and rock. And no one seemed surprised. No one even seemed to care. After they had raced their horses the several miles to the sheriff's office and breathlessly told him of their discovery, he took his time returning with them to the site. When he got there, he didn't even bend down, just prodded the woman's body with his toe. "Mexican," he said, turning away, "probably served her right."

Right? Right! Willa had been incredulous. They had been incredulous. And stunned by the lack of justice. No, stunned by the sheriff's disinterest in justice where that woman was concerned. During the next weeks of their stay he never bothered to discover her name and made very little effort to find out who killed her. She certainly had not died of natural causes.

And now this joke. John Dunn was a nice enough fellow, Edith knew, but his joke showed such a casual concern for life, for living things. Death as a way to settle disputes. Vigilante justice should be called what it is, violence and laziness and intellectual dishonesty, Edith settled the matter for herself.

This summer, she made a silent promise, this summer we must find out what happened to that poor woman. We must make sure that whoever did that to her is introduced to real, rigorous, honest justice. That's what Americans do. Well, Edith caught herself, that's what Americans must try to do now.

Having just come from Canyon de Chelly, Edith was reminded that only sixty years earlier, the army had ordered Kit Carson to round up the last of the Navajos and send them on their "Long Walk" to Bosque Redondo where they starved and many, many died before they were allowed to return. No, Americans have not always been a just people. And so it is imperative, Edith told herself, to insist on justice as soon as they were again settled in the pink adobe. Edith had a good two weeks before she had to take the train to New York and return to her job at the J. Walter Thompson advertising agency. Willa had even longer, perhaps a month, to work on her manuscript before heading for Denver and a visit with her brother's family.

—II—

After another forty minutes, John Dunn paused before plunging his taxi down the precipitous hairpin turns to the bottom of the Rio Grande Gorge. At the bottom they would cross the bridge he built over the Rio Grande and make the final turn north along the river toward Taos.

"Stretch your legs, ladies?"

John Dunn opened Willa's door first, then came around to help Edith out.

The ground felt good under Edith's feet. Solid, secure. A change from the anger and darkening thoughts that had threatened to take over her mood despite the pure, sage-scented air and endless blue sky.

The dark outline of the gorge had presented itself several minutes before. It was always a surprise. Unless you could soar like an eagle, Edith thought, the gorge would always hide itself. But when you did get close enough to the edge or high enough above, she remembered from the summer before, the view of the Rio Grande cutting its jagged path for miles and miles through the high Taos valley was stunning.

Today the sun traced patterns in the upper reaches of the gorge, but the rest was so filled with shade and shadows that it took a minute for her eyes to adjust. Trees at the bottom looked small from this height and so did the Rio Grande, moving swiftly now through the canyon it had taken thousands of years to shape and carve. It would spread out, Edith knew, to become deceptively lazy in the Española

Valley and farther south, where floods and quicksand could still prove its might.

"That river is a far cry from what it is at Alcalde," Willa mused.

Lush lawns spilled across Edith's mind, fields of corn and green chile reaching to the muddy banks of the Rio Grande where cottonwoods with their huge angular limbs spread a luxurious shade. The Española Valley, Alcalde, the Pfäffles' San Gabriel Ranch with its extensive pattern of irrigation ditches known here by their Spanish name *acequias*. The ranch had been their refuge for two weeks the previous summer while they corrected proofs for *The Professor's House* in the shade of the inn's *portal*. So beautiful Alcalde was that they thought briefly this summer about returning there until Mabel Dodge Luhan called to say they should come back to the pink adobe.

"A far cry, yes, it certainly is," Edith agreed, staring again at the narrow ribbon far below, running fast, deep, and dark.

"Breathtaking," Willa concluded.

II

"WE'VE BEEN HERE for just two hours and already we've seen absolutely everybody," Edith exclaimed, hanging the last of her blouses next to Willa's in the rustic Spanish wardrobe occupying the wall next to the small alcove where they would sleep.

"Everybody except Mabel." Willa's low laugh came from the little kitchen they planned to use sparingly during their weeks with Mabel Dodge Luhan and her husband Tony.

"I expect she's still working," Edith remembered how Mabel would remain for hours ensconced in her enormous four-poster bed surrounded by pens and well-covered pages. Writing her memoir was the reason Mabel said she invited them to Taos in the first place. Willa, she pleaded, must read her first volume and give her advice. And Willa did, with plenty of praise. She especially praised Mabel's directness and honesty, her refusal to back down from any subject, even her love as a young girl for her special friend, Violet. Must be close to finishing the second volume by now, Edith guessed. Mabel preferred to write in bed and could easily spend most of any day there.

"I'm sure she's glad to be home again. Tony, too," Edith changed the subject. They had had to delay their visit while Tony and Mabel were in Albuquerque where Tony had been hospitalized. Mabel never said why. No matter, Willa and Edith enjoyed the new La Fonda hotel and Santa Fe, where Willa found still more books about her priests, the two whose story was becoming her next novel, the one she was calling *Death Comes for the Archbishop*.

D.H. Lawrence Painting in the Pink Adobe

"I still love this," Willa was chatting to her through the wall as she moved about, changing the location of dishes and pots to clear a small table for use as a desk. Edith could picture the vase precisely, tall, thin and oriental with a phoenix painted on its side and a bright red chrysanthemum, whimsical with touches of yellow and orange, leaning from its mouth. It was not a real vase at all but one D.H. Lawrence had painted on the door of the room's only cabinet the year he and his wife Frieda occupied the pink adobe. Soon after their stay in the pink adobe they had moved to Kiowa, the ranch near San Cristobal that Mabel gave them in trade for the manuscript of *Sons and Lovers*.

"Yes, I do, too," Edith responded. "Maybe if Tony's feeling up to it we could arrange for another trip to their ranch this summer." She remembered the view of the mountains from the porch of Lawrence's small rustic ranch house near the tiny town of San Cristobal, eighteen miles to the north and five hundred feet above the seven-thousand foot elevation of Taos.

So many birds, that's what Edith remembered most about their visit. The sky above the ranch had been absolutely filled with motion and commotion. They had watched a pair of bald eagles diving, darting, floating, and even cartwheeling high through the blue. And in the trees below a pair of Steller's jays chasing a much larger Cooper's hawk, flitting through sun and shadow, the jays in unison uttering their full-throated complaint. But a much louder sound had come from a totally unexpected source—hummingbirds, hundreds of them, maybe thousands, careening together through a canyon below the ranch. Lawrence had taken his visitors on a short hike to the canyon where he knew they might hear the birds' thunderous hum long before they could see their tiny bodies hurtling through air.

Edith was amazed. They all were, and their visit with the Lawrences and the deaf young woman who moved with them from England had been delightful. Brett, Dorothy Brett, Edith remembered the young woman's name, a painter. Slight and blond, she used an ear trumpet and read lips. She seemed devoted to Lawrence, almost more than his wife Frieda, who clearly enjoyed a good argument.

But then, so did Lawrence, Edith chuckled. An odd threesome, not exactly Jack Spratt, but a skinny, talkative, red-bearded Englishman with a hearty wife whose gusts of conversation came in a German accent, and a slim assistant who simply did whatever she was told. Mabel brought them to New Mexico where they hoped Lawrence would find relief from the tuberculosis that ravaged his lungs, and where Mabel hoped Lawrence would write so brilliantly about Taos, the world would finally grasp its magic.

But Mabel had quarreled with Lawrence, and the Lawrences had gone off to Mexico with Witter Bynner and Spud Johnson, friends of Mabel's and in the case of Witter Bynner, or Hal as he liked to be called, an old acquaintance of Willa's and Edith's. Spud they knew from the previous summer, a truly nice young man, an aspiring writer with thinning hair and large glasses, but they knew Hal from twenty years before when the three of them had been at *McClure's Magazine* together. Edith remembered Hal as rude and flamboyant, a young man whose inherited wealth and early success made him impossibly self-absorbed. And, she recalled, he had no interest in working with women.

Bynner was just about to leave as poetry editor when first Willa and then Edith joined the staff at *McClure's*. In all the years since, they had heard nothing from him though they knew he had moved to California and was now living in Santa Fe. He had been out of town when they were in Santa Fe the previous summer, but they had gone to one of his famous parties just the week before while they were staying in Alcalde. They found Bynner twenty years older but otherwise unchanged.

When Bynner heard they were planning another stay with the Luhans, he began chattering away about his time in Mexico with Lawrence. Nothing of much consequence, Edith thought, but a great deal of noise about the beauty of young Mexican boys. He went on at such length, Edith neglected to tell him that they had already met the Lawrences and furthermore knew a great deal about them through Achsah and Earl Brewster, people Hal knew nothing about. Achsah had been Edith's college roommate and was still her best friend, and Earl was about to publish a life of Buddha. Lawrence had stayed with the Brewsters in India and they knew him well. Lawrence, after all, had lived many places in the world before he found Taos or travelled with Bynner.

It wasn't until the spring after the Lawrences left for Mexico with Bynner and Spud Johnson that they came back to Taos with Dorothy Brett and began to fix up the Kiowa ranch. Lawrence had hoped then to found a utopian colony, a new world in the New World, but Brett turned out to be his only colonist. The three of them, Brett, Lawrence, and Frieda, managed to make the ranch more or less habitable and lived there until British residency requirements forced Lawrence to return to England.

The Lawrences were now in Italy, temporarily, Edith hoped. But a trip to Lawrence's ranch with Tony was still a possibility. In the midst of the mountains, the ranch seemed greener and the mountains closer in than what they could see from the porch of their pink adobe. And where the ranch house stood in the shadow of an enormous ponderosa pine, their own porch overlooked rows of wild plum trees trained to arch over a wooden walkway that crossed through the alfalfa pasture between their pink adobe and Mabel's main house.

The pink adobe was pink, of course, only because of the paint that trimmed its windows and the porch that shaded its doors on the east, the traditional direction for doors at the pueblo, meant to face the sacred mountain and greet the morning sun. Aside from the Victorian gingerbread that decorated its porch and the Florentine door handles Mabel brought with her from Italy, it was a small and unpretentious house with thick adobe walls inside and out. Each room had multiple windows and doors, more windows and doors than Edith had ever seen in one dwelling. And the doors, even the front doors facing east, were like windows, their raised sills and low lintels required simultaneous climbing and stooping to pass from one room to another or move from inside to out. Tradition, Tony told them. From the pueblo. Keep everyone safe. No enemy can be strong when stooped.

Pueblo workers built the house under Tony's supervision, just as they had Mabel's main house, where the steps leading to the bedrooms upstairs required the same sort of simultaneous climbing and stooping. But the pink, Edith guessed, might have been Lawrence's addition. Adobe houses were always the color of the mud that formed them, and in Taos most of the doors were blue. Tradition, Tony told them again. Just like doors at the pueblo, blue to ward off evil spirits. Mabel's big house, one of the only multiple-story houses in Taos except for the five-story pueblo, was trimmed in bright turquoise.

—ıı—

"They're coming back. You heard?" Emilio shuffled papers on his desk in the outer office, then tipped his chair so it rocked on its front legs. He didn't look up. It was almost quitting time.

"Tony said. I heard." Unsmiling, William Santistivan, Sheriff of Taos County, dropped into his leather chair and slid open the bottom drawer of his desk. He paused to nestle one well-oiled boot against the other on top of the file folders stacked inside. The two women strode again through the door in his mind. He first saw them a year ago, when he was not quite seven months into his job, the older one fuming, the other a bit younger, a little less bold and hesitant in her speech but no less insistent. Anglos, from the east. They demanded that he arrest a murderer. Immediately.

The sheriff chuckled to himself. The two had burst into his office out of breath, as though they and not their horses had run a long distance to reach him. They had discovered a woman's body in a partially dug grave on a little-used trail not far from Arroyo Seco. The trail ran through pueblo land where he had no jurisdiction, but the body had been dumped just beyond. He had no idea where the actual murder might have occurred, but the location of the body put it just within his jurisdiction. So close to the line, the pueblo could give him trouble.

A woman had been murdered, he agreed with those women about that. A violent death. But he had no idea who she was or who the killer might be. Not then. Not now. The woman was not the only dead female found out there. And she wasn't the last. Two more bodies had appeared on a nearby trail in just the last month. And with these, the sheriff was more than twice as much at a loss about identifying the corpses. They were missing their heads.

Any number of possible suspects could have killed those women. There simply were too many complications and too many possibilities. The sheriff had asked Tony Luhan, a Taos Pueblo Indian, to explain to these women how that might be. They were staying with Tony and his wife, who always seemed to have a crowd of Anglo artists and writers at the house. Even Tony couldn't make them understand. And then they left. Their departure had been a relief.

But the sheriff had made no progress on the case since then, only empty speculation. Could the murderer actually have come from the pueblo? The sheriff didn't think so. All of these women looked like they came from Mexican families, not Indian or even old-Spanish families. They would have had no business on pueblo land. So the sheriff had speculated further, maybe the killer was one of the young whoremongers or gamblers who hung around Madame May's in Red River. A rough customer from the mining area around Elizabethtown. Lots of loose women and violent deaths up there, but also lots of out-of-the-way places to dump a body. Why haul the bodies all that way through the mountains, presuming they were all three killed by the same person? So if the murderer wasn't a Pueblo Indian, a customer of Madame May's, a gambler, or a miner, maybe he was that sorry excuse of a man, Arthur Manby. The sheriff hoped it was Manby.

Arthur Manby had been parading around Taos for years in his jodhpurs and tall English boots cheating people out of land and money, but no one had quite gotten anything on him they could prove. And he hung around women in the Mexican neighborhoods, especially Teracita Ferguson, who owned the tourist camp on the edge of town.

But mostly Manby was crazy. One of the local stories was that during the Great War, when that wealthy woman who married Tony Luhan first showed up in Taos and rented part of Manby's house, she could hear Manby on the roof at night listening through a chimney to conversations at her dinner table. Then he told federal officers she was a spy arranging for Taos to be invaded from

Mexico. Well, Tony's rich wife took care of that nonsense all right, but as far as the sheriff was concerned, all Anglos were strange, British or American.

From the outer office Emilio interrupted, "What are we going to do?"

"About these Anglos? Nothing," the sheriff sighed. "Nothing we can do."

—II—

Dinner that evening proved festive. The large dining room was specially decorated. The serving tables overflowed with flowers, and the wonderfully handcrafted furniture and bright red-and-black floor tiles gleamed with fresh polish. To celebrate Tony's return and welcome old friends, Mabel declared, and toasted Willa and Edith with a chardonnay made from grapes grown in vineyards near the Rio Grande.

The sun, resplendent in reds and golds, dipped below the horizon just as they finished dinner, its long rays reaching through French doors to cast its last bit of light across the celebrants. Dressed in burgundy satin softened by a shawl the color of cream, Mabel exuded warmth and welcome at the head of her long table. Her dark hair, cut straight at the base of her ears with bangs across her forehead, accentuated the shine in her eyes. Tony, at the foot of the table, echoed her mood and appearance, his long silken black braids woven through with ribbons of burgundy and cream.

Facing west, Edith and Willa with Spud Johnson between them turned a pale rose in the fading light of the sunset, while those opposite, Alexandra and Nicolai Fechin and their twelve-year-old daughter Eya, showed no change in hue. Recent immigrants from Russia, the Fechins were planning to build a house in Taos. The idea thrilled Mabel, who so loved to build houses she was getting ready to add a new one to her compound. Now with the

Fechins, she could be involved in two at once. His would be different from all the others, Nicolai declared, more like Russia. During their three short years in New York City, Nicolai had managed to build a national reputation as a portrait painter. Now tuberculosis forced his move to the Southwest.

"The light, look," Nicolai exclaimed, pointing at the three sitting across from him, "Beautiful, the light!"

"It is beautiful. Painters love the light in Taos," Edith agreed. She had spent much of her time during the previous summer sketching and drawing with several of the local painters, especially Mabel's friend Andrew Dasburg. Fascinated with the way the light in Taos fell on adobe walls, the many variations of colors it created, she used pastels to capture them as Dasburg had. She hoped this summer to try again, and with Nicolai here, to work with him and his brilliant use of color as well.

"Writers, too, love the light in Taos, yes?"

"I certainly do, yes," Willa nodded.

"Beautiful, the light," Nicolai said again, this time looking only at Willa. "I paint you like that. Serious, somber, striking in that light." Nicolai took Willa by surprise. She blushed. "You, too, Mabel," he turned to the head of the table. "I love to paint you, too, yes?"

Mabel did not blush. She simply said, "Yes. Yes, of course. And once you live here, you must paint whatever you like. Tony, too, don't you think?"

"All the Pueblo Indians. Yes, yes!" In his unexpected exuberance Nicolai made a toast first to Tony and his fellow Pueblo Indians and then to Mabel, his hostess, and finally to the famous novelist sitting across from him. Willa blushed again and tried to demur, but Nicolai would have none of that. "Yes, yes," he insisted, "I paint you, all of you."

Amused, Edith leaned forward to glance past Spud's lanky frame and catch Willa's eye. She hoped Willa was pleased and not about to slip away from Nicolai's praise. So often now Willa felt a need to hide from the fame that had attached itself to her once she won the Pulitzer Prize. She was happy, she said, that so many people read her books, but that's all she wanted, for them to read her books and leave her alone.

Edith was getting better at running interference so Willa could have the space and time she needed to write. Edith's job was simply to smile politely and turn the "gushers" away. If they managed to slip by her, they would be met with the Medusa mask that the Metropolitan Opera star Olive Fremstad had taught Willa to use, a look so empty and haughty as to frighten even the most forward of admirers.

Now when they travelled, Edith's was the only name to appear on reservations and hotel registers. Willa was simply nowhere apparent. Of course, here in Taos, in Mabel's house, Willa had no need for the Medusa mask or disappearance. This mountain town was protection enough, so remote and filled with people so accustomed to artists and writers that nobody seemed to notice individuals. As good, Edith thought, as Grand Manan, the island in the Bay of Fundy half a world away where she and Willa had chosen to build a summer cottage.

Ahhh, there were Willa's dimples and she was agreeing that Nicolai should paint her. Soon. Yes. Edith, off duty, settled deeper into her chair.

—II—

The stars were brilliant when Spud finally made his way home, a short walk cross lots from Mabel's to the adobe he was renting on the main road through Taos. Main road, he chuckled to himself, better call it a dirt track leading out of town. Exactly what he loved about Taos, its lack of everything. No macadam, no streetlights, no fast cars, no people racing for the top. No top even. What could be better.

At twenty-nine Spud was happy to find a quiet life in Taos after Santa Fe with Witter Bynner, sixteen years his senior and living in Berkeley when in 1922 he took Spud under his wing, as they said then. Spud had already caused a scandal at the university when he and a couple of friends published the satirical *Laughing Horse,* a magazine he later brought with him to Taos, and Bynner had cheered him on.

Before Spud quite knew what was happening, they had moved together to Santa Fe where almost immediately they met D.H. Lawrence and took off with him and Frieda for Mexico. Heady stuff that, Bynner opening his world to Lawrence, boys on the beach, barefoot in the sand, exhilarating, tempestuous, insane, and finally, finally, too much for Spud. Soon after they returned, Spud moved to Taos, a long and tortuous seventy miles north by car on a narrow, rocky dirt road through the Rio Grande Gorge and then up, up to the wonder of Taos valley.

Taos was also wonderfully quiet. Oh, plenty of uproar too, Spud chuckled to himself, but subdued, almost suppressed, until something lit a fuse and everything blew up. Like it had the summer before when Willa and Edith discovered a woman's body near Arroyo Seco. Spud and Tony hauled the body across pueblo land and into town on a buckboard. And they, not the sheriff, checked the area around the body and the trail as they drove toward town but saw no sign of unfamiliar tracks or commotion. Tony offered their help searching for the woman's killer, but once Willa and Edith left town, the sheriff seemed to lose interest altogether and neither Spud nor Tony found any worthwhile clues.

The excitement soon sputtered out as uproars in Taos usually did. In the intervals one could easily be lulled into thinking Taos the most peaceful place on earth. It was for Spud, though now that he had agreed to become Mabel's sometime assistant, he was constantly aware of underlying tensions and potential explosions. A current eruption, still smoldering, involved Mabel's protest against the United States government's policy of assimilation and recent attempts to sell Indian lands. Once Mabel discovered Taos and Tony, she wanted exactly the opposite to happen.

The country, the world, so broken after World War I, Mabel declared, should put itself back together and become like Taos Pueblo—communal, harmonious, living with land and sky the way Tony did—not combative, controlling, or for heaven's sake, distracted by Progress. Progress, Mabel sputtered, should move humans toward all that is natural and real, not away. Still, Spud chuckled again, his footsteps crunching gravel as he neared his front door, Mabel did buy Tony a Cadillac and on occasion she drove it herself.

Most newcomers, all the ones Spud knew, writers and artists recent to the Southwest, were generally ignored as long as they minded their own business. But Mabel never minded her own business. When Mabel and Tony became lovers and then decided to marry, Spud guessed they had no real idea what they were doing. Courageous and outrageous, as scandalous as Bynner with boys on the beach, but not the same.

Mabel, rich and Anglo, was a socialite and rabble-rouser with three previous husbands and one flamboyant lover. Tony, married and a man of tradition, was a spiritual leader in his pueblo. Mabel had often created scandals, living lavishly in Italy with her second husband, establishing a salon for labor leaders and intellectuals in her Fifth Avenue apartment, and in 1913 helping to organize demonstrations at Madison Square Garden and Paterson, New Jersey for the silk workers' strike. If that weren't enough, she was also behind the 1913 Armory Show in New York City that introduced modern art to the country and shocked all of America. And now she expected Taos to transform the world. Well, maybe it would. Spud wished her well.

But before Taos could change the world it had to catch up with it, Spud thought, at least a little and in certain ways. Last summer's murder, for instance, couldn't just continue to be ignored. Not now with rumors of two more bodies, headless and dropped unburied in almost the same place. The dinner conversation that evening had been pleasant until Spud mentioned the rumors. Edith in particular expressed shock and outrage. And she was right. Everyone agreed *mañana* justice in Taos had to end. Spud didn't know how, but he was determined to make that happen, to make Taos safe for everyone.

—||—

"Lovely. The evening. The day. All of it. Just lovely." Willa took Edith's arm to steady their way across the little bridge over the *acequia madre* that ran just above the wild plum trees lining their walk to the pink adobe. The fragrance of piñon burning in kiva fireplaces in the area invaded their senses and from a distance came the various pitched voices of dogs conversing in the cool night air. Oddly, their voices intensified the silence.

Edith felt compelled to pause, to breathe deeply, to let the sensation of well being and quiet exhilaration reach all the way to her toes. The unpleasantness at dinner about the uninvestigated deaths of three women finally gave way. Willa called out the constellations, Cassiopeia and the two dippers distinct among the thousands of stars above.

"Taos has to be the most beautiful place on earth," Willa pressed Edith's arm closer to her ribs. Edith smiled and nodded in silent agreement.

They had lingered after dinner, Mabel inviting them with Tony into what she called her Rainbow Room, her comfortable library a few steps up from the living room. Rainbow because the room's ceiling, made up of slender stripped-pine poles called *latillas* that crisscrossed above thick pine *vigas* in a herringbone pattern, were variously stained red, blue, and white, the colors of earth and sky, just as they were in the dining room. Like the rest of the house, the Rainbow Room was full of color and art representing a rich mix of cultures and religions from around the world.

Willa and Edith seemed always to be finding new things—sketches and paintings on whitewashed walls of birds, turtles, and other images sacred to the pueblos; an amazing variety of oriental and Navajo rugs, brilliant in their designs; gothic doorways with images sacred to local Catholics, including Our Lady of Guadalupe, carved or painted on the doors; huge portraits and landscapes by the most important artists of the Italian Renaissance interspersed with pieces by Cubists and other contemporary artists and with rustic *santos*, small wooden carvings and crosses that had adorned homes around Taos for generations depicting the images of saints; the wall of windows in Mabel's bathroom that Brett and D.H. Lawrence covered with geometric designs to provide Mabel with unwanted modesty; and the large collection of lovely pueblo and Italian vases, pots, and figures, including the large ceramic roosters Mabel distributed along the roofline of the western *portal* that explained why she named the house *Los Gallos*. A hodgepodge of everything lovely, Willa called it, just like Mabel herself.

"Yes, yes, a hodgepodge," Mabel laughed with delight, her voice then slipping into its lower registers, "just like Taos itself. Everything come together as one! That's as close as anyone has ever come to describing me. Jelliffe, Brill, Jung, none of them caught onto me as well as you. And you have done it in just one word. Hodgepodge."

Mabel poured each of them an after-dinner coffee and offered them a Lucky Strike from the carton they brought with them from Santa Fe as a gift for Mabel. Tony settled into his large corner chair, as he often did, and began to provide background music for their conversation, drumming and singing traditional pueblo songs. The unfamiliar words and quiet rhythmic sound drew little direct attention but radiated calm and peace. Jamie, the resident tabby, sauntered in to stare at the four of them, each in turn, and finally nestled in Edith's lap for his evening nap. The women lit their cigarettes, sipped their coffee, and sat for a moment before Mabel continued their conversation with a sly smile, "Hodgepodge, yes, but not always so lovely."

"Human then," Willa offered.

"Once again, exactly right."

Mabel had not always been so agreeable, Willa and Edith knew from the many stories they heard about her over the years. Rabble-rouser, suffragette, unionist, commie! Charges against Mabel had been loud and various and to some degree true. She had held salons in her Fifth Avenue apartment where labor leaders and anarchists fomented rebellion and plotted the Paterson strike. She had supported the crusades of people like Margaret Sanger, Max Eastman, Big Bill Haywood, and Emma Goldman. She had been in a well-known sexual relationship with John Reed. Several of Mabel's New York friends had at some point been arrested for their political activity or fled the United States. The rumors about Mabel herself had been no less startling. Insane, said some, a meddler who loves to disrupt relationships and embarrass even the most invulnerable, said others. Mabel sparked so much gossip over the years that Willa and Edith had been wary of accepting her invitations to Taos and once they did, tried to distance themselves by using formal terms of address, referring to themselves as Miss Cather and Miss Lewis and to Mabel as Mrs. Luhan.

But their reserve dissolved once they read Mabel's memoirs, spent days exploring the country around Taos with Tony and occasionally Mabel, and learning from them about the history and culture of New Mexico, both past and present. Kindred spirits, Willa decided, except for Mabel's desire to be the center of attention. Willa had wanted that kind of attention as a young woman but now she wanted that only for her work, not herself. Mabel had no need to earn a living. Willa and Edith did. They preferred to stay out of the limelight and let Edith's editorial work at the J. Walter Thompson advertising agency and Willa's short stories and novels speak for them.

—||—

Adam hung the ax on its pegs above the door and latched the door before carrying the new bundle of kindling to the box next to the stove. It was late. The sun had been down for quite a while and he was tired. Time to build up the fire so they could heat their beans and tortillas.

They would eat in silence, Adam at the table, Maria on her stool near the open shelves storing their few dishes. He expected nothing different. It had been a week since he arrived at Kiowa and found the ranch house broken into and still occupied by a huge young man with shaggy blond hair, an unshaven beard, and a dark scar that ran from the left side of his forehead to his right ear. Adam flinched when he said his name was Blade.

That's about all the man did say. Adam hurried to explain that the owner had sent him to live at the ranch as a kind of caretaker. His rush of words felt lame even to Adam, and Blade resisted leaving until Adam offered him a couple of dollars to clear out quietly. But once Blade gathered up what he had strewn about the few rooms and called to someone outside, Adam learned that his problem was larger than Blade.

Maria, blouse torn at the neck, skirt caked with mud and dried grass, sandals loose on both feet as though they belonged to someone else, emerged from the tiny cabin behind the house. Adam could not see her face because her long brown hair fell across it and she did not look up but pressed against the cabin's exterior and splayed her hands across its logs as if expecting to be hit. Adam moved toward her, but Blade spun him around and said just two words. "She's mine."

Stunned, Adam stood a very long time in what felt like a stupor until he came up with two words of his own. "Sell her?"

Blade dropped his grip. "Ten dollars." Exactly the amount Adam had in his pocket.

When Blade left, Adam fitted the doors with inside bars to serve as locks and gathered what scrap wood he could find to barricade the windows. Then he, with Maria, cleaned the two cabins. Maria said nothing. Adam could understand only a few words of Spanish and he was not sure Maria knew English. He was sure that she remained too frightened to speak. Adam would have to check this situation out with Spud when he finally went down the mountain for supplies. Spud would know what to do. Spud had, after all, sent Adam to the ranch so he would have a place to stay and paint his mountain landscapes until Lawrence returned.

III

EDITH LIFTED HER reins and nudged her mare into a trot. It felt good to be on Jesse again, a sweet-tempered bay with a smooth gait and quiet curiosity. Nothing rash or ill-mannered like the chestnut she had drawn for the ride into Canyon de Chelly. Sunny they called him, but there was nothing sunny about him. He was a cranky gelding with short pasterns and a choppy gait who tried to jerk the reins from her hands and trot quickly up and especially down the rocky trail. Edith's hands and arms ached from holding him back, and the muscles in her inner thighs complained for days.

But Jesse was happy to take notice of their surroundings and pick her way carefully along the trail. With her, Edith could relax and enjoy the mare's intelligence and the lively feel of her body even through several layers of leather. Willa's horse, a dark brown gelding named Jasper, was equally willing and sweet-tempered. Tony had his choice of horses from the pueblo and he chose well.

Riding was something Edith and Willa had grown up doing as a matter of course. Nothing like the feel of a horse, a good horse, Willa agreed with Edith about that. Like everyone else at dinner the night before, Mabel and especially the Fechins loved hearing Willa's stories about her childhood on horseback, visiting neighbors on the plains around Red Cloud, Nebraska. Immigrants all of them, from places as far-flung as Czechoslovakia, Sweden, Germany, and Russia, living however they could in dugouts, sod houses, and for the wealthier ones, single-story buildings with weathered clapboard siding. It was like taking a world tour of homes, languages, stories, and, for the young Willa, kitchens. Fragrant goulashes, warmed-over rabbit stews, and fresh-baked *kolaches* right out of the oven. Willa's memories were literally mouth-watering morsels.

Younger by nine years, Edith had spent her childhood a hundred and fifty miles east of Red Cloud in the bustling frontier capital of Lincoln, Nebraska. She grew to love many of the same newcomers and traditions Willa enjoyed, but her in-town life provided little of Willa's opportunity for day-long rides across the open plains. Except for a brief respite on her father's ranch near Kearney, Edith and her brother and sisters kept a pony and a cart in Lincoln and learned to ride properly and well. And her days in Lincoln were filled with social gatherings where she also learned to balance a teacup and practice manners.

When she became one of the recording secretaries of her local sorority, she was called upon to create flowery, if tongue-in-cheek, descriptions of such exciting events as the Naming of the Bulls, sponsored by a wealthy rancher whose daughter had also pledged Delta Gamma. After a pleasant luncheon, where everyone indulged in their favorite version of sophisticated chatter, the girls trooped outside to seats decorated with floral wreaths and arranged in a semi-circle around the side of a corral where young bulls were presented one after another to be formally dubbed by the girls and registered as *Sir Lancelot*, *Ulysses*, or *Zeus*.

Edith never ceased to be amused and a little embarrassed by her own youthful posturings, but Willa's spirited freedom and theatrical posings—as Pocahontas, a scientist, a scholar, a doctor, or actually on stage as a Greek goddess or the villain in a melodrama, mustache, top-hat and all—Willa's young self was downright exuberant and uproarious. Yet Willa, being Willa, never lost perspective. As easily as Edith, she would laugh at her young self and at the years they each spent actively smoothing their rough western edges.

For that, Edith had gone to Smith College in Massachusetts.

Willa, after gaining notoriety during her first year at the University of Nebraska by wearing her hair sheared into a flattop and calling herself William, finally accepted the advice of her elders and shifted to ladylike hairdos and dresses for the rest of her college career. But it took five years of living with the McClungs in Pittsburgh's fashionable and wealthy Squirrel Hill area for Willa to be really "finished." Her friend Isabelle McClung achieved that miracle. Or at least she moved Willa as far as possible into acceptability and for the first time Willa became comfortable in society. In trade, Willa taught Isabelle French and travelled with her in Europe.

Willa did manage to lure Isabelle into joining her for a few weeks of roughing it in Nebraska and Wyoming, but Isabelle preferred chamber music and Europe. Edith, on the other hand, enjoyed listening to music and loved going with Willa to the opera and concerts, but for her and for Willa, nothing could be better than a long hike or a day's ride across the mesa. What folly, Willa finally declared. Instead of working so hard to become ladies, we should have been teaching ladies how to become western women. How to live without fear in open spaces and accept the freedom to be anything we dare. At the time, Edith simply closed the book she was reading and silently agreed. Living well in society was fine, but growing up in the west had served them well. It was something they shared.

Their ride this morning held nothing from their youthful rides except the sense of space and open sky. In the vast emptiness around them now, mountains and mesas rose to define the horizon. Here the sky was paler and the earth lighter and more variegated in hue than the Nebraska plains. It held none of the fresh-plowed fields or waving grasses that sometimes reached higher than their stirrups. Instead of feeling small and sometimes alone in the magnificence of Nebraska, here one might feel small but not alone.

This grandeur carried with it a sense of animation and comfort from ageless struggles, Edith thought, not over nature but with it.

In Taos, ancient irrigation ditches bore the steady music and movement of mountain streams through tree-lined streets and green pastures. Here on the mesa, blue grama, sagebrush, and chamisa held tight just to keep the earth in place. Grasses seemed permanently bent by the wind. The sun warmed and clouds hung suspended or scudded in white puffs across the blue. Eagles, hawks, ravens rode the air, and comical magpies replaced sedate meadowlarks on low-hanging branches and twigs, echoing the jazzy black-and-white body paint and antics of the clowns in pueblo dances. Wind, wildness, warmth, and utter joy, that's New Mexico, Edith felt like laughing out loud.

"Glorious morning!"

Willa's shout matched Edith's own feeling about the day, and soon Willa was alongside, helping Jasper pick his way among the sage next to the trail. Just then Jesse's ears pricked forward and Edith noticed how the trail narrowed and clumps of piñon and sage began to thicken ahead. Tall ponderosa pines loomed in the distance. They must have come farther than she realized. They had to be close now, close to the spot where they found the woman's body the previous summer.

—ıı—

Spud began his day with a walk to the pueblo, his thinning hair safe from wind and sun under a wide-brimmed straw hat. In the far distance, he caught a glimpse of two people on horseback. They were just specks moving at a purposeful pace toward Arroyo Seco. He guessed they were Willa Cather and Edith Lewis.

It was unusual to see Willa on horseback this early in the day. The previous summer she had spent all her mornings writing. But Spud was not surprised. He was pretty sure he knew where they were going. At dinner last night, Edith asked Tony what had happened about the woman whose body they discovered last July. Tony said he had heard nothing, which Mabel explained meant that nothing had happened.

That wasn't exactly true and Spud said so. Edith gasped when he explained that this June he heard two new bodies had been found a little farther along on a nearby trail, both female and this time, headless. He watched as Willa placed her fork carefully on the edge of her plate before turning toward him to demand details. Exactly where were they located, how were they dressed, were they, like the first woman, of Mexican or Spanish descent, how were they found, what was the condition of their bodies, did anyone know what had happened to their heads?

Willa's questions tumbled forth in fully formed sentences, her voice low and steady, eyes intense. Spud found himself flustered. This Willa Cather was all business, direct and straightforward, so unlike the graceful woman with smiling blue eyes, charming dimples, and melodic voice he had come to know. Edith, always quieter and somewhat hesitant, also pressed for details. But Spud had little to offer. He hadn't thought to ask.

Spud was no stranger to forthright women. He rather expected women to be intelligent and inquisitive. It had been seven years since American women won the right to vote. They were flappers. They could wear pants. They could move their arms and legs freely and dance and drink in speakeasies. They had been going to college since well before the turn of the century. They had careers. Well, some had careers. And he was of the new generation, the generation some called Lost. He was not lost. He had found Taos. But Taos had suddenly produced the headless bodies of two women, women Willa and Edith adamantly demanded he describe in detail. What on earth, they wanted to know, was going on?

With that, Spud volunteered to go with Tony in the morning to find out what they could from the sheriff. Tony had first to go to the pueblo with John Collier, Mabel's latest wunderkind. Certain the Pueblo Indians would interest Collier as much as they did her, Mabel had invited this eager young social reformer from New York City for a visit. Once Collier caught hold, as Mabel knew he would, she and Tony helped him organize a contingent of artists and writers from Santa Fe and Albuquerque to persuade the Bureau of Indian Affairs and Congress to change their policies.

Hard to believe their most powerful foe was northern New Mexico's own congressman, Steven P. Cutlass. But there it was. Cutlass, a wealthy businessman and sometime rancher, wanted no changes in the way things were. He was known to be ruthless and his opposition to John Collier was formidable. Collier had recently increased the pressure on Cutlass by lobbying Congress with the American Indian Defense Association to convey exclusive rights to the Taos Pueblo Indians of the 48,000 acres of the Blue Lake mountain area on Wheeler Peak that was sacred to the pueblo. Cutlass was furious.

At dinner the previous night Mabel tried to explain all of this to the Fechins, insisting that any Anglo expecting to live in northern New Mexico needed to understand its history, its mix of races and cultures, and become actively involved in helping the pueblos once again defend their lands and customs. As Tony said, "My people cannot do this. Anglos must speak so Anglos hear." Nicolai was excited to learn. Willa and Edith were already well-informed. They had been in the midst of the activists in Santa Fe and Taos for two summers now, and though neither was inclined to political action, they understood the issues.

Willa rarely talked about her writing, but she often talked with Mabel and Tony about the mix of Pueblo, Spanish, Mexican, and Anglo cultures in northern New Mexico and the two French missionary priests, Jean Baptiste Lamy and Joseph Machebeuf, whose lives in northern New Mexico in the 1850s formed the core of her new manuscript. No less than Mabel, Spud was pleased with her choice of subjects, two gentle men who, because they stood apart from the culture they meant to convert, came to see clearly how to change both the culture and themselves to become one with it. Spud, an outsider himself, speculated about how like those men he was and now how like his new friends, Willa Cather and Edith Lewis.

Given current attitudes toward Pueblo Indians and Indian land, Spud thought Collier's project a long shot, but John could be very persuasive and Tony liked working with him. They might just pull it off. And this morning, Spud guessed, Tony and John would also be asking around at the pueblo to see who might know something about those headless bodies. Once he joined them, Tony could drive the three of them to the sheriff's office.

—ıı—

At the edge of the pines, Edith pulled up to have a closer look around. Jesse took the opportunity to stretch her head down just enough to get a nibble of blue grama grass. On the other side of the trail a rabbit froze, pretending to be a stone slightly larger and darker than the ones near the trail. A stream burbled just out of sight.

"I thought I knew exactly where that woman's body was, but now it all looks the same."

"Not here," Willa nodded after a moment. "She wasn't this close to water. And I think the trail was on a ridge of some kind."

"Yes, but which way?" Edith's words came out slow. She glanced back then rose in her stirrups to look farther ahead where the trail seemed to dip and turn into the trees. She needed to think back through the ride they had taken the year before. She couldn't remember the trail going through pines like these before they saw the woman's crudely fashioned grave, really just a hollowed trough that monsoon rains had revealed a few feet below the trail. But perhaps they had ridden through pines, perhaps after a bit the trail would circle back out of the trees.

Willa pushed Jasper past them, and Edith nudged Jesse into a jog to catch up. Once in the lead, Jasper's stride covered more ground than Jesse's, and Edith found it necessary to maintain leg pressure to keep Jesse from lagging behind. It was cooler and quieter in the woods with the horses padding along on the needle-strewn path. No rocks here. But Edith didn't have time to think about that. Once in the trees the trail dipped again sharply and soon they were crossing the creek they had heard. It was narrow and deep, more like an irrigation ditch. Jasper plunged right in and out again on the other side, Willa holding onto the saddle horn for support.

Edith felt Jesse's muscles tighten and her body prepare to jump. At the last second, Edith grabbed mane and barked a sharp "No." Jesse immediately changed her mind and slid deep into the swift water, then leaped up the opposite bank where she paused to shake herself dry, Edith still holding tight to her mane. Jasper was waiting for them a few feet away with Willa, hat pushed far back on her head, laughing. Then she pulled the bandana off her neck and held it out. Grateful, Edith used it to wipe her face dry.

"This can't be right, can it? I don't remember any of this."

"I don't remember you taking a dunking, that's true."

Edith leaned down to wipe off her boots, which were tall and tightly laced. They were both wearing outfits they bought more than ten years before from Abercrombie and Fitch, advertised as suitable for hiking and riding. They had used them all over the Southwest. Suitable, Edith grumbled to herself, but not waterproof.

"Do you want to cross the creek and go back?" Willa was still chuckling.

"No," Edith groaned, "but I have no idea where we'll end up if we go on."

"Well, then, let's find out."

—II—

Tony let out the clutch and the Cadillac jerked forward, its wheels headed down the dirt road that lead away from the pueblo toward Taos.

"Where did you see the riders, Spud?"

"They looked like they were going to Arroyo Seco. They were pretty far away." Spud pointed vaguely toward the northwest.

"Bad place to go."

"Why? What's wrong with Arroyo Seco?" John Collier obviously didn't know what to make of this hubbub about dead women and Willa Cather and Edith Lewis. "Do you think they're in danger?"

"I can't imagine they would be," Spud leaned forward to be sure Tony and John could hear him. "They're just riding pueblo ponies on pueblo land. Of course," he added, "they don't look like Pueblo Indians."

"Don't look Indian," Tony nodded, "and they are beyond pueblo land."

"How do you know?" John became almost plaintive.

"They are headed where the bodies were found," Tony glanced back toward Spud. "I think we'll go there, too."

"But if they're really in danger, shouldn't we stop by to tell Sheriff Santistivan first? Perhaps he should come with us."

"We three are strong." Tony's expression remained serene. "We don't need the sheriff."

"He has no jurisdiction here anyway," Spud raised his voice again to be sure it carried over the Cadillac's sputter.

"Not here, maybe. But in Arroyo Seco."

They passed the pueblo's San Geronimo Mission Church where three women, dark blankets draped loosely over their shoulders like shawls, dipped their heads and averted their eyes as pueblo women did. Another, wrapped in a white blanket, walked farther back along the stream that flowed through the pueblo, carrying buckets of water toward her home.

The stream, Spud knew, was a life source for the pueblo. They used its water for everything—drinking, washing, cleaning, bathing—and they had no electricity. *Primitive* is what the tourists who came to the pueblo called their way of life. Others said *traditional.* Either way, Spud mused, Tony with his Cadillac motorcar and electric lights, running water, and even a bathroom in his home, no longer fit. And his wife, the magnificent Mabel, certainly did not.

Until now Mabel's outrageous deeds had always been within the context of her own culture. But Spud knew her union with Tony was a challenge to both cultures. Tony might laugh, as he had

Taos Pueblo, 1920s

during dinner the night before, over Mabel's story about dropping into Tony's kiva at the pueblo early in their relationship because she decided he had stayed away from her too long.

But funny as her story was—she had, after all, literally "dropped in" since kivas are underground sacred ceremonial circles where men, only men, are instructed in tribal history and prepare themselves for ceremonial rituals and dances—it was also sad. After that, Tony, who had been an important drummer, singer, and spiritual leader, lost his place in the kiva and his status in the pueblo. As a member of the tribe, he still had tribal rights and a home in the pueblo where his former wife, Candelaria, lived, but Tony with Mabel was now an outsider. They both were.

—||—

Deep into the ponderosas, Willa held up her hand and signaled Edith to join her. The trail provided just enough room for Jesse to sidle alongside. In the clearing, ahead a crudely fashioned tent of canvas and ropes sagged between trees. The grass around it was thoroughly trampled and a narrow path trailed off toward a small stream, probably the same stream they had crossed earlier. Off to one side a large fire pit held chunks of burnt wood and ashes but showed no sign of flame or smoke. Several well-worn stumps circled the pit, and an ax nestled against blackened pots and utensils stacked on a large, flat rock on the other side of the pit.

"What do you think?" Willa whispered.

"I think it's time to turn around," Edith whispered back.

Neither of them moved. Jasper and Jesse seemed content for the moment to peer from a distance.

"Awfully quiet here," Willa ventured again. "Doesn't look like anyone is around."

"Can't be sure."

Jesse raised a hoof, ready to paw the ground or move on. Jasper reached over to nip her neck.

"Just take a peek?"

"I'm not at all interested in visiting with strangers," Edith offered in return. "Besides, we should be going back. They'll be wondering where we are."

"Oh, come on, a peek won't take long and it's probably just an abandoned hunting camp." Willa raised her reins and Jasper walked into the clearing.

Edith took a deep breath and let Jesse follow.

Nothing happened. No one was in the tent and aside from a few strips of venison drying into jerky on a rack behind, there were no signs that anyone would be around soon. But there were several coiled ropes and a few items of clothing strewn just inside the tent. And darkened blood, a lot of blood, stained a large stump and the ground around it at the edge of the woods on the other side of the clearing.

"Perhaps you were right," Willa finally whispered.

Jasper snorted and backed away from the stump. Willa kicked him in the ribs. Edith had no better luck with Jesse. She absolutely refused to move forward. Finally Willa allowed Jasper to turn back the way they had come. Jesse followed at a walk, but Edith noticed both horses had lengthened their strides and quickened their pace. Edith could feel the tension in Jesse's body. Was Jesse actually apprehensive, Edith wondered, or was Jesse's tension simply a reflection of her own? Either way, Edith was relieved to be following Willa and Jasper out of the clearing and she guessed Jesse was, too.

"Let's hope that whoever was there is not coming back on this trail."

"What an uncomfortable thought."

Edith reached down to pat Jesse's neck. She needed her to relax before reaching the creek where, Edith hoped, they could negotiate a smoother crossing.

—||—

Soon after they passed the pueblo mission church, Tony turned off on what looked to Spud like a simple path across the desert. Short cut. Wagon wheels, not car tires, made those tracks and their ruts didn't quite fit the width of the Cadillac's wheels. Fortunately, the monsoon rains hadn't yet made them deep or Spud guessed he'd be jostled right out of the back seat.

"There's no need to rush, is there, Tony?" John Collier gripped the edge of his seat.

Tony downshifted and the car gave an extra lurch, "Guess not. Don't know."

From his perch in the back, Spud scanned the open land before them. No sign of the women or anything else, just the usual blue-green wispy grass and occasional sage and cactus that the monsoons watered this time of year. Like everyone he knew, Spud had learned to love the monsoons that filled July afternoons in New Mexico. Most were gentle female rains, as the Pueblo Indians called them, refreshing showers that disappeared quickly after cleansing the sky and encouraging new growth in tender plants. But the monsoons could bring high winds, terrifying lightning strikes, huge balls of hail, and great rumbles of thunder. Those were the male rains, brief, heavy downpours that sometimes caused flash floods or wild fires that deepened arroyos and flattened forests.

Gentle peace or booming drama, it didn't matter, Spud loved the monsoons. Part of their charm was that they were visible from long distances, often several at the same time. Individual rainstorms dancing across the mesas and valleys, each distinct, their distant drops slanting through sunlight, rainbows glistening. There were two now behind them, hovering miles away near the Rio Grande

Gorge with Pedernal standing sentinel in the far distance beyond. Closer in, a hawk shot across the sky, two small birds in close pursuit. Must have stolen an egg or maybe a fledgling from their nest. Slim pickings when he could have grabbed a rabbit with a good deal less fuss, Spud chuckled aloud at the hawk's antics.

"Check it out, two o'clock ahead."

John's staccato words brought Spud's musing to an end. Two wisps of dust floating high in the air trailed two dots that moved with measured speed in their direction. They were still a long way away but wouldn't be for long.

"Must be them. That's about where I saw them earlier," Spud answered the unspoken question.

Tony eased up on the accelerator. No need to rush now.

—||—

"Arriving today by car. Samuel Dan, Special Agent, federal Bureau of Investigation."

Emilio's penciled note sat on top of the small stack of papers placed precisely in the center of Sheriff Santistivan's blotter. The phone call had come from Dan's secretary first thing that morning, long before the sheriff finished his fried eggs and coffee at Sadie's. Within minutes of the sheriff's arrival, a tall fellow with brown glossy hair strode through the door to the sheriff's inner office and introduced himself as Samuel Dan.

"Yes?"

"From the federal Bureau of Investigation. Albuquerque office."

"Bill Santistivan." The sheriff stood as tall as he could but watched his hand disappear into Dan's. "Haven't met anybody from the Bureau of Investigation before."

"We're fairly new, especially out here." Dan moved around to the chair reserved for visitors in front of the sheriff's desk. "My office called."

"*Sí*," Emilio burst through the door, then stopped short. His mouth open without sound, he stared up at Dan. "I mean, yes." He turned to the sheriff. "I wrote you a note."

The sheriff nodded and sank into his own comfortable chair.

"I'm here about the women." Dan folded himself onto the visitor's chair. "The three you found dead. Two without heads?"

"What about them?" The sheriff's eyes narrowed.

"We think they may have been killed by members of an international human trafficking ring. Something we're looking into."

"You are."

"Yes."

The sheriff picked up his pen and made a note on the small piece of paper Emilio had placed on top of the stack on his desk. Emilio continued to stand next to the sheriff's desk, hands slack.

"You may go back to your duties," the sheriff said without glancing up. Emilio half-bowed toward the special agent, backed to the door and closed it behind him.

Samuel Dan crossed his legs.

The sheriff leaned back in his chair and placed his fingers together as if he were about to pray. Samuel Dan was simply the biggest man the sheriff had ever seen. And he was wearing a suit with a white shirt and tie. No one in Taos wore a suit unless he was the doctor or maybe that odd English fellow, the skinny writer Tony's wife kept around for a while and then moved to a ranch near San Cristobal. Lawrence, that was his name.

After a moment, the sheriff offered, "Is there a way I can be of help?"

Samuel Dan cleared his throat. "Tell me what you know."

IV

"LADIES, LADIES. YOU must be tired. Thirsty. Hungry. You go to the big house, get burritos, no? It is late. I take care of the *caballos*."

Old José, refusing their objections, sent Willa and Edith away from the corral where he would see that Jesse and Jasper were thoroughly cooled down and brushed before turning them loose again to graze.

Edith expected as much. José did the same thing the previous summer no matter what time she rode, how many were in the party, or how long they were gone. Always, "Go to the big house, get burritos, no?" Like a refrain. But this time José was right. They were tired, thirsty, hot, dusty, and hungry. Except for a brief pause when a cloud of fast-moving dust came to a sudden halt directly in front of them and Tony's car appeared in its midst, it had been a long lope home.

When Tony, John Collier, and Spud got out of the car to greet them, Willa joked, "What is this, a search party, a posse, or are the three of you just out for a spin in soft sand?" Willa and Edith had many more questions for the men than they had for the two of them. Tony assured them that they had been travelling in the right direction but must have turned off to the northeast too soon. He knew nothing about a hunting camp in the pines but reminded them that anything beyond the stream would not be on pueblo land. He would have no reason to know about the camp unless its hunters poached deer or elk on pueblo land. And he had not heard of any poaching in that area. Tomorrow afternoon, he promised, he would drive them in his car to locate the makeshift graves. Right now, he told them, he was on his way with John and Spud to see what more they could learn from the sheriff.

"If there is anything more to learn," Spud frowned and they left.

Edith knew her smile had been grim in response, but Jesse didn't seem to notice any change in her rider and was anxious to start moving again. They waited until the car turned around and took its dust cloud with it. By the time they were ready to leave, Jesse had pawed a hole in the road deep enough to hold a small boulder, but Jesse and Jasper settled quickly into a comfortable lope and didn't slow until they reached their home corral. They, too, were thirsty and hungry and dripping with sweat. Women are supposed to glisten, Edith smiled to herself, but horses can go right ahead and sweat and then roll in the dirt to dry off. The thought amused her.

"Let's get cleaned up and find those burritos," Willa strode on ahead, fanning her face with her hat. Edith did the same while Charlie, Mabel's favorite among the household dogs, fell into step with Edith. Pueblo dogs all look alike, Edith paused for a moment to pet Charlie. His features seemed more heeler than the others and he panted as though he, too, had been with them on the long ride home. Their wide-brimmed hats and the constant breeze across the sage had kept them only relatively cool. They had expected to be done with their ride while it was still morning, but it was well after one o'clock when they reached the pink adobe. Just in time for a burrito in the kitchen of the main house and, Edith guessed, a relaxing *siesta* in the cool of their little house where they would talk over their morning's adventure and then, perhaps, read.

They usually did read in the afternoon, especially when Willa had manuscript pages or galleys to review. Then sometimes silently, sometimes out loud, they would read to each other and make notes of corrections or changes. That's how they had spent most of their time at Alcalde the summer before, working on the galleys of *The Professor's House.*

Now they were rereading Prescott's history of Mexico to be sure of dates and other particulars about the historical figures and places Willa thought she might include in what they were calling "the story of her priests." Edith made notes in her line-a-day journal, the same journal Willa sometimes used to sketch out a scene or two, though she would hold off doing more serious, sustained writing until she had a quiet month alone, as planned—after Edith left for New York and before Willa was to join her family in Denver—and even longer writing periods in their cottage on Grand Manan or in New Hampshire where Willa often spent the month of October at her favorite inn.

Not many places were peaceful enough to give Willa the kind of imaginative space she needed to write, and now that construction for a new subway meant that they would have to give up their quiet apartment in Greenwich Village, Willa was increasingly desperate to find such places. The previous summer they had been hopeful about Santa Fe and Alcalde, but neither provided quite the magic Willa needed for writing. Santa Fe fairly bustled with tourists, and the fact that they met interesting people and had friends in both places meant that Willa could never fully focus on her priests.

Taos proved perfect for both of them. Old friends of Edith's from Washington Square days, Ernst Blumenshein and Bert Phillips, were among the artists who settled in Taos years before Mabel. Edith was excited about how they had created community, a colony of artists, to publicize their work for an art market in New York that was unaware of the beauty of the Southwest. Serious artists, they were also serious about the business of art. And while they gave each other encouragement, they also gave each other space and welcomed the newcomers Mabel imported, like Andrew Dasburg and Nicolai Fechin. Nothing could have pleased Edith more or provided better working conditions for Willa. Here was a chance for Edith to sketch and paint with some of the most innovative and interesting artists in the country while Willa could focus entirely on her priests.

And the story of Willa's priests required her full attention. Willa determined from the outset this novel would be serene and simple on the surface. Below the surface, however, would stir a quiet but constant activity, an elemental journey through opposition — multiple levels of opposition in times, places, beliefs, cultures, natural elements, peoples, the forces of good and evil — a quiet turbulence that resolves itself not by overcoming or conquest but by yielding and accepting, by interfusing one into all.

Edith glanced at Willa, comfortable on the day bed next to the fireplace, a blanket tucked around her legs, a book lying open on her lap. The morning's ride had been long and the burrito filling. It would be only a minute before Willa slipped into sleep. Edith yawned.

They had eaten their burritos at a small table in the kitchen of the main house, enjoying savory odors from slow-cooked chili and beans and the quiet voices of Amelia and her young assistant cook as they moved about preparing for the next meal. The room was comforting and cool with doors and windows open to let in a breeze. The ride had tired them and so had the tension they felt at the hunter's camp.

"That place is somehow evil, don't you think?"

"Frightened me. Jesse, too," Edith responded without thinking.

"Almost elemental, that fear." Willa rose to refill her glass from a pitcher of fresh water on the counter. "I felt the same sort of stirrings when we were in the ceremonial cave Tony took us to last summer, though there were no outward signs of violence there."

"I did too," Edith watched Willa turn back toward the table with the glass of fresh water, but her mind was filled with their first sight of the cave, water spilling over ledges from above, hiding its dark recesses. A beautiful woodland scene as she remembered it, a deep ravine with a waterfall creating a blue pool that opened into a stream lined with cottonwoods and small pines, the sound of its water lively and inviting.

Once inside the cave, however, the light had dimmed and it took them a few minutes to see where they were. The cave was big but not huge, its sides, mostly dirt with a couple outcroppings of boulders, held small recesses that led nowhere in particular. The floor was firm, its dirt presumably hardened by feet following rhythms from ceremonial drums. Scattered ashes lined a fire pit. Nothing dramatic, really, but they both had shivered. The joyous music of the waterfall seemed to come from a great distance, their whispers were muffled, and they felt rather than heard distant stirrings, a subdued rattle, and then silence.

"Elemental fear, yes. I felt it, too." Edith rose to fill her own glass with fresh water. It was important to stay hydrated at this altitude. "That cave chilled me to the bone."

When Edith sat down again, Willa's mood had lifted. She chuckled. "That fear stayed with me until Tony's car fell into the ditch."

"What heroic effort that took!" Edith giggled in response. "A long walk to lord-knows-where and then four men and a horse to dislodge the car from the ditch."

"See," Willa said, still grinning as she pushed back from the table, "this morning's find was nothing by comparison. Nothing at all."

That conversation had eased their minds and now Willa was on the little daybed in their pink adobe, sighing in her sleep. Edith smiled at the open book rising and falling on Willa's lap. She closed the volume of Prescott she had been trying to read and reached down to cover her legs, resting now on the hassock, with a light throw they had found in the blanket chest. It had repeated zigzags and squares in multiple colors of earthen-dyed wool. She traced its pattern with the tips of her fingers. Its weave was nubby and soft. She particularly loved the browns and reds that lined and filled its squares.

Edith was tired but not yet sleepy. Good time to think through the topic they had discussed over breakfast early that morning. It was not their first discussion on the subject. More like the umpteenth. For the last year or so, they had been thinking aloud together about how Willa could structure her new narrative like a saint's legend, informed not by phallic ideals but by the archetypal Feminine Principle.

Willa wanted her priests to reflect universal mankind in a kind of updated and warmly human *Pilgrim's Progress*. Edith's college roommate, Achsah Brewster, well known in Europe for her religious murals, had achieved something very like that on canvas and masonry. But for Willa the question was which symbols, whose journeys, what archetypes, and which historical events she might draw from. There were so many. Willa had to be careful in the choosing.

One of the difficulties, they knew, was that readers had been inundated for so long with sensationalized tales of heroic action they would be slow to catch references to classical goddesses or serpent legends or the concept of compassion as an act of heroism. Zane Grey, that's what they expected in a novel about the West. Or anywhere, Willa had laughed. Not a couple of priests on a pair of white mules wandering around the desert. What readers knew beforehand about archetypes or the Feminine Principle might deepen their response to Willa's narrative, Edith knew, but the challenge Willa had set for herself was how to create meaning through a kind of elemental emotion. How to help readers grasp meaning without knowing what they understood. It would be a kind of felt knowledge.

Willa and Edith had talked evening after evening the year before with Mabel and the others around her table. Mabel, who had been in analysis for years, relied heavily on Freud but found Jung's theories intriguing, especially his interest in Indian traditions and archetypal patterns. Mabel knew a great deal about Jung even before he visited New Mexico and interviewed people at the Taos Pueblo the winter before Willa and Edith first stayed in the pink adobe.

And Mary Foote, the young painter who had been at *Los Gallos* the previous July and ridden with Edith almost every morning while Willa worked, was so interested in Jung's ideas she planned to travel to Switzerland in order to become his student and translate the concepts in his seminars for an American audience. By the time their daily rides ended each morning, Edith was eager to discuss Jung's concepts with Willa. It was fascinating, they thought, that Jung's ideas about archetypes were reflected in work Willa had already done. Clearly he was on to something. Or Willa was.

—ıı—

A bolt of lightning jerked Adam upright. He must have dozed off. His sketch pad slid to the floor with a thunk. Thunder followed almost instantaneously and the sound of wind thrashing nearby trees. The storm must be directly overhead.

"Maria!" he shouted. Adam had never called out her name before. He had always spoken it softly, gently, so as not to frighten her. But now with rain battering the roof and sliding down the windowpane facing her cabin, he sensed a sudden danger. A fear, not of her but for her. She had gone off alone, he remembered, to pick raspberries, had motioned with her empty bucket toward the bushes a hundred yards or so below the porch. How long ago? He didn't know. Minutes maybe. He had dozed off, he didn't know for how long, but he had seen no sign of rain when she left. Of course, monsoons could blow in quickly. The cabin faced southeast. Storms here usually blew in from the southwest. Adam had never known a place with such unpredictable weather. He had been surprised more than once by clouds scudding from nowhere to hide the sun.

"Maria!" He shoved open the porch door and shouted again. "Maria!"

The wind was so fierce, he had to brace the door open with his shoulder. He felt certain his shouts were ineffective, like whistling in the wind. With the roar of rain on the roof, Maria wouldn't hear him even if she were safely back in her own cabin. But he couldn't stop. He stepped onto the porch. "Maria!" he tried again. A huge bolt of lightning answered, the streak and sound coming together. Deafening.

"Damn!" A gust of wind knocked him against the porch door. Cold rain soaked through his pants below the knee. "Maria!" he shouted again. Where had she gone? Trees whipsawed against the side of the cabin, slashing back and forth, back and forth. Such violence. Trees could draw lightning or crack and come down. Maria wouldn't know what hit her. She had just meant to gather a few berries. "Maria!"

No answer. And then nothing. Nothing. No wind, no rain, no sound. The storm had blown itself out as suddenly as it had blown in. It was over. A rivulet of drips from the roof padded quietly against the grass below.

"Maria!" Adam renewed his efforts.

"*Sí, Señor* Adam. *Aqui estoy.*"

Maria's words reached Adam before he could see her, soaked to the skin, where she burst out from the woods below. She ran swiftly toward him, the bucket in her right hand heaped with berries. And then she was there on the porch and he was taking the bucket from her and telling her to go to her cabin and get dry. It was over, the crisis.

But it was no crisis after all. Maria had known to crouch away from her bucket and the flailing trees, to make herself small and safe from lightning. A survivor, Adam nodded to nothing in particular. He set the bucket on the kitchen table and prepared to heat water for tea while he changed into dry trousers. He could use something hot. And he expected Maria could, too.

If only she knew English or he knew more Spanish, Adam found himself wishing as he had how many times now? At least she had grown to trust him enough to speak a few words, the sort of words he knew, like *sí* and *aqui.* Mostly they communicated by gesturing or pointing, an awkward but effective kind of sign language. He often heard her hum and occasionally she sang quietly to herself. Happy-sounding songs from what he could tell. In fact, she seemed happy now. How quickly she had come back to life.

Were all women so capable of self-preservation, Adam wondered. He guessed not. Some seemed to crumple at the smallest slight. But those, he imagined, had experienced only small slights, handed out by men — and women — who thought of women as lesser beings. *Misogynists* some called them, the sort who for so long had refused women in America the right to vote. Perhaps they were misogynists, but they did not actively hate women, Adam thought, they simply held on to ignorant and old-fashioned views that demeaned and distrusted women.

Maria was different. Adam guessed few women had ever been treated as badly as she. She had run into a deep-seated hatred by a man who treated her as if she were chattel, something not human, something he could beat and barter like the lowest form of life. Adam could not imagine what Maria had been through. He still knew nothing about her, her past, her present, what she had been doing with that horror of a man who called himself Blade, or what she had survived before Adam happened along to free her.

Had he been Maria, Adam guessed, he could never have survived such violence as well. Blade had beaten her into submission. Submission would have thrown Adam into a state of depression. But submission, Adam realized, could do that only to someone who thought they were in control, in the right, equal, the same as others. Somehow Maria had survived despite all that Blade had forced her into and shown no sign of defeat or self-pity. Adam found that admirable. He wished he could tell her that, but all he could do at the moment was offer her a cup of hot tea.

—||—

Edith heard a light pitter-patter of raindrops on the roof. A female shower on the way, she thought, pleased with the way Pueblo Indians chose to identify gentleness as female. An essential, archetypal gentleness that nourishes and creates growth. Jung was certainly onto something there, Edith decided, and turned back to considering the differences between Jung and Freud.

Freud's preoccupation with sex and malaise had interested Edith and Willa enough for Willa to decide to portray the depths of depression and mental breakdown in her main character, Professor Godfrey St. Peter, in *The Professor's House*, the novel she and Edith had been proofreading in Alcalde the previous summer. But to depict the professor's condition, Jungian concepts had proven more useful. Like earlier doctors who labeled such depressions *neurasthenia*, Freud considered the individual and his unconscious solely responsible for his own condition. Jung, on the other hand, saw an individual's situation as reflective of a universal archetypal experience. For Jung a cure required something different and more than individual analysis. Cures involved an epiphany leading to a recognition and acceptance of one's place in the universe.

When she thought about it now, Edith realized that she and Willa had both witnessed breakdowns similar to the professor's. Isabelle McClung's father and Sam McClure, the publisher of *McClure's Magazine,* for whom Willa and Edith had both worked, had each been diagnosed with *neurasthenia*. Judge McClung's case was so severe that in 1908 he had had to resign his position with the court.

That happened two years after Willa left the McClung household and moved to New York, but Willa visited the McClungs often and actually spent part of the summer of 1908 abroad with Isabelle, just before moving into a new apartment in Greenwich Village with Edith. Because of the judge, Willa knew intimately the effects of *neurasthenia*, and she cast the professor's breakdown as a kind of internal lament for a world split in two, when romance and the certainty the professor felt before the Great War gave way in its aftermath to a profound sense of loss, a loss of love and belief.

Edith was pretty sure not only Willa but many others empathized with the professor's lament. After all Mabel was in Taos because she felt the world, having been violently severed from its past, made a wrong turn after the Great War. Once she found Taos and Tony in 1917, she wanted nothing to do with the masquerade of modern commercialism. This post-war world, Mabel declared, was not a fair and proper exchange for tradition and the certainty about universal truths that it replaced. In that sense, Mabel, Edith, and certainly Willa, empathetically understood the professor's breakdown.

To dramatize the professor's breakdown, Willa chose to interrupt her novel's conventional plot with a completely different story and character, a young man named Tom Outland. Then she made Outland's pre-war discovery of prehistoric ruins in the Southwest and his response to it as a lost civilization echo the professor's post-war realization that while loss is devastating, life goes on—if differently.

Edith thought it a brilliant strategy. Over several weeks Willa worked hard to adapt and integrate a short story she had written several years earlier about Outland's discovery of Mesa Verde. Outland would provide a counterbalance for the professor and Outland's death in the Great War a reason for the professor's malaise. In the depths of depression, Willa's professor is solipsistic, self-indulgent, and self-centered. He rises out of himself finally when he symbolically dies and rises again after gaining perspective and a stoic affirmation of his faith in life.

Of course, Willa being Willa, the professor's resolution was destined to be complicated and ironic, not romantic or heroic. Her professor's epiphany might involve such lofty Biblical archetypes as Eve and Mary, but Willa brought his experience down to earth by using a mummy to represent Eve and a dressmaker's dummy to represent Mary. Irony, Edith smiled at Willa, still slumbering on the daybed next to her chair. Irony and Willa's wonderfully sly sense of humor.

—||—

"Give me a hand here, will you?" John Collier squatted awkwardly next to the right rear tire and fitted the jack into place. He pulled his handkerchief from his pants pocket and wiped his forehead, which glistened with sweat.

"Just as soon as I block this wheel," Spud grunted. When he finished wedging a rock against the right tire, he rose and stretched as tall as he could. His back hurt. With Tony driving as fast as he could, Spud had been bounced several times almost out of the car.

"Good job," Tony cheered from the driver's seat.

Collier paused and glanced up. "You do have the brake set, don't you?"

Tony nodded, looking serene and regal with a shawl-like white blanket draped loosely over his shoulders. He set the brake.

Collier bent back to the jack handle and pumped several times before pausing to catch his breath and wipe his forehead again. "This heat is going to kill us if the sand doesn't choke us first."

"Could, but I doubt it." Spud made his way around the car to spell Collier. "Still adjusting to the sun and altitude, I see. You'll get used to it soon enough."

Distant thunder rumbled. Spud glanced toward the mountains before dropping to his knees for his turn at the jack.

"Rain would be nice. Cool us off." Collier stood and brushed sand off his knees.

"Not here yet. At San Cristobal," Tony pointed.

Near San Cristobal, the Lawrence ranch, and Adam. Spud glanced again at the mountains. The clouds there belched blackness with streaks of light. The whole sky boomed after each streak. Spud could imagine the downpour, wind shifting, churning trees, all directions at once. Adam can handle it, Spud decided. He's young but resourceful. Spud felt a smile form. Good painter, too. His smile grew. Once all this business about headless corpses and uncooperative sheriffs was over, he would look forward to a visit to the Lawrence ranch. Even before it was all over, he corrected himself. Edith Lewis said something to Mabel at dinner about visiting the ranch. He would make sure he could tag along. It was after all his friend who was looking after the place.

"That does it," Collier handed Spud a fresh tire. "You can put a tire on, can't you, my man?" Collier shook out his handkerchief and refolded it before stuffing it back in his pocket. He turned to Tony and glanced at the sky. "So odd how it rains here, a little here, a little there. Should be able to get to the sheriff's office before we get wet, don't you think?"

V

THE SOOTHING SOUND of light rain continued to fill the room where Willa slept and Edith nodded in thought. She found herself smiling. Willa's professor and now her priests. One never really knows where the impetus for a story begins, but Edith guessed Willa chose to tell the story of her priests because they endured a loss similar to the professor's, leaving their European old world in exchange for the New World. But their loss is different, the journey between old and new more definitive and deliberate, and the resolution, the final letting go, more joyous than stoic.

Everything Willa and Edith found at the historical library in Santa Fe and elsewhere—Machebeuf's autobiography, correspondence by Lamy with his sister in France, and many, many historical accounts—gave them all the details Willa needed. But how to tell the story, that was the issue. Edith was well aware that Willa wanted never to repeat herself. Willa loved to strike out into new territory, to experiment, and to create meaning through unexpected turns in structure or character.

In an especially silly moment, Willa declared that her *familiar spirit* was a wild turkey, a wily old bird that forsakes her feeding ground at the first sign of human footprints. Edith had laughed heartily when Willa gobbled loudly, flapped her elbows, pranced out of the room, and peeked back as if she wanted to be sure she wasn't followed. Trampled ground was not for her. Others could use conventional plots and characters. She would not. From then on if her disappearances were cloaked in decorum, they would still be disappearances. Critics and gushers would simply have to learn not to assume or anticipate what she might do. She would stay wild and free.

Edith chuckled again at the thought. Willa made a huge leap from the norm in the way she structured the story of her professor. She would jump even farther with the story of her priests, but the leap would be subtle and she would draw little attention to technique or herself. Willa may shun trampled ground, but she would never ignore tradition or the past. In fact she would choose to do exactly the opposite. She would tell the story of her priests the way the Catholic church depicted the lives of saints and martyrs through many centuries—appealing to senses and emotion, not knowledge or fact. Church missionaries consistently recast pagan myths and rituals as their own and appealed to parishioners through incense and art—music, paintings, carvings, rood screens, statuary, architecture. Worshipers who could never be expected to understand Latin would grasp meaning through their emotional response.

Willa would do the same. Plot, action, even accuracy didn't matter. Just as the church had done, Willa would fill the most static of religious forms, a saint's legend, with color, motion, rituals, scenes, images, symbols, and archetypes from all cultures and times. And just as the church had its converts, Willa would lead her priests and her readers to a similar kind of felt knowledge—a fusion of old with new, earth with sky, and life with death.

Readers might not understand Willa's experiment. In fact, Edith was pretty certain many wouldn't. Any more than critics understood modern paintings after the Armory Show. They simply accused Cubists like Andrew Dasburg of not knowing how to draw. Some might not even recognize Willa's novel as an experiment. Or as a novel.

Others might think she had lost her literary way or converted to Catholicism or was delving in mysticism. Certainly some, especially men, failed to grasp what Willa was doing linking her hero with Parsifal in *One of Ours*. Or rather, they failed to comprehend how Willa's Parsifal could be heroic. He remained much too sweet and inexperienced. Of course, those who did understand awarded *One of Ours* the Pulitzer Prize. Those who didn't attacked Willa for daring to portray a soldier in battle, a subject they declared no woman ever could or should know anything about.

Their attacks did not deter Willa, and Edith had cheered her on. After all, Willa had always countered romantic notions and played with literary references and nods to classical gods and goddesses. Just hints along the way, nothing too consistent or strikingly parallel. As she said to Edith at the time, she was not interested in rewriting Sophocles or Shakespeare or even church doctrine in modern dress. Her work should stand on its own. But of course she wanted it to last as long as Sophocles and continue to make meaning in new times. They both did.

Edith found herself suddenly wakened. The Prescott had slipped from her lap and made a loud clap on the floor, its pages closed. Raindrops still spattered on the roof. Monsoon, of course, female. How odd, she thought, the way male and female monsoons exist together, different rain falling at the same time, often in close proximity. Male, female, different but rain all the same.

Edith yawned. She hadn't realized she had nodded off. Willa's eyes were open, too. She looked startled but said nothing and her eyelids fell shut again. Edith glanced at her watch. Such woolgathering, she chuckled. The only real issue they had to deal with now was what to wear for the next meal. How lovely to do nothing productive and have no deadlines at all. Vacation. Edith let the word float in her mind until it flooded her consciousness. Then her eyelids fell shut again, too.

—II—

Spud felt a few raindrops when Tony opened the door to the sheriff's office and stepped back to let Spud and John Collier enter first. Tony had said little since they caught up with Willa and Edith. But then Tony usually said little. One could never tell what Tony was thinking or even whether he was thinking. Spud couldn't at any rate.

Tony was impressive, always neatly dressed and pleasant to be around. When loose, his shiny black hair fell to his waist, but he usually wore it in braids brightly decorated with colorful ribbons that draped down the front of his shirt. He had a special smell, a sweet smell Spud guessed might have something to do with the herbs and grasses in his medicine pouch. It was an odor Spud identified only with Tony. Mabel placed tiny bowls of cinnamon throughout the house to fill it with scent and chase away mice. But Tony's scent was entirely his own, and he always wore a little smile on his lips. His eyes reflected the same gentle kindness. But Tony rarely spoke or looked at anyone directly, not at Spud anyway. Inscrutable is a real word, Spud decided. Not a negative word, Tony was always pleasant, but a meaningful one.

"Sheriff's not available." Emilio glanced at the three of them when the door closed behind Tony.

"We'll wait," John lowered his body into one of the wooden chairs near the door. Spud did the same. Tony stood, his body lax and still. He seemed to Spud the model of patience.

Emilio shuffled papers from one side of his desk to the other. The process looked random.

John stirred in his chair and cleared his throat.

"What you want?" Emilio directed the question to Tony. Tony nodded toward John.

"We came to find out about the women who were discovered

near Arroyo Seco. The ones," John paused to clear his throat again, "with the missing heads."

"Nothing to know."

"Come, now, from what Spud here says the sheriff has had a month to investigate. Isn't that true?"

"Sí." Emilio opened the center drawer of his desk and took out a newly sharpened pencil. It was yellow and had a much-used eraser on the end. Spud could just make out the words Eberhart Faber on its side, the same brand he used. Emilio placed it next to the stack of papers to the right of his blotter. He glanced again at John and repeated, "Nothing to know."

"Well, is the sheriff in?"

"Sí."

"Then we'll wait."

The clock on the wall behind Emilio's head said 2:45. Its minute hand clicked. Spud began to anticipate its clicks. He let his index finger match the clock's movement, tapping on the arm of his chair. John crossed his right leg over his left. Spud did the same. Emilio picked up his pencil and put it down. Spud decided to try a little two-finger syncopation.

At 3:05 the sheriff's office door opened and an unusually tall man came out. He was wearing a suit. The sheriff was still talking behind him, so the man was half turned away from Emilio and the three men arranged against the wall in the outer office.

"That's really as far as we have gotten," the sheriff was saying. "You seem to know more than we do."

"I was hoping for more," the man cleared his throat. "A lot more."

"Excuse me," John rose, addressing the stranger and the sheriff at the same time.

"Oh," the sheriff said.

"Yes?" the tall man said at the same time. His eyes took in the three of them. "What is it?"

"We came to find out what you have learned about the three women who were found near Arroyo Seco, one last year and two last month."

"Three?" The tall man glanced at the sheriff. "Arroyo Seco?"

"Arroyo Seco, yes," the sheriff offered with a nod. He glared at John. "Why?"

"Well," John paused to gather his thoughts. "The women who found the first body last summer have returned and want to know what is happening. They were shocked to learn that two more bodies have been found and no one has been arrested for any of the murders." John's voice gained strength. He turned to the sheriff, "Just what have you found out about all this?"

"Details of such investigations are always confidential," the sheriff announced, his lips pursed.

Pink Adobe Porch

Spud found himself having to exercise control over his own lips. He wanted to guffaw but caught himself because there was really nothing funny about this conversation.

"Excuse me," the tall man interjected. "I am Samuel Dan of the federal Bureau of Investigation, Albuquerque office. I'm here to investigate those murders." He turned to John, "And you are?"

—II—

"Sorry to interrupt, Miss Lewis," Long John Dunn paused to scrape his boots back and forth across the doormat, two steps below the actual sill. The rain had stopped, but his boots still carried a bit of wet sand from the path. "I know it's growing late, but I thought I should stop by." His smile was polite and the stub of his cigar, almost hidden by his mustache, firmly clamped between his teeth.

"No interruption at all, Mr. Dunn. Miss Cather and I just spent the afternoon reading and dozing. Delicious, napping in the rain."

John Dunn's *yes* was a little uncertain and Edith realized he probably never took naps. For the first time Edith found herself looking directly into John Dunn's steel-blue eyes. Kindly eyes, Edith judged, but with depths reflecting more sorts of experience than she could quite believe possible for one man. Unladylike, her mother's voice echoed from the past and immediately she dropped her gaze. John Dunn didn't seem to notice.

A rustler, Mabel had assured them the previous summer on a drive toward Llano to look at property she wanted them to buy. A gambler and a desperado. Years ago when he was a young Texan, Mabel said, John Dunn shot a man to death and then ran until he got lucky with cards and finally made his way to New Mexico. He's been sort of honest since, Mabel shrugged. Once he reached Taos he started a livery stable, bought a stagecoach, and began hauling people and mail from the train at Tres Piedras. Wasn't long before he bought the first car in Taos and upgraded his service.

Of course, Mabel said, he's always made quite a lot of money on the side with gambling. The word is nobody can beat him at blackjack. And nobody knows how many casinos he owns. All around here. Red River, Elizabethtown, even Embudo. Partners with Al Capone, according to the rumors. Capone? Willa and Edith echoed each other's question. Al Capone, that's right, Mabel had nodded. He's supposed to be hiding out all around here. Anyway, whenever someone raises questions, John Dunn just closes his casino and opens a new one. The rumors may be wrong about Capone, but they are certain about John Dunn, Mabel grinned. That was one of his casinos a few years ago, she pointed to an abandoned adobe set back from the road. Now he's sort of honest and sort of rich. Better than most in Taos. Successful, you know. Mabel's rich laugh had ended her story.

Edith marveled that Mabel felt comfortable in such a world. But then, Edith did, too. So comfortable she and Willa had actually been serious the previous summer about buying a house. Just a little adobe to use in the summers, Willa had imagined aloud. Five rooms, dirt floor, no electricity or plumbing. Nothing to take care of, really. Simple and quiet with beautiful surroundings and a few friends nearby. The sort of place they both loved.

Taos still appealed to them, but this summer they felt less need. They were building just such a place on Grand Manan, the island in the Bay of Fundy where they had spent several weeks during each of the last four summers. Like Taos, the island was hard to reach. A world set apart. Away from the modern whirl insatiable in its appetite for everything noisy and new. But it was no longer clear, at least not to Willa and Edith, just how long Taos would remain a world away, not with Al Capone hiding out in the area and Fred Harvey's touring cars carrying daily loads of easterners to see pueblos, Taos first among them.

Mabel had found Taos in 1917, during the Great War. They

found Grand Manan in 1922, and as soon as the opportunity came up to build their own cottage they leapt at it. Only a few miles off the coast of Maine, they would be Americans with a Canadian cottage, not expatriates abroad like so many of the artists and writers they knew. They wanted to remain in America, to feel the pulse of their home country.

But like their friends, they also felt a need for distance from an America gone mad with Progress. It was, as Mabel said, like the world broke in two. The idyllic past had disappeared and no one knew quite how to be in the aftermath of war. America was all hustle and chaos. Everything had to be new and different and modern. It was difficult to find one's footing in such an atmosphere, especially for creative artists and writers. Perspective, Willa and Edith agreed with Mabel, that's what they needed. Distance bred perspective. The quiet of a world set apart, a world anchored in the traditions of pueblos and Hispanic households, would provide an opportunity to think and create. If only it would stay that way.

"These just came in the post for you and Miss Cather," John Dunn offered Edith a package containing books and a separate envelope with *J. Walter Thompson Advertising Agency* scrawled across the dotted lines intended for the return address. Its color and shape told Edith it contained the mock-up of a design she had been working on for Kodak and left for the editorial team to finalize in her absence. It pleased her that they were far enough along to send it to her for approval, but that also meant they were getting anxious for her return.

"Thank you, Mr. Dunn," Edith accepted the packages and stepped with them onto the *portal*. She wasn't quite ready for him to leave. "May I offer you a glass of water or some other refreshment?"

John Dunn removed his Stetson and backed to the edge of the porch before making a half bow, "Why, thank you, ma'am, no."

"Well," Edith felt her face coloring a little. "Would you mind if I asked you a few questions? About the murdered women."

"The murdered women? Oh, I know who you mean. Yes?"

John Dunn's *yes* was almost as drawn out and filled with syllables as his *yep*. Edith waited. If he was really the desperado Mabel claimed, he might very well have picked up information no one else could, least of all the sheriff.

"Yes," he repeated. His eyes looked thoughtful now. "The sheriff said the two of you might be asking around about them. Murders," he repeated after a pause. "Don't know much about them. Nothing really," he shook his head. "And anyway, you ladies don't need to get involved in all that. Not a right thing for ladies to get involved in," he shook his head again and replaced his Stetson.

"Well," Edith found it hard to continue. "Would you ask around to see if you know anybody who does know something? You know so many people we have no way of meeting. And I'd like to find out what I can. To be helpful, you understand."

—ıı—

"The sheriff was unbelievably difficult today," Spud addressed the diners assembled around Mabel's table that evening.

"So we heard," Mabel glanced at Tony, who smiled in agreement. They were again a matched pair, Mabel in blue satin, Tony with blue ribbons woven through his shiny black braids. "So we heard," she repeated.

"Difficult?" The question came from Nicolai Fechin, who ended a whispered conversation with Willa to ask it.

"Why difficult?"

"I'm not really sure."

Spud had been thinking about exactly that all afternoon. He didn't know Santistivan well. Hardly at all, really. But he had never seen him be so opaque. It was almost as though, Spud thought, the sheriff didn't want to have anything to do with those murders. And didn't want anyone else to have anything to do with them either. Certainly not John or Tony or Spud. Maybe not that special agent fellow either.

"Well, Nicolai, you can ask the man from the Bureau of Investigation the very same question tomorrow evening, if you like. Maybe he can give you an answer."

Mabel's words entered Spud's consciousness one at a time, slowly, as if he were hearing her under water.

"Tomorrow?"

"Tomorrow," Mabel assured everyone at the table. "When Tony told me what happened at the sheriff's office, I put a call into the Bureau of Investigation's Albuquerque office and invited their agent to stay here and take an occasional meal with us. They relayed the message to him and he accepted. He will be here sometime in the afternoon." Mabel said it as though it was the most natural thing in the world for an unknown special agent to join them at *Los Gallos*.

Tomorrow. Spud cut into one of the tomatoes nestled between the baked potato and large slice of roast beef that covered his plate. He had become a regular guest for evening meals at *Los Gallos* since Mabel took him on as her assistant. He thought of it as an unofficial part of his salary and he loved it. Not for the food so much as for the people, the conversation, and the constant intrigue.

Mabel was well known for arranging surprises, sometimes malicious, and for doing the unusual, whatever the *un*usual might be. Here were all in one. A special agent who was bound to have interesting things to say, a murder investigation, and Mabel's happy upending of the sheriff's recalcitrance.

Three murders, a special agent, and a sheriff who plays dumb. Spud couldn't help his grin. What fodder for a satiric piece in his

Laughing Horse magazine. He couldn't wait to begin. Of course, he caught himself, he would need to get the necessary facts first. What luck to have the special agent right here.

"Do you think this agent might need some assistance?" Spud ventured.

"What a good idea," Willa's delight and raised fork added force to her words.

"When you have the time free, I suppose he might, Spud." Mabel's reminder was less than subtle, but Spud knew Mabel would make up excuses to encourage his taking the time for adventures with the special agent. Spud would be the best conduit to information she could possibly arrange.

VI

THE SUN WAS high in a cloudless sky when Tony set the picnic basket in the trunk and ushered Willa and Edith into the back seat. Spud, whom Edith guessed was at least as curious as they were to see the haphazard graves where the women's bodies had been dumped, joined Tony in front.

Already Edith could see one small white puff hovering over Pedernal, a good fifty miles or more south and west of Taos. Clouds would begin to build soon with moisture from the Gulf of Mexico pushing north to bring the usual afternoon monsoon at this time of year.

Well, Edith thought, a little rain never hurt anyone and Tony would carry a tarpaulin to attach to the side of the car if they needed cover. They were late getting started because Mabel had invited them to her room for a second cup of coffee and then Willa, as promised, spent an hour with Nicolai Fechin to compare schedules and make plans for his portrait of her. His idea was to sketch Willa while they were in Taos and then arrange for additional sittings in New York to paint the full portrait.

"What a glorious day for a drive," Spud gushed from the front seat.

Willa opened her window. Edith followed suit. The breeze would feel good. Tony pulled out the choke and pushed the starter. The engine caught immediately. What a blessing to have electric starters. Turning a crank made starting cars both difficult and dangerous. Edith was glad neither she nor Willa ever had to learn to drive. They walked or used public transportation to get around New York

City and took trains everywhere else. Yellow cabs had been available in the City for almost twenty years, but they rarely chose to use them. They were skeptical, too, of Fred Harvey's new Indian Detour campaign to draw people off trains and into his Harvey Hotels. In spite of difficult roads, Harvey Indian Detours were popular. Worse, they had learned from Mabel, Taos Pueblo was already a favorite destination.

Cars are not safe, Willa had declared, with a statement that covered all New York cabs and Harvey Indian Detours. Especially unsafe, Edith thought to herself, with drivers like Tony who drove wherever he wanted regardless of whether there was an actual road. Tony also drove as fast as he could. But in a place like Taos, Tony and his car were gold. He was a wonderful guide. He had so much personal knowledge about the mix of people and their rich history in northern New Mexico. Without Tony they never could have reached the places he took them. And, Edith finished her rambling thought, his passengers usually arrived where and when they intended without injury. She smiled. At least the two of them had experienced only mud and inconvenience when Tony's car fell into a ditch near the ceremonial cave the previous summer.

Tony was clearly never timid about driving. Monsoons made no difference to him, even when the roads turned into deep slurry and threatened to carry the car into an embankment or slide it off into a ditch. Not everyone was like Tony, of course. They had had to wait for two and a half days at the Laguna Pueblo before anyone dared to take them to Acoma less than twenty miles away.

Caliche clay, the driver explained. Too slick, too sticky, too dangerous. He was right, of course. It rained hard for several afternoons in a row, and flash floods destroyed roads and cut new channels through arroyos. Even Tony might have delayed that trip. Caliche, sand, and rock seemed to be the only footing for roadbeds in New Mexico, and all three could prove dangerous. But no matter what was happening, Edith knew that when Tony took the wheel he would remain unperturbed and even serene. Tony loved his car and nothing pleased him more than an expedition. And a picnic. Without a picnic, this trip would be much too somber.

—||—

Adam set his easel under the canopy of the giant pine tree in front of Lawrence's cabin. Sun filled the valley below but he stood in shade. The tree was so huge nothing else dared grow there. He dipped the tip of his brush in linseed oil and swished it in quick little circles on his pallet to lighten the shade of green he meant to use next.

He no longer had to think about what he was doing with his hands or brushes, but landscapes always posed a puzzle. How to get the suggestion of detail and movement and depth in a painting that contained no tangible images and whose surface simply covered a flat board. Some days he wished he had been born a century earlier and could be content with capturing exactly the scene in front of him. But then he would just have had different problems to solve. There were always problems and he enjoyed his experiments, turning colors and shapes into images that were just suggestive, nothing concrete.

The sounds at his back were pleasant, Maria sweeping the porch and singing softly. So delightful after yesterday's fright. Maria didn't mean to be heard, and he couldn't understand her words anyway. A lullaby? Perhaps. Had she a child somewhere? A husband? Family?

He knew nothing about her. Not where she came from, how she got there, or who the brute was that brought her. Good riddance to him. Nothing had given Adam greater pleasure than hearing the sound of Blade's horse's hooves retreating down the trail and away from the cabin. His own horse and pack mule had nickered but not followed. He figured they knew evil when they smelled it.

To deepen the mystery, Maria had shown Adam a series of

scratches on the interior wall of the little cabin where Maria continued to stay. Maria shook her head vehemently when he pointed to them and looked at her. They were not hers. They were down low behind the door. No one would notice them when the door stood open.

He wouldn't have noticed had she not taken him by the arm and led him to them. One set with six vertical scratches, with a seventh scratch crossing through the cluster. Seven what, he wondered. Days? Why? When he looked again at Maria, she wiped her eyes as though she had been crying. But then she shrugged and so did he.

Seven what? Nothing occurred to him but an attempt to keep track of time. Why a need to track time? Had someone or some ones been imprisoned in that cabin? That wouldn't have happened when Lawrence was there. Spud told him that cabin had been occupied by Lawrence's friend and hanger-on, a deaf woman, a painter named . . . what. Adam had to think. So many *whats* in his mind. Brett, that was it. A bit odd, Spud said. Used a hearing horn. But surely not odd enough to scratch seven short lines on the wall near the floor of her cabin. For no apparent reason. She'd have had to do it on her knees. Adam found his thoughts coming in spurts. Then they stopped altogether.

Another sound had begun to interfere with Maria's song. This one came from the valley below. Adam could see nothing moving there, but the noise grew louder and closer and Adam finally recognized it as the rat-a-tat of a woodpecker. Probably a pileated woodpecker, he guessed, though he didn't think they inhabited this area. But banging like that could only be made by a large bird, a strong one.

Finally he saw a rustle of leaves in a distant cottonwood and caught a glimpse of red and buff as the bird burst out and flew to another tree. Not a pileated woodpecker but a flicker. Big, too, and with the same rat-a-tat. Birds of a feather, Adam smiled, but he also realized just how tight his nerves were, how much he was on edge. Noises, movements, minute changes in his surroundings. He noticed them all with a flinch.

Damn that Blade. This was supposed to be Adam's return to nature with freedom from people and material worries. He put down his brush and leaned against his stool to study again the scene below. Well, he would ignore the mystery of Maria and focus... *FOCUS*... on his work. He knew how to be disciplined. And he would be. That's all there was to it.

—||—

The trail had become increasingly narrow by the time Tony took his foot off the gas pedal. "Maybe here?" he finally asked.

Willa poked her head out the window behind him. "Up there," she gestured, "that's it."

The car tilted at a rakish angle and Edith had to raise herself up from her seat to see where Willa was pointing. She hadn't remembered that the trail ran along such a steep ridge. Maybe it was the perspective from horseback that made it seem different. But there it was. A shallow depression a couple feet below the car on the driver's

Tony Luhan's Car

side, with yellowish dirt and small rocks that clearly had washed there from higher up. And where Willa pointed, a deeper depression, one that had just barely held the woman's body the summer before.

Tony pulled the parking brake. The wheels on the driver's side rested on the trail, the high point of the ridge. The ground fell away quickly on the other side, where cascading stones also suggested a lack of stability. The Cadillac listed dramatically toward the passenger side. Clearly this was no place for a car to be. But there they were. Edith opened her door and slid out. Willa tumbled right behind, almost landing on top of her. Spud was already standing, his feet braced. He helped Edith and then Willa right themselves. Tony didn't move.

"You look." Tony rested his right hand on the steering wheel. That was his only motion.

They first had to edge their way along the side of the car and use its fender to help them reach the center of the trail. Once there they didn't quite know what to do.

"Well," Willa said, walking a few feet up the trail, "it's been a year. Probably isn't anything to see, really."

Spud stepped into the depression, squatted, and ran his hands through the dirt and stones along its sides. Edith watched him for a moment then let her eyes wander over the area beyond the depression and back down where they came from. Dirt and stones from the depression had surely washed that way. If anything had been left behind when they retrieved the woman's body it would be farther down the shallow ditch.

Edith moved slowly down the trail looking for signs of where rainwater might have created a runoff. A couple of tiny, dry rivulets ran off toward sparse bunches of blue grama grass, but they held only a few small stones that were indistinguishable from the rocks. She turned back. Willa had already returned to the depression where Spud squatted, still running his hands through the dirt. Willa was sitting on the side of the trail, her feet planted next to Spud's. Edith joined them and saw that Willa's eyes were closed.

"Meditating?"

"Shhh," Willa responded before opening her eyes. They were deep blue at the moment. She pushed a stray hair under her hat and brushed off her jodhpurs. "Just trying to get the feel of the place."

"Feels creepy," Spud stood up. His wide-brimmed hat shaded him to his knees.

"Not as creepy as I expected." Willa rose to her feet and stamped the dust off her boots.

Edith glanced at Tony still perched above them in his car. His eyes were closed. Meditating, praying, napping. Edith couldn't guess.

"I think it's time for lunch," Willa declared. "We can't very well eat here, so let's move on. What do you think?"

"I think we need to work our way back into the car first." Spud grinned. "Or would you rather walk until Tony finds some level ground?"

"No level ground here," Tony's eyes were open again. "Get in, please."

Easier said than done, Edith thought. Willa had to grab the back of Tony's seat but still couldn't pull herself all the way in until Edith braced herself and gave Willa a shove. Spud shut their door and asked Tony whether he would like him to stay outside and help steady the car.

"Too much danger," Tony responded, so Spud eased himself in next to Tony. Once the starter caught Edith realized she had twined her arm around Willa's and fairly clamped the side of her body against Willa. Willa was leaning uphill, too, with her head out the window and her left hand gripping the sill. Her right hand patted Edith's arm and then held it tight against her side. Edith heard the clutch release and bit her lip when gravel spun away from under the rear wheel on her side of the car. Tony eased up on the accelerator after what seemed a very long time and the wheel gained traction. The Cadillac crawled forward, but Edith didn't begin to breathe again until she could see the ridge widen ahead and felt the Cadillac begin to right itself. Then she took several very deep breaths and let go of Willa's arm.

—II—

Spud sat cross-legged next to Tony's car, a sharp knife in his right hand. Hope the next stops are on level ground was all he had said, but Tony's driving had unnerved them all. Spud carved a piece of white meat off the roast chicken Amelia packed for their lunch and offered it to Willa.

They had spread their picnic cloth on sandy soil next to the car. Sage and cactus dotted the sand around them. Tony had provided shade by stretching the tarpaulin from the roof of the Cadillac to a pair of poles he kept in the trunk. Now he sat cross-legged on the cloth next to Spud. No sign of rain clouds but also no trees nearby, and the sun had become increasingly brilliant and hot as it moved though its arc.

Shade and a gentle breeze were all they needed to be comfortable for the moment. Edith rested her back against the car's running board. From here they could see for miles in every direction. But there was nothing to see. Edith looked off to the south and east. Mountains in the distance, she corrected herself. Taos Mountain to be exact. They were actually surrounded by mountains, some relatively near, some far, some hiding behind others. And in between, Taos, Taos Pueblo, Taos valley and the invisible Rio Grande flowing so deep and dark through the gorge. With more mountains and mesas beyond. Vista, Edith sighed. Nowhere in the world is vista like this.

"You seem miles away," Willa interrupted Edith thoughts.

"Where did you go?"

Spud paused his chewing for a moment, apparently waiting for Edith's reply. Tony reached for an apple.

"Just admiring the view," Edith smiled at the three of them. "And enjoying this chicken," she raised her plate in Spud's direction. "I'll have another wing if there is one."

Amelia actually had sent the four of them off with two roasted chickens. "You'll work up an appetite and your day will grow long," she assured Edith. She was right, and of course, Edith guessed, Amelia wanted there to be food enough to feed the four of them and anyone else who might happen by. Chicken, tortillas, cheese, fruit, and fresh water. Perfect combination and so far today no one had happened by. Often men from the pueblo would show up miles from home. No explanation, no apparent plan, no hurry. And often as not, they would be on foot. Edith never could figure out what they were doing. Tony simply said *hunting* or *farming* with no elaboration.

Such an odd couple, Willa observed when they first met Mabel and Tony. Not only was their marriage in many places considered illegal—a white woman married to a Pueblo Indian—but Mabel was wealthy and garrulous, while Tony came from a culture where money meant little and using a lot of words showed weakness.

In Tony's world, words had power and should never be spoken without forethought and intention. Mabel liked more than anything to use words and loved a good argument. Words were her primary means of entertainment, whether she was pleasuring herself by writing her memoirs or listening to others in one of the salons she created and filled with visiting intellectuals and artists wherever she lived.

In Taos Mabel had resorted to importing guests for her conversations. Not unlike themselves, Edith had to acknowledge, though they paid their own way. Tony generally ignored Mabel's conversations. After dinner, while Mabel entertained guests in their living room or her library, Tony slept in his chair or drummed and sang quietly in the background. Yet he was never rude and Mabel and her guests took no offense. In fact, Edith thought, Tony's silence might well be the reason Mabel fell in love with him, and why she never got bored, as she had with her previous husbands.

"Dust cloud," Tony cut into Edith's thoughts. "Behind you."

Edith turned around to look.

"Horses? Wagon? Car?" Spud wondered.

"Too slow for a car," Willa shaded her eyes, "but faster than a wagon."

"Who on earth would be coming this direction?" Edith asked. "So far out of the way. We've been off any kind of road for quite a while now, haven't we?"

"Whoever it is is coming the same way we did," Spud squinted. "May even be following our tracks, I'd say."

"Trail," Tony reminded them.

"Mmm," Willa nodded, still shading her eyes, "but a little-used trail. I'm beginning to see now that it was last year we made a wrong turn, not yesterday. This trail looks barely used. Yesterday's seems like a major thoroughfare by comparison."

Tony shook his head. "This trail is not used. The road is close," he offered by way of explanation, "no need for trail."

"But there are trails all around here," Spud objected.

"Once a trail starts," Tony's smile was kind, "it never dies. Sometimes elk make trails."

"I see," Willa's hand dropped to her lap. "No rain, no vegetation."

"Whenever anyone crosses through, a trail appears and simply stays put whether others follow or not," Edith finished Willa's thought.

"Yes. And I suppose it's impossible to know just how fresh a trail is or how frequently used."

"Good trackers know," Tony assured Willa.

"All trails must go somewhere," Willa was thinking out loud now.

"Trackers know where and what," Tony added. "Trackers know elk, deer, cattle, coyote, horse. Human, too."

"Yes, of course."

Edith wondered with more urgency just who used the trail to the camp they found yesterday, when and how often. This trail, too, she glanced ahead. It had become almost impossible to see the tracks now that they were in sand. No rain, no vegetation, yes, she thought, but wind and sand can make a trail disappear, too. So could rocks. She remembered the many outcroppings they crossed this morning on the way to the first burial site. Still, Tony always seemed to be able to pick up the trail again. Good trackers know, Tony's words repeated in her mind.

The distant rider was much closer by the time Spud began to gather their plates and pack up what was left of their meal.

"Here, let me help you," Edith offered.

"Not now," Tony touched Spud's arm. Spud settled back on his heels. "Rider comes here."

"I thought perhaps we should leave before he gets here," Spud appealed to Willa and Edith with his eyes. "We don't know who he is. He may not have the best of intentions on this trail."

"No," Tony reiterated, "special agent."

"You can see that far?" Edith shaded her eyes. The rider, well beyond the first burial site where they had seen him pause to look around, had urged his horse into a jog trot again. Edith could just make out that he was wearing a ten-gallon Stetson like the one Tom Mix made famous. She had enjoyed meeting Tom Mix. He was nicer than some of the movie stars she had to deal with in arranging advertising photo shoots for J. Walter Thompson. And Tom Mix's horse Tony was a gem.

"Yes, I can see, too," Willa also shaded her eyes. "Big man, isn't he?"

"With a hat like that he should be one of the good guys," Spud nodded. "Guess we should wait and see what he's up to," he closed the picnic basket and returned to his earlier sprawl. He didn't have long to relax.

"Second rider." Tony announced, indicating the opposite direction from where the special agent was once more carefully picking his way toward them. "See her?"

Edith did her best to suppress a smile at Tony's use of pronouns. Gender clearly meant nothing to him.

"Who on earth?" Spud leapt to his feet.

Willa and Edith turned in unison. They stared in silence. This rider was moving rapidly, standing in his stirrups, his horse moving at a brisk trot, the kind that would throw a rider high in the air if he were to try sitting it. A Remington rested in the scabbard strapped beneath his stirrup leathers, and a large dog ran along side, a German shepherd, Edith guessed, with markings like Rin Tin Tin's.

This rider was closer than the special agent but moving toward them from the opposite direction and on a different trail. The riders would pass each other before the special agent reached their picnic site, but they probably would not see each other. Nor would this new rider see them, Edith decided, because he was on a trail well below their own. Neither he nor his dog or horse looked up. They were aware only of what was directly ahead of them.

"Downwind," Tony said, his voice flat.

Unlike the special agent, this man wore jodhpurs and rode with a certain stiffness. Older. Edith guessed his joints must ache with that fast trot. He wore his low-crowned hat pulled down tight. Edith couldn't see his face.

"Isn't that Manby?" Spud wondered aloud.

Tony nodded.

"Manby?" Willa shaded her eyes.

"Manby," Edith repeated.

VII

AFTER THE SPECIAL agent caught up with them and they made their introductions, they decided to join forces to locate the second burial site. None of them had seen it before, but the sheriff had given Agent Dan directions. Tony had a more exact description from friends of his from the pueblo. The sheriff had drafted Tony's friends to haul the two women's bodies out in a wagon. Agent Dan asked Tony what his friends at the pueblo felt about hauling the headless bodies out. Tony seemed not to hear. He turned his back to Dan.

"Not many wagons come through here," Spud ventured. "Cars either," he glanced at Tony.

Edith nodded.

Tony explained that they had to leave the trail they were on and drop about half a mile below to pick up one that meandered through scattered grasses, prickly pears, and occasional junipers.

"Not many cars through there either, I wager," Spud observed. It was the trail they had seen Manby using. When they reached it they would turn east, away from the direction Manby travelled.

They finished packing their lunch wares in the car and prepared to follow Agent Dan to Manby's trail. Tony had named Manby but said nothing more. Once reminded, Edith recalled seeing Manby strut about Taos in his old-fashioned, high-laced British boots. He was certainly a character and quite out of place. What made him memorable was that he had come from England with the singular purpose of turning Taos into his very own kingdom. He had almost pulled it off. Mabel told them that no one took him seriously until they found out he had gained control of thousands of acres through speculative dealings and fraudulent land-grant transfers. Then, just as unexpectedly, he lost everything except his twenty-room house, the same house Mabel had rented part of when she first moved to Taos in 1917.

Manby had also given his name to some hot springs on the Rio Grande where he built an odd stone bathhouse next to the river and drew up plans for an enormous hotel and spa. Mabel had taken Willa and Edith there when she knew Manby was elsewhere. The three of them hiked down to enjoy a long soak, but they really hadn't learned many details about Manby. Mabel seemed to think he was more humorous than dangerous. Tony was even more tight-lipped than Mabel. But Spud's *bad business, that one* stayed in Edith's mind. She wondered what he was doing on the same trail where the two bodies had been found. Finally, to change the subject, she shook her head and pressed hard against the back seat of Tony's car.

Agent Dan cantered ahead of the Cadillac and within half an hour pointed to what was left of an empty grave. Before they could get out of the car, he dismounted and dropped his reins. Edith took that as a good sign. He knew his horse would stay put, ground tied. Not all pueblo ponies were well trained but most knew how to ground tie. Not all outsiders knew that about them either, but Edith did and Agent Dan did. She approved.

Edith's only acquaintance with the Bureau of Investigation was through increasingly frequent newspaper articles documenting sensational arrests where special agents in business suits and felt fedoras arrested infamous criminals. Well, this one might be a special agent but, Edith guessed, he was no stranger to horses or the Southwest. A good sign.

The ground here was more forgiving than the ground where the first body was located. This grave was larger and deeper and had no stones to mark its location or disguise the depression it made. Spud was first out of the car, then Tony. By the time Willa and Edith joined them, Tony was heading up the trail to join the special agent who crouched down about twenty yards ahead.

"Nothing here." Spud shoved his hands in his pockets and watched Tony join up with Agent Dan.

"Probably not." Willa tested the dirt with her toe. It was pliable. "Wonder where Manby was going?"

"Or coming from." Edith could just make out the tracks his horse made. Shod. She didn't remember many shod horses in the area. Maybe Manby rode on steep trails where rocks were a problem. She glanced up, her eyes following an imaginary trail north up the mountain. A pass near the top suggested a way through to some of those mining towns, Red River or Elizabethtown, places she hadn't yet been. Another cut to the northwest looked like a trail could angle toward San Cristobal, the tiny town near Lawrence's ranch. A long way from here, Edith guessed. She wondered how long it would take on horseback.

"Found something," Tony returned holding a silver cross about two inches long, its bottom oddly angled and smooth as if it had been worn off.

Willa took the cross from Tony's palm and held it up for a closer look. "Wonder what happened to the bottom of it," she passed it to Edith, who rubbed its smooth base with her thumb.

"How did it get there? Pretty far from the grave."

"Do you think it belonged to one of the women?" Spud looked over Edith's shoulder.

"It must have had a chain." Edith examined the small loop at the top of the cross. It was intact. "Did you see any sign of a chain there?"

"Just that," Tony indicated the cross.

"Maybe a bird stole its chain?"

"Bird? What kind of bird would do that?" Willa took the cross back from Edith.

"Magpie maybe."

"They do like shiny things. Could also have broken loose from the body," Willa guessed.

"If the body was a body then," Spud latched on to the idea. "Or maybe they were still alive and one of the women pulled it off to help someone find them. Like Hansel and Gretel with bread crumbs, you know?"

The four of them stood silent, stumped for the moment.

"What on earth happened to those women?" Edith ended the silence with a shudder. "And the one, the woman we came across last summer."

Agent Dan rejoined them, and Willa turned to him. "You do think these deaths are connected, don't you?"

"Too soon to think anything."

"Yes, of course, too soon."

"You take the cross back with you." Agent Dan gathered his reins and prepared to mount. "I'll ride on a bit. See if I find anything else."

—||—

Willa and Edith lingered in the rocking chairs on the porch of their pink adobe before crossing through the plum trees to the main house for dinner. As he often had the previous summer, Charlie showed up to keep them company. Large and longhaired with a perpetual grin, Charlie was especially fond of Willa. This time he placed a large bone at her feet. When she didn't reach to retrieve it, he picked it up and settled down next to her, as close as the chair's rockers would permit. Then he placed the bone on his own paws and stared off into the distance as if to announce he would protect them from the rain. The brief shower that had greeted them on their return ended just as the sun was beginning its slide into the valley below. Wisps of rain clouds in the distance were turning a lovely peach.

Spud had asked to be dropped off at his house so he could get cleaned up after their expedition. It would be a while before he could join them for dinner. It would probably take still more time for the special agent, though his horse loped about as fast as Tony could drive. A big, handsome bay José had pulled out of the pueblo herd for the agent to use, appropriate for such a tall man. Edith appreciated the way horse and rider moved together. Agent Dan knew how to ride. Edith decided he was a good man for the job at hand, though she doubted many of the locals would trust him. She wasn't sure she trusted him either, though she couldn't say exactly why. But she knew why the locals wouldn't.

To be considered trustworthy in northern New Mexico, your family had to go back at least six generations and even then you had to be on the right side of things, Edith chuckled at the thought. Spanish Americans who traced their lineage to the conquistadors preferred to be called Hispanos. They did not want to be confused with the Mexicans who came later and were generally much poorer. It was the Hispanos who owned the haciendas, held positions of authority, and derived pride in land grants deeded to their families at the time of the conquistadors. Now, whatever side Hispanos took *was* the right side, they would say, and so it had been for centuries. Indians, Mexicans, Anglos, well, unless they agreed with Hispanos, they would be in the wrong.

Edith and Willa had had long conversations about this cultural happenstance, sometimes with Mabel, sometimes alone. Local Hispanos would be offended by the way Willa planned to portray Padre

Martinez in her new novel. Padre Martinez was much beloved in northern New Mexico but not by the French-born Archbishop Lamy, the subject of her novel and the center of its moral universe. Padre Martinez may have been the first to create education opportunities for northern New Mexicans and the first to bring a printing press into the state, but his interpretations of canon law, defiant lifestyle, and political activism brought him into direct confrontation with Lamy. Lamy first distrusted Martinez, then condemned him. The clash between the two was public and fierce, and in 1858 Lamy drove Martinez from the church and excommunicated him.

Many northern New Mexicans never forgave Lamy for that. Now, Mabel pointed out, those same New Mexicans would think Willa mistaken to tell her story from Lamy's point of view, even if her story was meant to show how Lamy's view changed and grew. Willa had no choice but to stay true to her character's perspective, though Edith agreed that doing so was like dangling her toes over a bear trap.

Now, with these murders at hand, if the locals were to trust him, Agent Dan would have to avoid taking sides of any kind. Yet here he was staying with Mabel and Tony and their Anglo friends. Clear evidence, Edith guessed, of starting out all wrong.

"I think Tony is magnificent, don't you?" Willa picked up the conversation they had begun while changing into their dinner dresses a few minutes earlier.

Edith welcomed the shift in subject.

"And I understand his adherence to pueblo cultural codes," Willa paused. "But sometimes it seems to me Tony could be a little more forthcoming. Not to say more about Mr. Manby," Willa seemed to be searching for words, "and then to ignore Agent Dan's question about his friends at the pueblo."

"I suppose Tony might have said he couldn't answer because he is a Taos Indian." Edith glanced at Willa and tried a tentative smile.

"He could have," Willa rocked forward in her chair, deep in concentration. "Tony has often said his pueblo believes that speaking of evil draws evil. I am beginning to understand how he feels," she added with a grimace.

Willa's response surprised Edith. She tried again. "I guess Agent Dan should have known better than to ask Tony about headless bodies."

"He might as well have asked Tony if he believes in witches. The answer would have been the same. Nothing."

"Yes." Edith hesitated. "Beheading is one of the greatest evils to them."

"Just to haul those bodies to town must have been extremely difficult for those men, given their taboos and fear of witchcraft." Willa tipped her chair back and began to rock again.

"Well," Edith shifted her focus, "I for one don't think anybody from the pueblo could have beheaded those women except a witch."

"I for one don't believe in witches." Willa stood and brushed her hands down her skirt to smooth out wrinkles.

"Well, I for one can't imagine witches in the pueblo, so I don't think anyone from the pueblo killed those women."

"And I want no more talk of witches or murders now." Willa took a step off the porch and shook her shoulders as if to loosen a spell. "Let's cross over. It must be time for dinner."

—||—

"A New Mexico dinner tonight!" Spud greeted them at the main entrance from the *portal*. "Blue corn enchiladas and calabacitas," he exclaimed. Agent Dan rose from his chair and made a slight bow as the women entered the living room.

"Enchiladas," Willa echoed with enthusiasm. "Wonderful."

"*Sí.*" Edith said out loud and immediately felt silly. She usually kept her enthusiasms to herself, especially in a foreign language.

"The Fechins are spending the evening with the Blumensheins." Spud explained their absence. "And Mabel and Tony will be a bit delayed. John Collier will join us for dessert. But we have been invited to sit," Spud made a flourish with his hand.

Spud and Willa led the way down the few stairs into the big dining room. Agent Dan offered his arm to Edith. The formality made Edith feel even sillier, but she put her hand lightly on his arm and followed suit.

"I think we clean up rather well, don't you agree?" Spud turned to Agent Dan as they reached the bottom step. "Nice shirt," he touched the starched white of the agent's shoulder. Dan took no notice of the gesture.

"You look quite fetching yourself," Willa patted Spud's arm and smiled at his bow tie and red suspenders.

Once Agent Dan had seated Edith and Spud had seated Willa, Spud settled into his own chair and opened the conversation with a question. "So, Agent Dan, what do you make of all this? Three dead women, two without heads, all found within, say, four or five hundred yards of each other?"

"I was about to ask the same question of you. Each of you." He did not smile and paused to look each of them in the eyes.

"That was skillfully done, switching the focus back to us," Willa chuckled, dropping her voice to its lowest register. "But we have no clue, as the saying goes. Edith and I discovered the first body a year ago, but we are not from Taos and until three days ago we were not here. When we returned we were shocked to find that no one had made any progress in solving that murder. No progress at all."

"And then *this*," Edith surprised herself by interrupting. "Two *headless* women. And discovered so near the first one," she was almost breathless when she reached the end of her sentence.

"Surely the same person killed all three," Spud broke in.

"Don't you agree?" Willa turned the conversation back to the special agent in their midst. "You're the expert in these things."

"Perhaps," Was all Agent Dan offered. "We must not jump to conclusions, you know. This is only the beginning of the investigation. I personally haven't seen the bodies and know little about the victims or their circumstances. I don't know much about Taos or the surrounding areas either. In those ways, you know more than I do." The special agent's glance took in the three of them but settled longest on Spud.

"Perhaps," Spud offered in return, "but we don't know what to do with what we know. How to connect the dots."

"That's probably because there are no dots," the special agent nodded. "It's too soon for that."

After a long pause, Willa agreed. "I suppose."

"But I want those dots," Edith insisted.

From the kitchen they could hear a salad being tossed, and the rich aroma filling the large dining room in which they sat suggested the enchiladas were about to appear.

"Water, everyone?" Spud rose to pour.

Edith guessed there would be no wine tonight, not with a federal officer at the table. Local officials Mabel could handle, but not federal officers. Prohibition, after all, was a large part of a special agent's job. Most people simply ignored the new law and drank whatever bootleggers supplied, but bootleggers and gangsters had recently become such popular heroes that newspapers chased after their stories while special agents chased them. Sometimes the agents even caught them, but most often gangsters just seemed to kill each other in highly dramatic ways. None of which seems to have anything to do with any of us, Edith decided. Especially not here, in Taos, in the midst of such tranquility. But even here, Edith glanced at Agent Dan, violence prevails. And unnerves. A vision of the scabbard on

Manby's horse proved her assertion to herself. We are an unlawful nation, half drunk on denial and the fear it produces.

Unnerved by her own thoughts, Edith placed her hands in her lap and waited silently for Spud to fill her glass with water.

"Actually," Agent Dan studied Spud's face and nodded his thanks for the water, "I have an easier time saying what I don't know than what I do. For instance, I have no idea who those women were, where they died, or what killed them."

"Or whether they knew each other," Willa added to Dan's list. "And whether the same person killed all three."

"Or why," Spud finished filling Edith's glass just as the kitchen door swung open.

With the dish too hot to pass, they waited to be served, then ate in silence. Lost in the savory mixture of spices in the enchiladas or lost in thought, Edith wondered. Both, she decided, and reached for her glass. There were no answers to any of their questions anyway, not yet.

VIII

MORNING BROUGHT A peach-colored sky over Taos Mountain. Puffs of cloud billowing above tapered off to the northeast. On the porch, Edith stretched her arms as high as she could reach, then let them descend slowly until they reached her sides. One way to ease the stiffness in her arms and back from the previous day's outing. Not that she had done anything strenuous or travelled all that far, but Tony's choice of off-road trails kept her tense and at times breathless, and that night gangsters and special agents had invaded her sleep. She took special pleasure in knowing this day would bring no explorations or frightening adventures.

After they finished dinner the night before, John Collier had joined them for dessert and they decided among themselves that Agent Dan would try another visit with the sheriff and take with him the small silver cross Tony found. Collier, who as usual would spend his day at the pueblo, agreed to see if he could pick up any rumors about strangers or odd activities in the area. Spud would stay at his desk catching up on Mabel's correspondence. Mabel declared herself vaguely interested but not yet caught up by the mystery. She wanted details, lots of details, especially details about sexual misdeeds, then she would be happy to pay attention. For today she would work on her memoir while Tony checked on his crops and cattle. Willa and Edith were free to do as they liked.

The morning air was so inviting, Edith stretched again as tall as she could reach, then let her body sink into the closest chair. Willa would be along shortly so they could have a leisurely breakfast before starting out. Willa had planned to read for an hour or so and then meet Nicolai Fechin in his makeshift studio. Edith expected to join them later but first she wanted to go to the pueblo with Andrew Dasburg, who had sent an invitation through Mabel for Edith to spend part of the day sketching with him and Ida Rauh.

Edith had enjoyed several pleasant hours the previous summer sketching with Andrew. Sometimes she managed to entice Mary Foote to join them, and Ida, who lived in an open relationship with Dasburg, often made it a foursome.

"Open relationship!" Edith's mother had scoffed, all the while shaking *The New York Times* in Edith's face. Ida Rauh's picture had jigged with each shake across its front page. "You know her? How could you!" Her mother's voice rose and fell. "She's a tramp, that's what we call women like her. When we are being polite." Edith's father had laughed and said something like, "Now, now, Mother, our little Edith is all grown up. She edits one of the most important magazines in New York City, after all. That is how you know someone like Ida Rauh, isn't it?" Edith remembered her father squinting a little when he said that. It all passed in a moment and it had been years since she edited *Every Week Magazine,* but Edith never laid eyes on Ida Rauh without also seeing her mother and hearing those words. She hadn't even had time then to respond.

Edith first admired Dasburg's subtle use of colors and Cubist forms in the 1913 Armory Show in New York. She either knew or knew of Mary Foote and Mabel and Ida by then, too. Mary Foote, a successful portrait painter, set up her studio very near where Willa and Edith first lived on Washington Square. Ida Rauh, actress, lawyer, union activist, and now sculptor, had lived nearby and been as public as Mabel Dodge about her private life and as strident in demanding better conditions for garment workers after the devastating Triangle Shirtwaist Factory fire.

The Triangle Fire happened on Washington Square on March

25, 1911. One hundred forty-six young immigrant women flung themselves off ledges and out of windows on the eighth and ninth floors of the Asch Building. They had no choice. Employers had locked all the exits to keep workers from taking work breaks. There was no way out. Many who jumped were already ablaze. Others simply jumped to their deaths. Hundreds of people watched. It was horrendous, the deadliest industrial disaster in the nation's history. And it happened where and when Edith, Willa, Mabel, Ida, and Mary lived right there in Greenwich Village.

They weren't all acquainted then, but they knew first hand about the Triangle Fire and about the garment workers' strike that followed. They also knew that something else had happened, something like a miracle. Women were united in protest. Not just Ida Rauh and Mabel Dodge, who were already involved in protests and the demand for women's voting rights. Edith and Willa and even Mary Foote, none of whom were the least bit political—professional, yes, Edith acknowledged, but not political—even they felt the need for immigrants to be treated better and for women to gain equality with men. After all, Edith and Willa agreed, we are all human. And within months of the Triangle Fire, Willa set to work creating her strongest female characters, both immigrants, first in *O Pioneers!* and then in *My Antonia*. And what a miracle those novels proved to be. Edith smiled at the memory.

—||—

A narrow beam of light touched the edge of Adam's blanket. He had overslept. He was about to yawn and stretch when the beam jolted his memory. He turned his head to stare at the window. The makeshift shutter he had built was still in place. He rose on his elbows to check the rest of the room. It was as it had been when he fell asleep—window shuttered, door barred, ax snug on its pegs above the door.

Maria lay on a pallet near the door. She smiled at him.

"You slept?" Adam complimented himself for making the words sound normal.

"Slept?" Maria asked.

"*Sí*," Adam made his hands into a pillow to show her what he meant. She nodded.

He slipped out of bed and skirted Maria's pallet to reach the window. With the shutter open, he could see that as usual sunlight and shadow danced together beneath the tall pine. Grasses swayed. The day was already beautiful. When Adam removed the bar from the door and stepped out onto the porch he took several breaths and exhaled slowly. All clear, he announced to himself.

But it hadn't been so during the night.

Maria had awakened him in total darkness. She had already dropped the bar into place on the inside of the door, closed the shutter, and crouched next to Adam's head. He felt her hand on his mouth and her whispered "shhhh" brushed against his ear. At first he could hear nothing, not even the familiar night yip of coyotes or the soft hoot of a screech owl. Then he, too, heard hooves on the trail below. They were approaching. Slow. At a walk. Then voices, male, conversing. Two, maybe three. Adam couldn't hear their words. He felt Maria clutch his arm. He reached for her hand and held it. The sound of hooves came to a halt.

"Blade!"

Adam felt the shouted name reverberate through the room. It bounced from wall to wall to wall. Then he realized the person shouting had been repeating it, louder each time. Maria's nails dug into his hand.

"Blade! Open the door, damn it. Blade!"

Adam rose from the bed, Maria's hand still in his. They crossed to the window. Through the narrow slit in the shutter, moonlight allowed him to see what seemed to be enormous shadows at the edge of the porch. The riders were still mounted. Then a horse stamped and backed. Getting restless, Adam thought. Soon the riders would dismount and try the door.

Terror struck Adam's knees. He put his free hand on them to stop their shaking and dropped his voice to its deepest register. "Blade's gone!" It was the loudest he had ever shouted. "I'm the caretaker! You need to leave!"

"The hell, you say." The sound of restless stomping increased. One horse began to paw. "Where's Blade?"

"Gone! You need to leave!"

"Gone! The hell. Where'd he go?"

Adam released Maria's hand, sidled to the door, and reached for the ax above it. He would be no match for these men, but he would have to try.

"Oh, what the hell." This time it was a different voice. "Let's head for the Hole. Blade'll turn up."

"Blade left." The first voice again, softer. A saddle creaked. Then loud again, "Anyone with him?"

"No, nobody." Adam felt his throat contract. He saw Maria crouch lower by the window.

"Don't sound right." A horse stomped and shook its head. Its bit jingled.

Oh, God, don't do any thinking, Adam almost said it aloud. His fingers tightened on the ax and he pressed his free hand over his mouth. Beneath his fingers, he felt the tight clench of his teeth. His jaw began to ache.

"What the hell." The first voice muttered this time. His saddle creaked and he turned his horse away from the porch. "Let's head for the Hole."

Adam crept to the window to watch the shadows recede. "That's right," he whispered aloud as the sound of hooves retreated, "and crawl right into it, wherever it is."

Adam didn't expect Maria to understand his words, but it made him feel better to say them. Unaccustomed to his own bravado, he decided he liked it.

Once the sound of hooves faded, Adam removed the bar from the door and, with Maria alongside, slipped out to check on his own horse. In moonlight dimmed by clouds he lit no lantern but found nothing amiss. Smokey nickered from the corral and Adam and Maria went to the fence. The big gray strode over to press his muzzle against Adam's cheek. Feeling the horse's warm breath against his neck, Adam shuddered and leaned against the fence. He patted Maria's shoulder and found that she too was leaning into the fence. When Maria started for the house, Adam waited a minute, then followed.

Standing on the porch in the morning light, Adam could hear the muted chunk of a log and clink of a stove lid. Maria was building up the fire. Soon he would smell coffee brewing and beans heating and it would be a morning like every other morning. Only it wasn't.

For the first time since Blade left, the thought crossed Adam's mind that he really should get word to Spud about what was happening at the ranch. Until now he hadn't felt any sense of serious danger. After all, once the prospect of money presented itself, Blade seemed almost eager to disappear, leaving Maria behind. But last night's visitors changed the odds. Adam couldn't leave Maria and now more men knew Adam was at the ranch. It probably wouldn't be long before the two riders from last night would know he was there with Maria. Alone. Adam didn't want to bet on the outcome.

If only he knew the identity of those men. Why were they there? Why was Blade there with Maria in the first place? Where was this Hole? Why did they ride off down the trail rather than up? Adam knew the way up. He had come from there, cutting through Arroyo Hondo toward San Cristobal before angling over to the ranch. But he had never gone down the trail. Could the Hole be down there? It must be. Adam felt the back of his neck begin to tingle like a dog's hackles rising to signal his own growing fear.

The aroma of fresh coffee brought Adam back to the morning before him. His horse and mule dozed in the corral. Two mourning doves in the woods sang their sad, comforting tune. Adam rolled his shoulders to relax. He had no answers and no plan for how to reach Spud, but for the moment he allowed himself to feel comforted. No motion or noise came from the trail, the sun continued to move through its arc in the sky, and the aroma of coffee reminded his stomach that it was time to eat.

⊣II⊢

After breakfast Spud hunched over his desk in the windowless office nestled among the small warren of rooms near the east entrance to Mabel's house. He piled several poems together and made space for them to the left of his desk mat. He would take another look at them later. It was time to continue editing Mabel's memoir. He had reached the section where she described building her house.

Blue Sky and Rainbow

Funny that we call this Mabel's house, as though Tony had nothing to do with it. Tony, who designed and built it, gets no naming rights. Well, Tony didn't actually do the physical work himself. He supervised a crew from the pueblo. But still, he created this home for Mabel, really a whole new world for her, for them, one in which they both felt safe.

Spud remembered Tony stretched tall near the door to Mabel's room, a paintbrush extending his reach as he added a small kneeling figure to the top of a broad arrow that covered the sky below. The arrow was rounded like a rainbow over the sky, its blue dotted with little puff clouds. The dark kneeling figure held a small arrow pointed down like a quill pen or a knife. Spud wondered if Tony meant for the kneeling brave to be creating a universe or protecting it. Maybe both. Tony often painted symbolic figures throughout the house. The week before, he had sketched two buffalo in the same hallway as the new sky, one red, the other earth-toned with a large black blanket circling its body and covering its hump. The red

Buffalo

buffalo was hidden behind the earth-toned one, its features vague. The legs of both ended in hooves that hooked back. Spud guessed Tony meant the hooked hooves to suggest that the buffalo moved forward together. The earth-toned buffalo in the foreground also sported a penis. Spud decided Tony meant that to suggest they were a pair.

Tony and Mabel, such an odd couple. The oddest part was that they were married. They lived together for several years before marrying, so, Spud wondered, why marry? He couldn't imagine. He knew that Mabel sent her previous husband packing in 1919 and arranged for some kind of divorce for Tony from his pueblo wife. But who proposed to whom? Most likely, Mabel simply told Tony to marry her. But maybe not. Maybe others told them to marry, even insisted they do. Hard to believe that Tony would have brought up the subject. Not the sort of thing that would have occurred to him. White man's laws. Just as hard to believe that Mabel cared one way or the other. She had already had her fill of husbands, Spud smiled at the thought. And lovers, too, his smile broadened. Mabel believed in free love, that was a fact. And, from what Spud had seen, she exercised her belief on a regular basis. Though, he had to grant, not everyone succumbed to her charms. Lawrence resisted and certainly Spud had. Mabel was a generous and loyal friend, Spud long ago learned, and it was better to keep her that way.

But marriage to Tony? Spud let his chair settle onto all four legs. He had to acknowledge that he really didn't understand all the fuss about marriage anyway, never had. Such an uncomfortable custom. Man as head, woman as helpmate. Not mate, helpmate. Not something Spud wanted to be. Marriage, so unequal. The kind of inequity that led some men to think they could do anything with women, even kill and behead them and leave them half buried in dirt. Spud tilted his chair back, his mind filled with three shallow graves. Those women had been helpless and cast aside.

Spud caught his breath and gripped his head with both hands. He so rarely experienced anger he didn't quite know what to do. He felt his head was going to explode. He wanted to hang the men who did that. Not necessarily by the neck. Sudden death would be too swift, too easy. He wanted those killers to dangle. He wanted fear to seep into their bones. He wanted their pain to become excruciating. Then maybe death. Spud exhaled slowly, a long, measured breath. He settled his chair square on the floor beneath him. Those women deserve justice, atonement, a restoration of balance in the universe. But hanging by itself wouldn't create balance, except as an eye for an eye. Only a world in which women were equal to men would do that. The suffragettes had convinced him, but now that women had the vote, what really had changed?

Even Mabel seemed to think women should be subservient to men—plenty of evidence of that in her memoirs—but surely she didn't think she needed marriage to accomplish that. So why marry Tony? And if Tony hadn't proposed, then the rumors might well be true. Maybe Mabel and Tony agreed to marry in order to prevent the scandal of their relationship from endangering passage of the Pueblo Lands Act. How romantic, Spud scoffed, but important to them all the same. John Collier and his Indian Defense Association had sponsored the bill to protect Taos Pueblo lands and water rights. Collier, with Tony's and Mabel's passionate help, fought to keep Indian lands from falling into the hands of the non-Indians who had settled on them and now claimed ownership.

Spud knew both sides of that argument all too well. Hal Bynner had joined the opposition, feeling more sympathy for the settlers than the Indians. Hal pressured Spud to join him, but Spud decided to remain neutral. He wasn't married to Hal, after all, and chose not to do his bidding. Without Collier's bill those lands would simply disappear into the hands of developers, men like Manby. Spud didn't want that to happen and he didn't want anything to interfere with his relationship with Mabel and Tony, either. He knew they would do whatever was necessary to keep those lands in Indian hands.

But marriage? Marriage was a big step for Mabel and Tony, even bigger if they did it as a concession to political forces. Or maybe he was looking at it backwards. Spud rearranged Mabel's papers, placing the pages he had not yet edited squarely in the middle of his blotter and moving the rest to his right. Maybe for them it was simply one step toward passage of the Pueblo Lands Act. Spud selected a freshly sharpened Eberhart and tested its eraser.

Andrew Dasburg could set him straight on all those rumors about the marriage, Spud guessed. Andrew Dasburg and Ida Rauh had been present at their wedding, the only guests who were. They would know what actually happened. But he probably wouldn't ask. Andrew and Ida weren't about to get married, at least Ida wasn't. She had been vocal about how marriage entrapped women. But there she was, standing up with Mabel and Tony. Well, Andrew was one of Mabel's oldest friends and her staunchest supporter. He would do whatever she asked of him. Apparently Ida would, too.

Spud wasn't about to pry into Mabel's life beyond what she revealed in her memoirs. But he liked to know things. He was curious. He enjoyed gossip for exactly that reason. And exactly for that reason, he also wanted to know everything there was to know about the three women who had been murdered. Violently murdered and their bodies mutilated. Spud placed his Eberhart to the left of the manuscript and picked up the top page. How awful that must have been. He couldn't imagine.

—||—

It was well past nine and already reaching high into the eighties when Edith joined Andrew Dasburg and Ida Rauh for the drive to the pueblo. Ida handed her an umbrella to keep the sun off. It was going to be a hot day. Edith had prepared for the sun by wearing the wide-brimmed hat she used for riding, but who knows, by early afternoon they might get another monsoon rain. She climbed into the back seat of Andrew's Ford and balanced the umbrella with her sketchpad on her knees.

Andrew laughed and said, "That umbrella won't protect you from the sun any more than your hat and jodhpurs, but it might keep tourists from asking if you are one of their girl guides."

Edith laughed along with Andrew. She and Willa did dress a little like the female tourist guides for pueblo tours. But she wouldn't be mistaken for a tourist guide much longer. During breakfast Mabel had mentioned that when Fred Harvey took over Koshare Tours, his Detour guides might still be female but they had to trade their smart uniforms of jodhpurs, white shirts, and ties for Navajo skirts and jewelry. Well, Mabel declared, with all the dirt and dust at the pueblos, Fred Harvey's laundry bills will soar. And they would, Edith chuckled, seeing in her mind the twenty or so Detour Cadillacs regularly lined up in front of La Fonda Hotel in Santa Fe. Fred Harvey would have to add a whole new wing to the hotel laundry.

The drive to the pueblo had become so familiar Edith barely needed to look up to know where they were. It was as though the previous summer had etched the road in her bones, a little swing to the right then a long straightaway, then another swing. Even the bumps were the same. It felt good to be going to the pueblo to sketch. And it felt good to be with Andrew and Ida again.

"How was your expedition with Tony and Spud?"

"Yes," Ida broke in before Edith had a chance to answer. "We heard you bumped into that special agent guy and saw that horrible Manby person trotting down the mountain by himself. And you found a little silver cross near where those women's bodies were dumped?"

"Well, whoever told you knew what they were talking about."

Edith leaned into a curve then placed the umbrella and sketch pad on the seat next to her. "It was an interesting excursion and we found both burial sites. But other than the cross I can't say we succeeded in finding anything new. And I'm not sure the cross has anything to do with those bodies."

"I suppose." Ida sat silent a moment, then glanced back at Edith. "This probably doesn't have anything to do with those bodies either, but Angelica has been telling me about rumors her Mexican friends heard. They say a lot of women in Mexico have disappeared, maybe killed or kidnapped. Nobody knows."

"Angelica?"

"My housekeeper. You met her last summer."

"Disappeared in Mexico?"

"In Mexico. Like I said, this probably doesn't have anything to do with those women, but we heard they did look Mexican. Their clothes and all?"

Edith settled more deeply into her seat.

Andrew parked the Ford under a cottonwood tree near the Rio Pueblo, where shade and running water promised to keep it cool. The three artists spread out, choosing their spots according to what they wanted to sketch. Andrew strode to the top of a small rise where he could take in the whole façade of the building that housed most of the pueblo. Edith was familiar with the way his sketches turned into paintings with blended colors and softened squares suggesting rather than depicting the actual pueblo.

Ida, who preferred sculpture to painting, leaned against a low adobe wall close to where three women were grinding corn. Ida's sketches would trace the shape of the women's faces and the strong, strong hands that shoved their grinding stones up and down, up and down, crushing corn against the *matates* positioned tight against their kneeling limbs. Just the faces and hands, Edith guessed, nothing else. Her mind slipped back to the face and hands of the woman she and Willa found the previous summer. Mexican, yes. Not Navajo. Not pueblo Indian. Mexican. And, Edith remembered, her wrists and ankles were bruised as if she had been bound.

Edith put the memory aside. She would think about it later. She chose to sit on a flat boulder from where she could see close up the shadows and patches of sun as they picked out the angles and curves in a single adobe wall. Adobe bricks, made from the sand and clay underfoot and annually coated with mud, created walls that were never even. They undulated, swelling or falling away as the hand or tool spreading mud rose and fell following the bricks beneath. Soft and warm, the color of the earth around them, the muted shapes and hues of the walls responded to light and shade in slow motion, almost as if they were alive.

As he had the previous summer, Andrew loaned her a box of pastels. She would try juxtaposing their colors to catch the sense of life, the shape-shifting in the wall before her. It's magic, Andrew said, when she asked him how he created the aura of motion in his pueblo paintings. Not all Cubists did that, but Andrew did. Focus on color, on shades of color and lines, he said, and the magic just happens. Edith placed the flat side of an earth-toned pastel against her sketchpad and with a firm hand drew it down. She wanted nothing less than magic. Takes practice, she reassured herself, and chose a deep blue for the first stroke of shadow.

IX

"THE SHERIFF IS not here."

"Doesn't have to be." Agent Dan dropped the small silver cross on Emilio's desk. "Ever see one like this?"

Emilio touched the cross with his index finger. He shook his head.

"Local made?"

Emilio shrugged.

"Know who sells crosses like this one?"

"Many places. Don't know this one."

"Could it be local? Pueblo? Mexican?"

His face expressionless, Emilio looked at Agent Dan.

"One edge is worn, maybe it's been used to cut something?"

Emilio stared at the cross. His face remained expressionless.

"Right." Agent Dan picked up the cross. "Where does the sheriff keep his evidence locked up?"

"Evidence?"

—||—

"That's amazing, Nicolai!"

Willa's raised eyebrows added force to her exclamation. Edith watched as Willa adjusted the sleeves on her peasant blouse and slipped off the stool Nicolai had placed so that she would be flooded with sunlight in his makeshift studio. Willa was so excited she hugged Edith. "I'm glad you came back in time to see this. It's a triumph!" Ignoring Nicolai's reticence, she hugged him, too.

Nicolai Fechin, Sketch of Willa Cather

Nicolai pulled away saying, "No, no. It's you! You are the triumph! Look," he extended his arm toward the charcoal sketch on his easel, "this is *you*. This is a woman who has lived fully and well. This is a writer thinking, a serious writer in command of her art, a powerful artist." Nicolai paused, stepped back, and repeated, "*This* is you."

"It's perfect."

Edith loved the sketch. Nicolai was right. He had caught Willa the artist. Not the one who would giggle and dangle her toes in a mountain stream, but the one who thought deeply, researched thoroughly, and honed her craft until it had become hers to use as she chose. This Willa, Nicolai's Willa, brimmed with life. And she was powerful, almost overwhelmingly so. Palpably so. Edith stepped forward for a closer examination. Nicolai had included only Willa's head and the upper portion of her body, but her energy flowed from the sketch as if the paper were charged with electricity.

"The peasant blouse is perfect," Edith continued. "That flowing, deep-throated collar," she pointed to the material near Willa's throat. "Lovely. Just lovely."

Nicolai had provided the peasant blouse. Genius, Edith thought. Willa loved posing in costume. She always had. It was like acting, and Willa loved the theater. Loved everything theatrical. Edith guessed that's why Willa had been drawn to Leon Bakst, the Russian painter and set designer for the *Ballets Russes*, for her first portrait. The Omaha Society of Fine Arts had insisted on a portrait after Willa won the Pulitzer Prize. They wanted to celebrate her success by hanging her portrait in the Omaha Public Library. They told Willa to pick the artist. Willa was visiting Isabelle and Jan Hambourg in Paris at the time, and Isabelle suggested Bakst.

When she returned to New York, Willa described to Edith the endless days she spent sitting for Bakst in his Paris studio. How his studio overflowed with rich colors and plush textures and how delightful he had been. But the final portrait proved to be a disaster. Despite all Bakst's efforts and the modern cut of her dress, her seated body was out of proportion, her hand holding a book too large, and her eyes, eyes that stared disconcertingly forward, followed a viewer from every direction. And they were opaque, vacant, almost as empty of expression as the eyes of the woman whose body they found last summer. Edith shook her mind loose from that vision and returned to the image Bakst had painted of Willa. His Willa appeared sad, listless, and somehow stiff, as if she were a tired pear a little off-center in a still life.

How can a dress so stylish be made to look like such a limp sack, Willa had protested. She was embarrassed and the women of the art society disappointed, but they hung the portrait in the Omaha library and paid Bakst's bill. The whole experience made Willa so uncomfortable Edith couldn't resist teasing that Bakst made her look like one of the club ladies who ordered the portrait. That's not funny, Willa said, and Edith promised never to mention the portrait again.

But now Willa was ecstatic. No question about it, Fechin had caught her essence. "Such a sense of life. Of emotion. And it's *me*," she exclaimed. "But how serious I look, how stern, almost imperious. Do I really look like that?"

"Often," Edith smiled.

"You do to me," Nicolai nodded. "It is a magnificent expression, no?"

"I suppose," Willa paused to examine the sketch again. "And you finished this in just one afternoon."

"Yes," Nicolai laughed. "But you will sit for me more, yes? In New York? In my studio? It is a real studio. All my things are there. Bright, bold colors. And in the midst of those colors, I will frame your face in the white of the peasant blouse. Light against dark. A few sittings and you will be vibrant. You like?"

"Yes," Edith responded quickly.

"Oh, yes," Willa agreed.

—||—

"I love that man. I just love him."

"Oh, Willa, I was sure you would." Mabel's laugh was low and comforting. "Look how he's painting me. Colorful and majestic, like a queen." Mabel poured chilled wine into two empty glasses on the low table before her.

The three of them, Mabel, Willa, and Edith, were sitting on the covered deck at the edge of the patio, waiting to be joined by the others before dinner. A *ramada,* Edith had learned to call it, a rustic structure covered by brush to provide shade and in this case built so that it straddled the main *acequia* with its stream beneath rushing to irrigate the alfalfa field below. Edith visualized the image Nicolai had painted of Mabel, dressed in black and seated in a wealth of plush purples and reds. Nicolai had gotten the proportions right, and touches of white set off her face. It was an excellent likeness. Edith pushed back with her feet so the double swing she shared with Willa rocked gently. She felt confident Nicolai would do as well for Willa.

"Seated on your throne, surveying all of *Los Gallos*, like now. Yes, I see it." Willa took a sip of her wine. "Chilled to perfection," she declared and raised her glass to salute Mabel. "Your Majesty."

"I'll never understand Prohibition." Edith tasted the wine in her own glass. Excellent. "Why keep us from enjoying something so fine as this?"

"Inconsiderate of our government, to say the least," Mabel agreed, "and a bad policy for New Mexico, which has always produced fine wines. Fortunately I make my own rules. My kingdom, my rules. Some of the best grapes come from the Rio Grande valley, and a little village named Corrales, not so many miles from here, has a wonderful vineyard. That's where this came from."

"Yes," Willa nodded. "We managed to try their wine when we were in Albuquerque. It was lovely. Do they also supply the gambling halls we've heard so much about in, where is it, Red River?"

"Red River, Elizabethtown, and all along the road that drops south to Las Vegas and the lovely Harvey hotel, the Castañeda. You have stayed there? It's right next to the railroad tracks. Fred Harvey knows how to build fine railroad hotels," she raised her glass in a side tribute to Fred Harvey and his hotels. "You might find good wine at the Castañeda when nobody's looking, but you won't find any kind of wine in Red River or Elizabethtown. That's Al Capone's secret world. Whiskey's more like it. Rye whiskey, believe it or not, from a little town in Iowa called Templeton, I believe. Whiskey, women, guns and gamblers. And lots of money. That's Red River."

"What kind of women?" Edith wanted to know.

"What kind?" Mabel laughed. "Well, the kind your mother never wanted you to hear about, of course."

"Yes, of course, but what do they look like, these women? Where do they come from?"

"Not Iowa," Mabel giggled.

"Why do you want to know?" Now Willa was curious.

"Ida said something odd this afternoon. I don't quite know what to think of it. She said her housekeeper told her she had been hearing rumors about women in Mexico disappearing, maybe kidnapped, maybe killed. Ida seems to think they might have something to do with our women's bodies."

"Interesting," Mabel allowed, "but Mexico is a long way off. Why would anyone kill them and bring them here?"

"I doubt that they'd be dead before they arrived," Willa observed.

"I suppose." Mabel laughed at her own blunder.

"But why would anyone kill them once they got here?" Edith frowned. "That doesn't make sense."

"And how on earth would they get here?"

Mabel sipped her wine. "Yes. How on earth."

—||—

Spud worked late before joining the others for dinner. Mabel was a good writer. Not wonderful and a little gushy at times, but good. And fearless. Spud admired that about her. There were things, revealing things, he advised her to take out, not because they were revealing but because they took her narrative in too many directions.

Complexity in simplicity, he preached. Don't clutter a manuscript. Look at how your friend Lawrence works. Or Willa. They may have plots and subplots and characters upon characters, but everything moves the story forward. Nothing distracts. Mabel generally heeded his reminders, but she would say, she had so much to tell. Life is not fiction. It goes on and on, mostly without form. Clutter *is* its form. Perhaps, he agreed, but memoirs are not life, only an echo of life. And as it is, you'll require several volumes to record yours. Ah yes, she replied. I've lived so many lives. You have no idea.

Spud laughed at the memory. Mabel had lived many lives, all of them different and all of them undisciplined. Once her first husband died, she was freed from convention, which never had interested her or served her well. What she got out of her first marriage was a solid financial base and John, her son, who was all grown up now and married himself. She also got the freedom to do as she pleased. Which is exactly what she did, son or no son. So it was that, Spud decided, that made her marriage to Tony different. As a woman with freedom, she was Tony's equal. She might believe in subservience to men but she never practiced it. Certainly not with Tony, who never expected it from her. That's not how they connected. The irony is, Spud grinned at the thought, their union is considered unequal because they mixed the red race with white. But exactly that difference balanced them. Mabel respected Tony as he did her, and they learned from each other and together whole new ways of being in the world. What a concept. Spud pushed his chair back from his desk. He was done for the day.

—II—

Tony and John Collier and the Fechins entered the room together, John in the lead. Finding only Spud there, they seated themselves and prepared to wait. Mabel was often late and sometimes never appeared, preferring to eat alone in her room where she could think. Think, she would say in a way that made the word linger.

John rose to pour wine for the others. Tony closed his eyes and began to hum one of his pueblo songs. Nicolai sipped his wine and whispered to his wife, who whispered to their daughter. Spud spread his napkin on his knees. Surely, he thought, Willa and Edith will be along soon. They were always prompt. Sometimes even early. And that special agent fellow, he should be joining them, too.

A shout came from the kitchen.

Spud reached the kitchen just ahead of Mabel, running in from the patio with Willa and Edith. Amelia stood at the kitchen door clutching her apron in her hands. Within seconds they were all standing in the driveway outside the door, staring at the buckboard coming toward them at a brisk pace. The lone rider who preceded it shouted "Agent shot, Agent shot." A second rider cantering just behind led Agent Dan's horse. The horse was slathered with sweat and dirt. Its saddle listed to the right.

For a moment after the buckboard stopped no one moved, then Mabel yelled "Call Doc Martin," and everyone reacted at once. Amelia ran into the house to make the call, Spud grabbed Agent Dan's horse, John Collier caught the bridle of the one of buckboard's team and helped the driver turn his exhausted horses toward the kitchen door. Agent Dan, immobile and unconscious had been placed on a makeshift stretcher of loose boards and blankets and tied in place with ropes. While Willa and Edith loosened the knots holding his legs, Nicolai and his wife worked on the rope that crossed his chest. Tony and Mabel climbed aboard to look beneath the blood-soaked rags covering the upper reaches of Agent Dan's chest and left shoulder.

The bullet had gone through not far from his heart, but it had gone through, Mabel declared, and missed his heart. Tony replaced the rags and added pressure to slow the oozing blood. Agent Dan began to moan.

After the men settled Agent Dan into his bed and Amelia began to wash his wound in preparation for the doctor, the others returned to the dining room.

"Once Doc Martin sees him, he should be fine," Mabel decided. "Doc has fixed many, many gunshot wounds."

"Lost lots of blood," Tony sounded doubtful.

"Seems it was a while before he was discovered." John Collier, along with Spud and Tony, had taken time to talk to the men who brought Agent Dan in. "Two fellows from the pueblo saw his horse and backtracked after they caught it. Found Agent Dan unconscious on pueblo land."

"Took time to get the buckboard, more time to get him on it. Big man." Tony added to the narrative while helping himself to green chili. He turned to Edith, "Found Agent Dan lying under sage near the trail to hunting camp you saw."

Willa's sharp intake of air startled Edith.

"That hunting camp? But you said you'd never seen it. What were those men doing there?"

"I sent them to look where Edith said. Never found the camp. Found Agent Dan."

Edith again felt Jesse tremble between her legs and smelled the scent of dried blood and dead ashes. The horses had been as anxious to leave that place as she and Willa had. How frightened they all were. But why? They had found no one there. No one or thing actually threatened them. But they felt it. They felt terrified.

"Sounds like we'd better have another look." John Collier's voice was steady, his expression grim.

"Perhaps the sheriff would . . . ," Spud's voice trailed off.

"A posse . . . ," John Collier tried again.

"What is posse?" Nicolai wanted to know.

"Tony will call on more men from the pueblo." Mabel's tone was decisive. "That's all the posse we need."

"But this camp is beyond the boundary of pueblo land. I think Spud's right, perhaps we should ask the sheriff." John Collier ladled beans onto his plate and began to eat them using his tortilla as a scoop. "Or at least inform him," he spoke around a mouthful of beans and tortilla.

"Inform him, then."

"You don't trust him to do the job?" Willa turned her full attention to Mabel.

"Hardly." Mabel responded. "He may intend to do it, but he just can't seem to get it done."

"Dishonest, you think? Or incompetent?"

"May depend on the circumstances. I am sure he does not care about victims who are female and Mexican. Of course, that's pretty typical around here. This sheriff doesn't care much about victims who are American, either. The female part goes without saying. It's just a good thing he doesn't have anything to do with the pueblo."

Edith noticed that John Collier had continued to eat in silence but he nodded now, agreeing with Mabel about all things related to the sheriff.

—II—

When Adam sat down to eat his beans and tortillas, his appetite surprised him. Muscles ached throughout his body and he was fully aware of how tired he felt, but he had ignored hunger. Now here it was, waiting for him. Dinner and sleep would restore his energy. He was sure of that and thankful for it. He saluted Maria with a raised fork filled with beans and gave her his broadest smile.

When she returned his smile, Adam realized the bond between them. They had earned each other's trust. Earned, not just given. They were equal, partners, in this together. Amazing, he thought. They couldn't even talk, couldn't have a conversation, but they could eat and work together in comfort. Adam felt the day's tension drain from his shoulders while the food eased his hunger. A good day's work was behind them.

Adam and Maria had spent the day doing what they could to add to the security measures Adam had installed immediately after arriving at the ranch and meeting Blade. He was glad he had the foresight to bar the door and cover the windows that first day with what loose boards he could find. Flimsy barricade but it worked. Without it the previous night's visitors could have walked in with no warning. He was pretty sure if they had, neither he nor Maria would be alive now.

How the two of them might have died or why, Adam had no idea. But he felt it with a certainty that made his skin prickle. Those late-night riders were no rowdy boys or young fellows on a lark after a long night at the saloon. They were clearly serious and experienced trouble, and they were looking for Blade. Were friends with Blade. Expected Blade to be there. There, in the very house where Adam was to sleep.

Thank heavens for Maria. But how did Maria know to wake him? Know they were approaching in the night? Know they meant

D.H. Lawrence Ranch House

to harm them? Had she seen them before? Did she know when Blade left that they might arrive? Adam wished desperately Maria could answer his questions. *Spanglish* was far from enough. But *Spanglish* and smiles were all they had. At this point all Adam could do was say *Gracias* and smile as Maria placed his coffee next to his plate.

Tonight the ranch house was tighter, and they had moved Maria's bedding from the little cabin into the ranch house. She might use the cabin if she liked during the day, but Adam didn't want to chance their being separated at night when it would be almost impossible to keep watch over both places. Maria had made him understand that she heard the intruders' horses when she was starting back to her cabin after using the outhouse. There was enough moonlight so she could find her way without using a flashlight, and she had managed to slip into the ranch house without their seeing her.

It was just luck, then, that Maria was able to wake him when she did. Luck and guts. She must have been very frightened. It was late when she heard them, too late for anyone to be on that trail. That had to be unusual and unnerving and frightening even before she recognized who they were. And Adam guessed that she did recognize them, though she couldn't tell him that she knew them any more than she could tell him who they were. The fact that Maria chose to enter the ranch house and shake him awake told him how frightened she must have been. Terrified, actually. Adam appreciated her courage and her good sense. She could have run off and hidden, but she didn't.

Instead Maria had trusted him. And now they really were in this together, and they had taken what precautions they could for staying, but Adam knew that wasn't enough. He needed to do more, needed to figure out how to get word to Spud, to get help, to get them to a safer place, and then to deal with Blade and his friends. It was a tall order.

Adam pushed at the few beans still on his plate with the remains of his tortilla. Maria had already risen from her stool near the shelves. She was getting ready to wash their few dishes, and then she would save some of the heated water for each of them to use getting ready for bed. Adam must think through all that he had to do. Spud would have no way of knowing what was happening at the ranch. Nobody in Taos would. It was up to Adam to let them know. He realized that he knew where to start, but he didn't quite know how to begin.

X

When Willa and Edith crossed over to the main house before dawn, Amelia met them at the door to the dining room.

"Mr. Dan slept through the night," she told them. "He is still asleep and so is everyone else except Tony and Spud."

Spud, they learned, had stayed up to watch over Agent Dan, and Tony, up well before dawn, had gone to the pueblo to raise a posse. Now that Willa and Edith were there, she told them to help themselves to coffee and she would fix breakfast. Amelia knew exactly how to cook Willa's eggs and took special care to do her bacon underdone, precisely the way Willa liked it.

"What would you think of asking Long John Dunn to take us to Red Rover?" Willa carried her cup to a table near the kitchen.

"Red River."

"Pardon me?"

"Red River. You mean Red River." Edith spread butter on a piece of toast. "Why Long John Dunn instead of Tony?"

"Mabel said John Dunn owns at least one gambling place in Red River and has owned others. He would be a more knowledgeable guide than Tony in a place like that, don't you think?"

"I suppose," Edith considered. "But why do you want to go to Red River? I thought our next excursion might be to the Lawrence ranch. We talked about asking Tony to take us back there."

"Yes, I know." Willa took a sip of her coffee. "But I can't imagine that we would find a number of Mexican women at the Lawrence ranch. I can imagine them in Red River. Just seems a likely place to have a look around."

"Mexican women?"

"Well, yes. Isn't that why you were asking Mabel about the women in Red River? And where else would we find the three women we know about if, in fact, the rumor Ida's maid mentioned turns out to be true?"

"I didn't realize you were getting so interested in this mystery."

"Why not? It needs a bit of prodding, and from what we heard last night everyone *but* the sheriff might well be the ones to do the prodding."

"Well then, I suppose you think *we* should stir some up some action?" Edith took a sip from her cup. "Mmmm, too hot." She blew on her coffee. "Don't want to stir up much in Red River, though. Despite Mabel's story, that place sounds dangerous."

"I agree," Willa nodded. "And especially for women. But we managed that awful hunting camp all right. I'm sure we can manage Red River. Don't you think?"

"Mmmm." Edith put her cup down. She preferred not to think about Red River and its dangers, at least not until they finished their breakfast.

—||—

When Doc Martin finally arrived, he took forever treating and bandaging Agent Dan's chest and ribs. The bullet, from a fairly large caliber rifle, had passed through the upper left side of Agent Dan's chest.

Agent Dan moaned but remained more or less unconscious until Doc Martin finished, and even then Dan hadn't been able to tell them much. He kept passing out. He'll be himself by morning, Doc promised, though it'll be at least a day before he's up and around. He's strong and Amelia's good food will do the trick. Just feed him and let him sleep. Best medicine there is.

And sleep Agent Dan did. Spud volunteered to stay with him through the night. He knew nothing about wounds or the wounded. But he stayed all the same, just in case. Just before dawn Agent Dan's moans grew louder and he tried to sit up. Spud had to hold him down while telling him he would be all right soon.

At first Agent Dan didn't seem to understand why he wouldn't be all right *right now*, but then his pain must have kicked in and he fell back against the pillows. What happened, Spud and Agent Dan asked each other in unison. Then Agent Dan began to remember. In snippets.

Agent Dan still did not seem to remember everything, certainly not in chronological order, but he did remember that he had been shot. He had counted several rifle shots but couldn't return fire because special agents were never armed. And he saw no place to take cover. When the searing pain hit, it sent him sprawling. Two riders stopped to make sure he was dead. One of them kicked him so hard in the ribs it was all he could do to roll with the kick and stay loose. Play dead, he chanted in his mind, play dead. One rode a bay, the other a sorrel. The one on the bay had a beard, a dark beard. He couldn't see the sorrel rider's face. Then he passed out.

"Pain," Agent Dan whispered now.

"Take it easy. You'll be all right." Spud put his hand on Agent Dan's good shoulder and repeated it over and over. Agent Dan's shoulder felt warm and solid to the touch. Agent Dan really would be all right, Spud decided, despite the fact his face was so pale each whisker stood clearly delineated. Spud admired the strength of that jaw. When Agent Dan slipped back into his own oblivion, Spud sat with his hand on Agent Dan's shoulder until an hour before dawn, when Amelia patted Spud on the back and sent him off to get coffee.

Spud never failed to take Amelia's advice or her coffee. He carried a large cup to his little office where he could kick off his boots and lean back in his desk chair and smoke his pipe. His chair rocked comfortably on its hind legs. Spud sat quietly at his desk, savoring what was left of his coffee and rubbing Jamie, one of Mabel's resident cats, with his big toe. Jamie rolled over and stretched in obvious pleasure.

Spud pulled out a Big Chief tablet and prepared to jot notes in two columns. One he labeled *Know*, the other *Need to Know*. He stared at the headings for several minutes before he wrote under *Know*, *Three Women Dead* and then *Two Decapitated*. Below that line he wrote *Mexicans*. Next, *Shallow Graves on Trail Near Arroyo Seco*. Finally, *Small Cross*.

Spud paused to think whether he had left anything out.

Jamie loved belly rubs almost as much as Spud loved Amelia's coffee. Both helped Spud think. But this whole business was just too much. What did he know about women and murder? He knew words, that's what he knew. Prose, satire, poetry. Give him words and he could do anything.

But human decapitation? No. He felt queasy just thinking about it. Mexican women? Well, he knew something about Mexico. During his months there with Hal and the Lawrences he had absorbed as much of the culture and history of the place as he could. Which meant, Spud caught himself mid-thought, that he had learned a great deal about Mexican men, especially young Mexican men. Hal saw to that, one of the reasons Spud had chosen to break it off with Hal and move to Taos. But Spud knew almost nothing about Mexican women. Actually, when he pushed his thought a bit, he knew very little about women. Period. So his *Need-to-Know* list might be a little longer than others.

Still, Spud picked up his pencil again. He must be able to think of a few general *Need-to-Knows*. *Who Were These Women*, *Where Did They Come From*, *How Did They Die*, *Who Killed Them*, *Where Did*

They Die, and *Why*. Spud put his pencil down. *Why*. He let the word linger in his mind. Jamie jumped onto the desk and nudged Spud's hand, then pushed his head under Spud's fingers. Spud was all too happy for the interruption.

Why indeed. That's what detectives mean by motive. Know the motive and solve the crime. But no motive presented itself to Spud. Not for two sets of murders in two years, even if all three victims were Mexican women and they were found in close proximity to each other. None of it made sense. Jamie's purr turned more determined and he shifted his position so that the back of his head rested on the desktop while his body remained as it was. Going to rain again soon, Spud thought. Cats know. Wish this cat could identify motives and predict the outcome of mysteries as well as he can predict rain.

—ı ı—

Edith heard the hoofbeats before Willa did. A lot of hooves, a posse's worth. Edith and Willa slipped from the dining room out through the kitchen to hear the latest from Tony. Amelia put down the eggs she was about to crack open and joined them. Tony had driven his car back from the pueblo to saddle a horse for himself and collect a couple of dogs from the pack that seemed always to be hanging around *Los Gallos*. He chose two known to be good trackers and shut the others in a side yard, asking Amelia to release them when the posse was well away from the house.

Six riders waited for Tony in the dim light of predawn. Edith recognized them as some of the pueblo dancers who often performed at *Los Gallos*, sometimes for Mabel's fabled parties, sometimes for no apparent reason. They were Tony's friends. All were well armed. Edith was impressed. Two of the younger men wore headbands, the others wore braids draped over their chests like Tony's. Their horses fidgeted in anticipation, and before Tony could mount his gelding, several began pawing the ground and one of the young men's horses reared high in the air.

"Whoa," Willa exclaimed. "So eager."

Tony's gelding ignored them and stood patiently waiting for Tony to swing into the saddle.

"You'll be all right?" Edith put her hand on the nosepiece of Tony's bridle as he mounted.

"We'll find them," Tony declared once he was in the saddle. He, too, had placed a rifle in his scabbard.

Spud, John, and Mabel hurried out of the kitchen. Still in her dressing gown, Mabel saw nothing but Tony. The door slammed behind them. Tony's horse flinched.

Mabel went immediately to Tony and put her hand on his leg. "I don't like this, Tony. You haven't ridden much lately. There's no reason for you to put yourself in danger. Let the sheriff take care of it."

"Sheriff no. This happened on pueblo land."

"All the same, no need for you to go."

Tony urged his gelding in front of the posse. The young man's horse reared again and then they were off, cantering easily toward Arroyo Seco, the two dogs trailing behind and Tony in the lead.

"Tony will be all right," Willa reassured Mabel. "And he's right to take the lead. He's level-headed. He'll make certain they stay safe."

"I suppose," Mabel conceded, "but Tony doesn't know who these men are or why they shot Agent Dan. Nobody does, not even Agent Dan. How can Tony keep the posse safe?"

"He'll find a way." Edith joined Willa next to Mabel. "Tony is resourceful."

—||—

As the others turned to follow Amelia back to the kitchen, Mabel joined them, declaring that until Tony returned she would spend the day in her room. Willa and Edith paused to watch puffs of dust rise lazily upward, marking the riders' route until the posse disappeared into the shadow of Taos Mountain.

"You do think Tony will be all right, don't you?"

"I hope so. Oh, I'm sure he will."

Edith turned to follow the others inside, but Willa called her back.

"Look," Willa pointed toward the mountain. "So beautiful."

Willa's voice sounded like a breath exhaled. She put her hand on Edith's arm to draw her attention to the top of the mountain just as the sun crested its ridge. Gold shot high into the sky and spilled down the mountain's face. Rose and peach tinged the clouds above and the ground below. Wisps of sage scattered along the desert floor grew into individual plants, gray and soft-green. Some wore crowns of gold.

"Glorious, the light, yes."

For no reason Edith could think of she found herself focused not on the light, the rose and gold, but on the mountain's dark face. Trails there rose to the hidden heart of the mountain, Blue Lake, revered as the source of life, the place from which the Taos Pueblo people came. Sacred. Spirit-filled. Source of inspiration and renewal. Edith knew from Tony a little about the ancient rituals the pueblo practiced there. She also knew that little bit was all she would ever know. The pueblo chose not to share those rituals as they did their feast day dances and celebrations with the church. Catholic priests over many generations had managed to reform some of the pueblo's rituals to include Christian symbols and church ritual, but the pueblo kept the most ancient to themselves.

Funny how that works, Edith mused. Taos Pueblo wasn't the only group practicing religious rites on that mountain. Last summer Edith and Willa had been wakened in the middle of the night by low moans and the sharp sound of lashes. At first they were terrified. Then they learned they had been hearing the *Hermanos Penitentes* trudging along the trail that ran next to *Los Gallos* to their place of worship, *La Morada de Nuestra Señora de Guadalupe.* One of the first *moradas* in New Mexico, this one was founded under the guidance of Padre Martinez, the same powerful padre Archbishop Lamy excommunicated. Willa and Edith had learned a great deal about both of those men and the *Penitentes.* Archbishop Lamy became Archbishop Latour in Willa's novel, but she had not changed the name of the character representing Padre Martinez. He became for Latour as he had for Lamy, a sign of corruption and violence and misdirection.

What struck Edith now as she contemplated the dark face of the mountain were parallels in the practices of Hispanic *Penitentes* and members of the pueblo kiva societies. Both were restricted to men, and both kept their sacred rituals secret. But there, as far as Edith could tell, the similarities stopped. *Penitentes* seemed to want to put to death whatever was earthly in them. The kiva societies were all about life, about fecundity in humans and nature, about the natural rhythms of living and dying.

Instead of the *Penitentes*' moans and lashes and the dragging of heavy wooden crosses, Edith thought, kiva societies' public displays were symbolic pageantry. They repeated tales about deer and buffalo and corn over and over on individual feast days, made lively with costumes, drumming, and ritual dances, and edged with the ribald humor of *koshare*, the sacred black-and-white clown dancers who teased and disrupted the others in order to admonish bad behavior. The kiva societies are like satirists, Edith guessed. They would welcome Spud with his *Laughing Horse.* He would fit right in. But, she thought, Spud's brand of irreverence would never find favor among the *Penitentes*. No, Spud would not be acceptable among the *Penitentes*, Edith decided, nor would anyone else at *Los Gallos*. Such a different understanding of the world around them, the kiva societies and the *Penitentes.* And, she finished her thought, of life and death.

—ıı—

The sun was already casting morning shadows when Adam set up his easel next to the porch steps. Not an ideal location and Maria might consider him frivolous, but he needed to think what to do next and that meant he needed to paint. Words interested him and he loved to read, but he knew himself to be a visual thinker. His ideas always came in images, sometimes in mid-image. When he prepared a canvas or picked up a brush he might be expecting to work on a certain scene or experiment with juxtaposing an orange and a red, say, but when he actually put brush to canvas, something quite different might happen. And when it did, he knew he was thinking inside the painting, not imposing ideas on it but letting them happen. Those were moments to celebrate. And repeat.

A few years ago, when he was just beginning to paint and found himself paralyzed, staring in apprehension at an empty canvas, a fellow painter told him not to think, just to put a mark on the canvas. Any mark, anywhere. And let it tell him what to do next. He tried it and it worked, worked amazingly well. After that he forgot to be apprehensive. He forgot everything except what was immediately before him. Every morning the marks on his canvas would take him somewhere interesting. And the morning after that he would tidy up what he'd done and move on, always letting the marks on his canvas tell him where to go next.

Maybe focusing on the colors and shapes in the canvas before him now would free his thoughts of clutter and fear. And maybe then he could give rein to new ideas, not just about the painting before him but about what to do next. Adam could hear Maria moving about in the house, sweeping the floor and putting things away after breakfast. Comforting sounds, but sounds he needed to let fade from his consciousness. At this point, he wanted to empty his mind entirely. A deep breath, slow intake, slow exhale should do it. He let his arms and hands go limp in preparation. Then, keeping the colors and shapes on the canvas fixed in his mind, he closed his eyes and breathed deeply, and again deeper still.

But nothing came. No new idea. Just a visual image of Blade holding out his hand to take Adam's ten dollars. That was a lot of money for Adam. He had expected it to get him through the summer, especially now that he was staying at the ranch. He would have to borrow from Spud. If he ever got to see Spud again. Those men who came looking for Blade had really frightened Maria, and Adam was sure Maria didn't frighten easily. But he had felt her hand tremble on his shoulder and heard the relief in her voice when they rode away. If Maria was frightened, he should be, too. He wished he had seen them, those men, wished he knew more about them. He was sure Maria knew them somehow. How? For Adam they were random visitors. They were not random for Maria. If only she could tell him what she knew.

Adam picked up his pallet and a tube of paint. He had slept well, amazingly well considering the circumstances. No nightmares of Blade or riders in the dark. He knew when he fell asleep that he had to come up with a plan to leave the ranch before those men returned or at least to get word to Spud and others who might help, but he remembered no dreams about any of that. In fact, he remembered no dreams at all. Still, he did feel refreshed. And hopeful. The tube he picked up was bright green. He squeezed a dab next to a dusky blue already on the pallet and picked up his brush. The day before he had begun to catch the upsweep of the enormous ponderosa that hovered over the ranch house. What he wanted to capture now was its motion and its towering height. Once he swirled the colors on his pallet, he looked again at the canvas and this time did not look away.

—||—

Edith smoothed the Two Grey Hills rug they were using as a blanket to cover Agent Dan's chest and placed a fork in his free hand. Spud had already propped Dan up so he could eat from the bowl of scrambled eggs they brought him from the kitchen. Sustenance, sayeth the doctor, Edith smiled to herself.

Dan scooped a forkfull of eggs. "Feel much better already, thanks," he spoke with his mouth full.

"You should," Spud grinned. "Those are Amelia's eggs."

"You certainly look better," Willa mirrored Spud's grin. "You were a ghost of yourself when they brought you in last night."

"Deathly pale," Edith nodded. "Lucky to be alive."

"Guess it *was* luck those fellows from the pueblo found me," Dan agreed around another mouthful of eggs.

"Where did they find you?" Willa asked.

"And why? Why were you there?" Edith added before he could answer.

"You know, I have no idea where I was when they found me. I was following hoof prints from a hunting camp near pueblo land. Might have been the camp you saw," Dan nodded at the two of them. "Two horses, fresh prints."

"How fresh?"

"Fresh," Dan responded with emphasis. "Fresher than I think your tracks would be. But say again when you were there?"

"It was the second day after we arrived," Edith recounted, "so three days ago."

"And it's rained since," Willa reminded them.

"But why were *you* there?" Edith wanted to bring him back to her original question.

"Got curious." Dan handed his empty bowl to Willa. Spud gave Dan a glass of water and told him to drink. He did.

"What did it look like, the camp you found?" Willa looked hopeful. "Maybe it wasn't the same place."

"I bet it was," Edith grimaced. "I've never been so frightened. Did you see the blood? The chopping block?"

"We really were frightened half to death," Willa acknowledged. "Even our horses were spooked."

"You should have been scared, too," Spud turned their attention back to Agent Dan, "going around unarmed the way you do."

"The Bureau doesn't allow guns and we're not really part of the Wild West, you know. I'm here because of Capone and reports about human trafficking. I didn't plan to do anything that would get me shot."

"Why *did* get you shot do you think? Were they out to get you or were you just in the wrong place, wrong time?" Willa asked.

"You mean the hunting camp?" Dan's voice fell to a hoarse whisper. "You never know when death comes. But you two were right to leave that place when you did." He closed his eyes.

"You saw the blood?" Edith insisted.

"I saw it. Left to track hoof prints. Followed them for maybe three quarters of an hour back onto pueblo land, then north and west again." Dan let his head sink deeper into his pillow. His voice grew more hoarse then sank to a whisper. "You were right to leave that place."

Spud took the bowl from Dan's hand and straightened the rug on his chest. "Guess that tired him out. But I'll bet he's back on his feet tomorrow. He's plenty strong, this man."

"I do think it's time we let him sleep," Willa whispered.

Edith could tell Agent Dan had already drifted away, but his words about the hunting camp lingered, sending a chill all the way down to her toes.

XI

"WHAT DO YOU think?" Edith watched Spud carry a tray to where they stood near the fireplace in the dining room. "Will he live?"

"Oh, Agent Dan'll live all right. He'll be up before you know it." Spud shook his head. "Question is, will he be able to help Tony catch those men and can he help us figure out what is going on? Hope so. The sheriff is useless."

"That seems about right," Willa pulled out a chair and sat down.

Spud lined up three glasses and began to fill them with lemonade.

"Do you drive, Spud?" Willa accepted the glass he handed to her.

"There's a nonsequitur for you," Edith said.

"Never have." Spud sat down. "Can't afford a car. You?"

"No need in New York City. Neither of us drives. We walk most places and occasionally take a taxi or the subway. A car is the last thing we need."

"I expect if I had one, I'd be more dangerous than Tony. I'm anything but mechanical." Spud laughed at his own joke. "Why do you ask?"

"I was hoping since Tony's not here you might drive us somewhere." Willa's smile became mysterious. Edith thought Willa was probably determined to convince Spud that he could drive after all.

"Where do you want to go?"

"I've been thinking about an excursion to, where is it again?" Willa turned to Edith.

"Red River."

"Red River." Willa turned back to Spud. "I really want to go there. I thought of asking Long John Dunn to take us, but I expect we'd have to wait days for him to find the time. And I thought of John Collier, but he has work to do at the pueblo."

Willa paused but Spud didn't speak. Edith smiled. Willa's persuasive techniques seemed a bit rusty. At least they weren't working on Spud.

"John Dunn does have a lot on his plate, and John Collier is busy with pueblo leaders."

"Yes. Well, we also want to visit the Lawrence ranch," Willa tried another tack. "We had such a pleasant afternoon there last year we'd like to see it again. I've forgotten what they call it," she turned to Edith.

"Kiowa."

"Kiowa," Willa nodded.

"I wish I could drive you. A friend of mine, a painter, is taking care of the place." Spud smiled encouragement despite his refusal. "But why do you want to go to Red River?"

"Curiosity. It sounds amazingly lawless with all those gambling establishments and houses of ill repute. And Al Capone. Exactly the sort of place that would harbor whoever killed those poor women."

"You may be on to something," Spud agreed. "But Red River strikes me as exactly the sort of place I never want to go. And I'd advise you to stay away from there, too. It's enough that Agent Dan has been shot. You don't have to go tempting the fates as well. You already did that once with the hunting camp."

"You think there's a connection between Red River and the murders?" Edith wanted to be sure she was following Spud's logic.

"Could be."

"What about that man we saw near where the bodies were buried? He had a rifle."

"Manby? I'd never put anything past Manby, but two men shot at Agent Dan."

"And we know nothing about them except that one has a dark beard," Willa reminded him.

"Manby doesn't have a beard."

"We're jumping pretty far ahead here," Edith interrupted, placing her empty glass on the table. "We don't know why those men shot Agent Dan. We don't even know whether they were at the hunting camp. All we know is that Agent Dan was there and after he left they shot him."

"Logic is a hard taskmaster," Willa sighed.

"Do you suppose Manby has a bearded friend?" Edith wasn't ready to give up that line of thought.

"Don't believe everything you might imagine," Spud responded. "We can hope Tony will tell us more before long."

"Patience, that's what you recommend?" Willa's sigh ended with a smile.

"Yes. But in the meantime, remember, Mabel knows how to drive."

—II—

Adam had no trouble pausing for a second cup of coffee. Sunlight still topped the trees and a quick break could only help at this point. He stepped back from his easel.

The tree filled his canvas just as he intended, tall and hazy and full of motion as if a turbulent wind were about to carry it off. Not that anyone would know it was a tree. It simply appeared to be colors and swirls with the hint of a tree. Now to pull the eye down, to anchor the image. Perhaps something dark, a different shape near the trunk. Nothing distinct, just the suggestion of something, something alive perhaps, something moving and drawing attention to itself, an ephemeral presence near the base of the tree. Adam took a sip of coffee and looked away from his painting. His glance fell on the horse and mule dozing in the corral. Adam put down his cup and reached for his brush.

The larger of the two would be dark, a bay perhaps, the mule darker still. Adam stirred the colors on his pallet, the image of horse and mule filling his mind. The horse in front but only by a shoulder. The mule close, offering to pass but not. One would not lead the other. They would be paired beneath the tree, a team. Adam touched his brush to the canvas. The image continued to shape itself, growing taller and accommodating riders, one male, the other female. The male, bareback with a loose rein, would let his mount take charge, alert but careful in the wind. His partner would cling to her saddle with determination and, in Adam's mind, an air of grave serenity. Despite the wind in his tree, this would be no runaway but a stately procession. Just for fun, he picked up a smaller brush and added in a hint of blue atop the mule. It didn't matter that no one could tell that the blue adorned a rider or that the rider was Maria.

Adam stepped back and picked up his coffee, cold now but still good. Tension had slipped from his shoulders, his forehead relaxed. He liked what he saw. It was the idea he had been waiting for. He and Maria could ride out together if they were brave and careful. The fact that he had never ridden bareback gave him pause, and he was sure Maria had never been on the back of a mule, saddle or no. But it could work. At least he had ridden Smokey and he knew enough about horses to think after the long ride up from *Los Gallos* Smokey would carry him quietly. He just didn't know about the mule or Maria. But they could practice this afternoon and, if all went well, leave tomorrow or the next day. All they had to do in between was live through another night or two at the most.

—II—

Spud put his feet on the hassock in his little office and leaned back, still smiling from his conversation with Willa and Edith. Willa had almost shouted "Of course, Mabel drives!" before Willa and Edith rose in unison and ran off to find Mabel. Spud wondered how

Mabel would react. And if she agreed to drive, where would she take them?

Mabel had been to the ranch often. That would be no chore. After all, it was Mabel who gave the ranch to Lawrence. And Lawrence, who hated to be indebted to anyone, least of all Mabel, paid her back by giving her the original manuscript for *Sons and Lovers*. Tempestuous relationship, that one, a constant tug-of-war. Of course Lawrence did owe Mabel. She brought him and Frieda to New Mexico and made it possible for them to stay. Spud guessed that at least for Lawrence, *Sons and Lovers* evened the odds enough to allow them to remain friends. Mabel might even enjoy seeing the ranch again, Spud reasoned. It would give her an excuse to write to Lawrence.

But Red River? As far as Spud knew, Mabel had been there only once. Spud heard about it from Andrew Dasburg, who omitted no detail. Andrew and Mabel often went off together during their early days in Taos, when Mabel was falling in love with Tony and Andrew with collecting *retablos*. Andrew was one of Mabel's closest friends, and Mabel was using every excuse to stay away from home and her husband at the time, the painter Maurice Sterne, her one serious fling into the art world. Once divorced from Maurice and comfortable with Tony, Mabel didn't care so much about excursions with Andrew, but by then the two of them had visited just about every village in the area.

Red River didn't offer much in the way of Mexican folk art, but Andrew said Mabel wanted to see outlaws and prostitutes in the raw so off they went on a bright sunny morning to Red River and Elizabethtown, both close enough to Taos to make it a day trip. As soon as they arrived they realized morning was the wrong time of day. In one saloon they did encounter several men too drunk to leave but found no prostitutes. In another they saw two men huddled together in a corner snoring and one woman seated in a single ray of sunlight near the door, cradling her cup of morning coffee. She was neatly dressed, almost prim Mabel said later, and engrossed in the papers spread before her. Ledgers. She was the proprietor.

"Pull one up," she offered and they did, sitting gingerly on chairs across the table from her. "Name's May," she nodded. When they said yes to coffee, she signaled someone in the back and pulled her papers together. "Sorry about the mess. Busy night. Had one cowboy go flying over the bar. Broke twelve bottles of whiskey. Expensive rye whiskey," she emphasized with raised eyebrows. "Well, that's business," she sat back and sighed before either of them could respond. "Still," she smiled at Mabel, "beats teaching."

Andrew recited their whole conversation, all about how difficult it was for women to earn their own way in the world. "Easier in the west," May claimed. "Don't get stuck in factories or schoolrooms, and husbands are ripe for the picking. Don't have to worry about lawmen, either. They just fit right in."

Andrew had felt increasingly naïve but Mabel was right with May, egging her on. They could have been back in New York City listening to the union organizers and suffragettes who just six years before had won the right to vote. Madame May didn't care about the vote and she didn't want a husband. She wanted to earn her own money and be her own person. When Mabel asked if the women she employed felt the same way, May responded, "They will."

That was pretty much that. No dance-hall girls, no gambling men, no gunplay. They were disappointed. But before they left May told Andrew to come back on his own. "New girls all the time. Someone to suit you for sure." Andrew wondered what she meant by "new all the time" and now Spud did, too.

—II—

Three riders came in fast from the open fields behind *Los Gallos*. It took Spud a few minutes to reach the kitchen door where Amelia was already speaking with the riders in rapid Spanish. Spud caught several words but not enough to understand until Amelia translated for him.

The posse had tracked two horses up the mountain on trails heading toward Red River. A third horse joined them, but the trackers lost the hoof prints on hard ground. When the dogs picked them up again, the two riders who shot Agent Dan had apparently split and gone in different directions, one with the new third rider, the other on his own. The posse split up to follow both. The three posse members with Tony and the dogs continued heading toward Red River. The other posse members followed the tracks heading toward Taos. But when they reached a road near Arroyo Seco, those tracks simply disappeared in the mix of others. Since none of the posse members had any idea what their quarry looked like, they decided to go back to *Los Gallos* to see if Agent Dan could give them a description.

Amelia asked Spud what to do. She didn't think Agent Dan would be able to tell them anything, but Spud said he would go with her to Agent Dan's room and, guessing the posse members spoke Spanish and their native Tewa but very little English, he asked Amelia to translate for everyone. They found Agent Dan sitting on the edge of his bed.

Agent Dan told them all he knew. One man rode a bay, the other a sorrel. He thought both horses were shod. The bay, tall and stout, might have a blaze. The sorrel, on the thin side, had no markings that he saw. The rider on the bay had a dark beard, not long but longer than stubble. Both were wearing gun belts and chaps. That much Agent Dan had been able to see, but he had only a hazy impression of anything above the bearded man's waist and nothing at all about the rider on the sorrel. That man never dismounted.

Agent Dan wasn't even sure which of the two shot him. Could have been either one. The man with the beard wasn't carrying a rifle when he got down to make sure Agent Dan was dead. All Agent Dan could remember was that the man's boots were black and badly scuffed. But that description was no help, Agent Dan acknowledged, because it would fit just about anyone around Taos.

When the posse members left, they took another dog with them, hoping it could pick up the scent of the single horse and separate it out from the mix of prints in the road. Slim chance, Spud thought, returning with Amelia to the kitchen.

News of the third rider surprised them. Not even Agent Dan knew what to make of that. He'd never expected to watch for armed men on horseback around Taos, he said. He thought he would be identifying cars or trucks used to transport the victims of an international human trafficking ring.

"What on earth is going on in this Godforsaken place?" he asked. When neither Spud nor Amelia answered, he shut his eyes and insisted they had to get him back on his feet. He had work to do. When nobody moved to help him, he shrugged, put his head on the pillow, and promptly fell asleep.

"Tomorrow," Amelia whispered, "tomorrow he will be strong. You will see."

—II—

"Tomorrow. Let's go tomorrow," Mabel promised Willa and Edith. "As soon as we know Tony's all right."

"Surely he will be." Edith wanted to be cheerful. Spud had joined them in Mabel's bedroom to fill them in on news from the posse and ease their fears. Mabel was especially relieved. Tony was still in charge and Spud assured her the posse would have little real trouble tracking those men, even if they were now dispersed.

"By tomorrow Tony will have captured them, don't you think?" Willa picked up on Edith's cheer. "I have complete faith.

We'll know a lot more when they do catch them and then we won't have to worry about where we go."

"I'm not worried, not worried at all," Mabel said.

After Spud went back to his office, Mabel rose from her favorite writing place, her four-poster bed, to join them on one of the lounge chairs arranged in front of her fireplace. "I'm sure Tony is fine and we will be perfectly safe whether they've caught up with those awful men or not. But they might not catch them today. Those men don't want to be found."

"Yes," Willa agreed, "but we should be perfectly safe in Red River anyway, don't you think?"

"Probably safe. We'll know more when we hear from Tony. But I think we should go to the ranch instead. Spud said the men Tony is tracking seem to be heading toward Red River. Can't imagine why. That town is about as un-dangerous as any place can be. Beautiful but boring."

"Beautiful?" Edith asked.

"Boring?" Willa's face expressed surprise.

"Beautiful, yes, with the river and glorious aspens and ponderosas. Promoters are starting to rent out abandoned miners' cabins and calling the place a 'mountain playground.' Maybe it is at night, but nothing happens there during the day except a little fishing. Last year when Andrew and I drove up there, we wound up drinking coffee and chatting with Madame May. The Madame part makes her sound exotic, but she's just a woman taking care of business. Her profession may be a little on the wild side, but she wasn't. She seemed completely practical and down-to-earth. She didn't even wear a fancy dress."

"What about other women? There should be a lot of women." Edith tried to visualize all that Red River had to offer.

Mabel shook her head. "Probably sleeping."

"Well, yes," Willa agreed. "But there are a lot of women in Red River, aren't there?"

"We need to know what they look like. Whether they look like the three who were murdered."

"Mexican, you mean?" Mabel shook her head again. "We weren't looking for anything in particular that day and no one was around. Just Madame May, who is definitely not Mexican, and a couple of drunken men asleep on the floor."

"Perhaps you're right," Edith nodded. "Red River would tell us nothing."

"Though Madame May might." Willa's smile lingered.

"I don't think so. She's not the sort to tell you anything you really want to know."

XII

CONVERSATION IN THE main house became tense as the afternoon wore into evening. No one had heard another word from any member of the posse and Mabel had become increasingly apprehensive. With the sun still high there was plenty of light and would be for several more hours so no one expected the posse to give up their search. But Mabel was disappointed Tony hadn't managed a speedy capture or at least to send more news. Both segments of the posse were by now well beyond the limits of legal pueblo jurisdiction.

"Tony should never have gotten involved in this," Mabel declared. "He knows nothing about criminals and guns. If his posse does reach Red River they're likely to be the ones who get killed and no one will be the wiser. Red River may be boring in daylight but it has always been dangerous for Taos Indians off pueblo lands. For armed Indians chasing white men into the den of notorious *gringos*, well, think about it. It's time for Tony to let the sheriff handle things."

Those had been Mabel's final words before Willa and Edith retired to the pink adobe to dress for dinner where their speculation about Red River turned less sanguine.

"The sheriff," Willa scoffed in the privacy of their own room. "What Mabel actually means is that it's time to give up the chase. Nothing will be done. Nothing at all. Those women are dead and their killer or killers will go free."

"I'm afraid you're right," Edith agreed. A vision of the lone corpse they had found invaded her mind, the disheveled body half buried in rocks and sand. Edith felt her own body tense. If only they could do something, anything, to help catch the killers. She took a deep breath and forced her attention back to the present and Willa's mirrored image.

Scowling, Willa jerked a brush through her auburn hair until the strands fairly sizzled with static electricity. Soon, Edith knew, Willa would arrange her hair loosely at the base of her neck and once again appear tidy, serious, and wise. Amused in spite of what they had been talking about, Edith watched Willa's reflection in the full-length mirror that tilted on its own legs. It often chose its own angle and like a fun-house mirror caught the person standing before it in absurd reflections. Now Willa's head appeared enormous and her hands flared large with each stroke of the brush.

Medusa hair. Edith patted the back of her own head to find her short sculpted bob calmly in place. Much easier to care for, a professional woman's hairdo. Modern, tailored, designed for successful women. No hint of Medusa here. Willa had admired Edith's bob but exhibited no interest in updating her own appearance or hiding gray strands that were beginning to show, even though Edith teased her about beginning to look dowdy.

Willa didn't care. "Just you wait. It'll happen to you soon enough. Say, in about nine years." That was the age difference between them, nine years. One of their few real differences. Willa was now over fifty and an established writer of fiction. With no demanding job and no office to go to once she'd left the top editorial position at *McClure's Magazine*, Willa decided no one would care what she looked like. She no longer did. Comfort was Willa's goal now, with flat-soled shoes, no corset, and no particular effort to look anything more than presentable.

That had always been closer to Edith's goal than Willa's. Too shy to call attention to herself as a young girl, Edith had dressed as other girls did during her early years in Lincoln, and once she enrolled at Smith College she became adept at wearing shirtwaists, long belted skirts, and a soft chignon, just like her fellow students. Moving to New York City and into the world of publishing meant little change. Smith had prepared Edith well to be a Modern Woman, although she would never break as free from tradition as her Smith roommate Achsah Brewster. A painter now living as an ex-pat in Italy with her husband Earl and spending increasing amounts of time with Frieda and D.H. Lawrence, Achsah had created her own style with flowing robes and colorful veils. Edith admired Achsah but could never imagine herself or Willa doing anything like that, although she had taught them how to meditate, a facility they found as useful as most people seemed to think odd.

Willa had been as unconventional as Achsah in her youth, adopting a variety of personae, mostly male—doctor, writer, actor, drama critic—to establish her own identity and independence. That early spurt of rebellion ended during Willa's freshman year at the University in Lincoln when it became clear that while she could revel in dramatic poses for theatrical roles in college, she would have to dress and act like a conventional woman if she wanted to be taken seriously. Now that, Willa declared at the time, was truly ironic—a conventional woman being defined as someone to take seriously.

But Willa did want to be taken seriously, to be noticed, heard, and respected. She stopped calling herself William, grew her hair long enough for an Edwardian pompadour and took on the Gibson Girl look. Not only conventional, she meant to be stylish. And smart, too smart to be ignored.

But it wasn't until Willa moved to Pittsburgh and became a member of the McClung household that she learned how to dress and behave like an intelligent woman of a certain class. Willa was to tutor Isabelle McClung in foreign languages, but Isabelle, who adored Willa, singlehandedly became Willa's finishing school, her tutor in gentility. Where Edith had Smith College, Willa had Isabelle. An arrangement Edith thought went a little too far.

With Isabelle, Willa learned to tamp down her enthusiasms, reform her western ways, and choose among the silverware the proper fork for salad. Congenial companions, Willa and Isabelle travelled widely and together enjoyed each other and the great operas, symphonies, and plays. They read the great works of literature and viewed the great art in museums. Edith found no fault with any of that. She too enjoyed travel, music, theater, literature, and art, and she knew her silverware. But she did find fault with Isabelle and, more recently, with her husband. Specifically with their condescending attitude, which they rarely displayed toward Willa but almost always, Edith felt, toward herself.

Isabelle was just being herself, Willa had pointed out. Of the three of them only Isabelle had grown up with Old World charm and expectations of wealth. But now, forty-eight years old and ten years into her marriage to Jan Hambourg, a Jewish Russian-Canadian violinist with a great deal of charm and few real prospects even in the world of music, Isabelle's money and their patronizing attitudes had worn thin with Edith.

After all, Edith thought, the Hambourgs were living near Paris rather than in Pittsburgh because Isabelle's family home had been sold after her father's death. And while Isabelle's money might buy Jan a Stradivarius, to live graciously they had to stretch every dollar as far as it could go. Joining the ex-pats in France had made that more possible.

When Isabelle had decided to marry Jan, both Willa and Edith were appalled. Of course, Isabelle had to do *something.* Isabelle's younger sister had trained as a nurse, married, and moved to upstate New York, and her brother had married one of the Mellons and taken a banking position in New York City. Isabelle had no occupation, no husband, and once her father died, no home.

For years, Edith knew, Isabelle simply worshipped Willa and did all she could to further Willa's career as a writer. When Willa was finally established as a novelist and living with Edith in New York, she feared that Jan, with little social standing, was an opportunist who, rather than taking care of Isabelle, would take advantage of her. But when it became apparent that Jan did have some standing in the world of music, a world Isabelle had always loved, and that he would care for Isabelle, Willa warmed to him. Edith did not.

With Isabelle, how they dressed and wore their hair still mattered. With Isabelle and Jan, what they did for a living mattered, too. Isabelle was enormously proud of Willa. No one could have been more enthusiastic about Willa's success or more encouraging than when Willa dropped her reservations about Jews and shifted publishers. At the time, Edith had pointed out how Harcourt Brace, the Boston-based company that published Willa's first three novels, never provided adequate marketing support. When Willa agreed and gave *One of Ours* to Alfred Knopf, Knopf nominated the book for the Pulitzer Prize, which made Willa famous and finally stable financially. Edith's fortunes too improved when she left her editorial job at *Every Week Magazine* to join the staff at J. Walter Thompson. Less exciting work, but her position was more secure and the company valued her expertise. Isabelle and Jan were polite about Edith's success, but neither was effusive in their praise and Jan, at least, seemed to think women in professions were not to be encouraged.

At times Edith envied the no-office part of Willa's working life, but she enjoyed her job in advertising. And while Willa had finally become financially stable, even verging on wealthy, Edith's income had always been enough to pay the rent. Recently the J. Walter Thompson agency had given Edith a thousand-dollar raise and assigned the accounts of such important companies as Jergens and Kodak to her. Usually, teams handled accounts at J. Walter Thompson, but despite the added workload and responsibility, Edith was delighted. The assignment meant she had more control over her schedule. She could take off whatever time she needed to travel with Willa. Together they had created a perfect life—never dull, always creative, with lively companionship and plenty of freedom to roam and think and write.

—ıı—

When Tony did not return in time for dinner, Mabel sent word that she would take her meal alone in her room. The Fechins planned to be out for the evening.

"Spud should be along soon, don't you think?" Willa settled into the chair next to Edith at the big dining room table.

"I hope so," Edith nodded. "I'm starving."

"Me, too." Agent Dan, taking one step at a time, came down the stairs leading from the living room. Spud followed on his heels.

"And me," Spud exclaimed. "I could hardly be hungrier or more pleased that Agent Dan feels strong enough to join us."

"What a nice surprise," Willa clapped her hands together.

"Wonderful," Edith half rose, thinking Agent Dan might need an extra hand.

"Please, please, stay seated," Agent Dan waved Edith off. His face was pale and his body stiff, but he was steady on his feet and had no trouble taking the seat opposite Willa's. "Nobody and nothing is going to keep me down. Bandages are all I need to hold me together, and I've stayed in bed too long as it is."

Spud let Amelia know Dan was joining them and then pulled out a chair for himself across from Edith.

"I told Agent Dan you were talking about driving to Red River. Are you still planning to go?" Spud directed his question to Edith, but Willa picked it up.

"If we can convince Mabel to take us. She seems to think the place is too dangerous, especially now that we know at least two of those killers are headed in that direction."

"We don't know for certain that's where they're going," Edith corrected. "It's really just a guess."

"That's what most detective work is," Agent Dan smiled. "But don't tell anyone. People think we're awfully intelligent."

"Well, we think *you* are. But it's just a matter of logic isn't it, after all." Willa was stating a fact, not asking a question.

"If Mabel agrees to drive, would you join us?" Edith asked Agent Dan. "If you can. Mabel would feel safe with you along. She'd have little reason to say no."

"Great idea, Edith. Yes." Willa's enthusiasm gathered steam. "She would surely agree to take us if you go."

"If," Spud broke in. "If Agent Dan feels up to it in the morning."

"Of course," Willa spread her napkin on her lap. Edith followed suit.

"He will be fine. His worst problem was losing so much blood. Now he has blood again." Amelia carried a sizzling platter of beef-steaks in from the kitchen. She placed the platter in the middle of the table. "Don't let it get cold." She glanced at Agent Dan. "Eat. You're a big man. You need to eat. Food will give you strength."

Mabel changed her mind when Amelia, fresh from the dining room, told her the agent was up, having dinner with the others in the dining room, and they were all talking about going to Red River tomorrow. Within minutes Mabel joined everyone down-stairs and arrived in the dining room just as a courier from the pueblo arrived with word that the posse had returned empty-handed. Tony was on his way home.

"That decides it, then," Mabel declared. "Who wants to go to Red River with me tomorrow?"

It was almost ten o'clock when Tony joined the others in Mabel's Rainbow library. Mabel had already finalized arrangements for the next day's drive to Red River. Neither Tony nor Spud was to be invited. Tony would be too conspicuous and Spud too nervous,

Mabel declared. Instead, once Agent Dan said he was strong enough to make the trip, the intrepid four—Mabel, Willa, Edith, and Agent Dan—would comprise the scouting party. The women would present themselves as harmless tourists, with Dan, who turned out to know some Spanish, as their guide in the wicked world of Red River. The women they hoped to find would speak only Spanish.

"Sleep in a bit," Mabel advised. "Agent Dan can use the rest and it won't do much good to arrive early in the day. Red River is definitely not a morning town."

—II—

Using gestures and pantomime, Maria tried to show Adam how dangerous she thought their situation was. Inside the tiny cabin where she was living before Adam arrived, she pointed again to the seven scratches low on the wall behind the door, a cluster of six and another single one. Maria put her head against her hands as if she were sleeping and then simulated yawning and waking up before pointing to the scratches again.

"Days?" Adam guessed. "Nights?"

"*Sí. Dias y noches.*" Maria nodded.

"Did you make the marks?" Adam pointed to the scratches and then at her.

Maria shook her head no.

"*Seis mujeres.*" She held up six fingers.

Adam frowned and shrugged. He didn't understand.

"*Seis mujeres,*" Maria repeated. This time she pointed to herself and held up seven fingers.

"Six *señoritas, señora*?" Adam gave her a hopeful look.

"*Sí. Sí. Seis mujeres.*" Maria nodded and gave him an encouraging smile.

Six women, Adam repeated to himself. Six women and Maria was one of them. He shook his head. Seven days. Stuffed into this little cabin, hardly bigger than a jail cell. How on earth. But Adam had no time for wonderment. Maria held up two fingers and drew them slowly across her throat.

"*Dos mujeres asesinadas.*"

"What?" Adam choked out the word, drew his hand across his own throat and mimicked falling on the floor.

"*Sí.*"

Adam flinched at the word and the terror in Maria's eyes.

"*Que descanse en paz.*" Maria bowed her head and made the sign of the cross. When she raised her eyes again, the terror had given way to intense determination.

"Yes." Adam let the word slide into silence and bowed his own head for a minute. He had been thoroughly frightened by his encounter with Blade and his friends, but he never imagined anything like this. Had Maria actually seen them slit the throats of

Brett's Cabin, D.H. Lawrence Ranch

those poor women? What about the others? Were they dead, too? Why had Maria been spared? Why had Blade kept her at the ranch? So many questions still and all the possible answers were terrifying. Adam had no idea how to ask or what to do next. But he hardened his resolve. He had to get the two of them out of there as soon as possible.

Adam had expected to begin the day by familiarizing Maria with mule and saddle, but once he haltered the mule and prepared to put the saddle on, he realized how complicated his plan was going to be. The mule had no problem with a packsaddle but wanted nothing to do with saddle and rider. Adam spent the rest of the morning negotiating with the mule. Finally around noon the mule decided that carrying a rider was not all that different from hauling a sack of beans or transporting firewood. Despite his sense of imminent doom, Adam took time to ride a victory lap around the corral.

When it was Maria's turn, she mounted easily and giggled when *la mula* lurched into a fast trot. With the lead rope still in his hand, Adam had to run to keep up. "Grab the horn," he shouted and tried to demonstrate. But when he tightened his fingers around the saddle horn, he found his body levitated and his feet paddling air until the saddle tilted to accommodate his weight. He dropped to the ground and, again running alongside, righted the saddle with Maria in it. Maria grabbed the horn and remained upright and easy. Her giggle became laughter and *la mula* brayed happily. Adam felt giddy with delight. Thank God, Maria is not afraid, he thought. Almost immediately the reality of their situation jerked Adam free from giddiness, but his delight remained. Hope had returned.

After dealing with *la mula*, riding Smokey bareback proved to be simple. The trick would be leading *la mula* with Maria aboard. The mule didn't like that idea any more than she liked the notion of carrying a saddle and rider. But Maria just laughed and dismounted to search the small barn attached to the corral for another lead rope.

She tied the rope to the mule's halter to use as reins. She might not be able to stop *la mula* with such makeshift reins but they could help Maria steer her, and that would help Adam. He felt blessed by a sensible woman. Now he was sure they would be able to reach Taos before the next nightfall.

Adam made a final round before bedtime that night, checking again the lock on Maria's cabin and the gate to the corral. The image of Maria's fingers drawing slowly across her throat had tormented his mind all day. She must have been terrified seeing that. Must have been terrified the whole time he had known her. She had shown him the scratches on the wall before but until now hadn't let him know the number of women imprisoned in the cabin or that at least two of them had their throats slit. Adam could make no sense of any of this. He felt as though he had been in shock the whole day, though he was proud of all they had accomplished in spite of their fear and anguish. Now that he knew more of Maria's story, it was a fear and anguish they shared.

Maria would stay with him in the house, that had already been decided, but he wanted no intruder to be able to look for her in the cabin and find her missing. And he closed Smokey and the mule inside the small barn to make sure they were also hidden from uninvited visitors. He considered locking them in the large woven-wire pen attached to the back of the barn and covered by a shed roof. He had no idea what sort of animals might have been kept there. It was more secure than the barn but would not keep Smokey and the mule hidden. Adam decided hiding them was the better option. He wanted no surprises and nothing to happen to the animals. They were still the best means he could think of for their escape to Taos.

XIII

THE SHERIFF DROPPED his eyes and leaned back in his chair when the federal agent strode through his office door. Tony Luhan and that young man they called Stud followed on his heels. *Spud*, not Stud, the sheriff caught himself and snickered before looking up. They were still there.

"Sorry, so sorry, Sheriff." Emilio scuttled through the door. "They would not listen. I tried to stop them."

"You're interrupting." The sheriff glared at Agent Dan. "You can see I'm busy," he pointed to where John Dunn lounged in the chair next to his desk, Dunn's long legs crossed at the ankles, his boots scuffed. "You need to wait your turn."

"Can't wait." Agent Dan stood tall, his voice firm. "Need to let you know I've been wounded. Two men on horseback shot me the day before yesterday on pueblo land near the road to Arroyo Seco. Tony and his friends from the pueblo went after them. Saw they were joined by a third rider, then split up. Two headed toward Red River and one toward Taos. I'm going to Red River now. You need to keep an eye out for the other rider here."

"Yes, Emilio, I'm sure you did try to stop them. Thank you. I'll handle it now." The sheriff nodded to Emilio before turning his full attention to the federal agent. Emilio backed out of the room.

"Heard something about that from Doc Martin yesterday." The sheriff tilted his chair on its hind legs. "Said he taped you up and told you to stay in bed. That about right?"

"I'm out of bed now." Agent Dan took a step forward.

"So I see." The sheriff eased his chair back to the floor.

"Red River?" John Dunn removed the cigar stub from below his mustache. "Been thinking about going there myself tomorrow."

"What do you think you're going to do there?" the sheriff interrupted, looking hard at Agent Dan.

"God damn Harvey tourist cars going all over the place these days." John Dunn uncrossed his legs and turned to look at the federal agent.

"Beg your pardon?" Agent Dan turned to Dunn.

"Heard they were even in Red River. Not civilized enough for them there," Dunn shook his head. "I was just telling the sheriff here he ought to check into it. Might be dangerous, tourists and all." Dunn returned the cigar stub to his mustache and took a minute to study Agent Dan from his boots to his hat before finishing his thought. "Might be dangerous for you, too."

"Yes, well," the sheriff intervened. "No reason you shouldn't go, I suppose. You're not a tourist."

"Right," Agent Dan responded. "Just letting you know. Soon as we gas up, I'm going." Agent Dan turned on his heel and nodded in the direction of John Dunn. Tony and Spud brushed past Emilio on the way out.

—||—

The drive to Red River was longer and more difficult than Edith expected, but it was also breathtakingly beautiful. Once they reached Questa and turned east toward Red River, the river itself rushed alongside, glinting in the sun and tumbling over mineral-laden rocks. The higher they rose, increasing numbers of ponderosas and aspens danced in the breezes and sheer cliffs towered above. Mabel's car protested the climb and the roughness of a road pitted and rutted by huge trucks hauling mining equipment and ore. Many of the early gold, silver, and copper mines around Red River and Elizabethtown were already played out, but a molybdenite mine had recently roared into business in Sulphur Gulch and created chaos on the only road.

Massive trucks flew past on their way down the mountain, spewing gravel and dust, but Mabel pushed on. "That idiotic congressman of ours." Mabel pumped her fist at a truck. "He's the reason these trucks are here. Representative Steven P. Cutlass, such a fancy name. He won't let the pueblo have their own sacred Blue Lake back, but he'll let mine owners do whatever they want. Just look how they're tearing up this road. A little money under the table, that's what I think." Mabel glanced at Agent Dan. "You should look into him," she suggested. "I'm willing to bet Cutlass is at the bottom of most of the corruption in New Mexico."

Agent Dan looked interested. "John Collier said something about him. The Blue Lake land was one thing, but he also said Cutlass might have money in one of the brothels in Elizabethtown. I will look into him. And that other man Collier mentioned? Manatee? Manby?"

"Manby, yes, our famous Britisher. Another evil man," Mabel chuckled, "though he never personally bothered me except when he tried to have me arrested for treason. Nonsense, of course."

"And another fellow I heard has run a whole mess of gambling houses all around here." Agent Dan paused to think. "He owns the livery stable and has some sort of taxi service. Dunn, that's it. Saw him in the sheriff's office this morning. Don't know what he was doing there."

"Long John Dunn?" Mabel laughed. "He does run gambling houses and, yes, he is the taxi service in Taos. I think he was a little crooked in the past, but he's a straight arrow now. Clever and enterprising but not corrupt."

"Seems like a good man to us," Willa spoke up from the back seat.

"If you like him," Agent Dan twisted in his seat to address Willa, "then he's probably all right."

"I like him, too," Mabel agreed, "but you never really know, do you?"

Just then one of the big trucks careened around a hairpin curve and aimed straight for them, ending their conversation. Mabel skidded the car to a stop and they watched the truck speed by. Willa surprised Edith by grabbing her hand and holding it so tight Edith could feel the edges of her ring sharp against its neighboring fingers.

"Do you mean to tell me they bring tourists up this road?" Agent Dan burst into the silence after another particularly tight turn.

"What makes you think that?" Mabel asked, as though Agent Dan were simply starting a new topic of conversation. "All we've seen so far are mining trucks."

"Something what's-his-name, John Dunn, said when we stopped in to see the sheriff. Something about touring cars going all over the place these days."

Mabel glanced at Agent Dan but said nothing. Another truck passed them on its way down.

"Harvey touring cars are taking people just about everywhere now," Willa spoke up from the back seat. "You just have to tell them what you want to see." She relaxed her grip on Edith's hand and settled deeper into her own seat. "They were lined up three deep outside La Fonda when we were in Santa Fe. We thought about taking one of their pueblo tours, but they fill up fast. So crowded, you know."

"Amazing, isn't it, how many people are coming to the Southwest these days? Not like it used to be. Just proves the power of advertising, I suppose." Edith smiled.

"Of which you are rightly proud," Willa nudged Edith.

Willa and Edith had watched with interest when the railroads first laid out their campaigns to encourage people to take in the sights on the way to California. It wasn't enough to get people to California. Once the Atchison, Topeka, and Santa Fe Railroad built hotels with Harvey restaurants and gift stores along the route, Fred Harvey began to entice people to take long and expensive vacations. And people did. People, Willa and Edith guessed, who would want to read Willa's new novel about New Mexico even if no one else did. But, Edith settled deeper into her own seat, others would, too. After all, Willa's earlier forays into the Southwest in *The Song of the Lark* and *The Professor's House* had been well received. Willa's new book would be, too, Edith was sure of it. But tourists in Red River? Edith wasn't so sure about that, not if they had to get there on this road.

Once past Sulphur Gulch, Edith changed her mind. The car stopped complaining, Mabel and Agent Dan visibly relaxed in the front seat, and the scenery grew ever more striking. The drive now began to remind Edith of the road to San Cristobal on their way to the Lawrence ranch the previous summer. Similar elevation, she guessed, and once again she decided they needed to include another trip to the ranch, whether or not that trip had anything to do with catching killers. This one did and that fact alone made her apprehensive. But Red River turned out to be as beautiful as the scenery on the way there. How could it be as dangerous as its reputation? Saloons, most of them unpainted but wearing large signs, dominated the main street, but Edith thought she saw a church ahead as well.

Mabel parked the car in front of one of the grander saloons, barn-red with black trim and gold lettering that spelled out *Madame May's.* Edith took a deep breath and held it for a minute before exhaling in a slow, controlled sigh. She would do whatever she could to calm her nerves. Fear never helped anyone ever, she told herself and squared her shoulders. Willa, she noticed, also squared her shoulders before getting out of the car.

"I doubt we'll learn anything in here," Mabel announced when the others joined her on the boardwalk, "but it's as good as anywhere else to start."

Agent Dan held open one of the swinging doors to Madame May's and Mabel led the way. Inside the light was dim, but Edith easily made out a long bar backed by gold-trimmed mirrors that flanked an enormous painting displaying a Rubenesque figure sprawled across a red velvet chaise lounge. Crowned with golden ringlets that flowed over and down her shoulders to hide fulsome breasts and reached just to the edge of the narrow red shawl tossed carelessly across her hips, this lush presence dwarfed the myriad of empty liquor bottles lined up below and dominated the room. A portrait of Madame May, Edith decided.

But no, Mabel was already introducing them to a dark-haired, middle-aged woman sitting alone at a table near the door. Madame May, conservatively dressed in nondescript beige, looked decidedly dowdy next to Mabel, whose purple crepe dress and paisley scarf spoke eloquently of casual wealth and tourist status. Amused by the comparison between Mabel and May, Edith fingered the pearls draped around her own neck and hoped that she and Willa were equally well disguised as tourists. As for Agent Dan, his suit and tie suggested that he, too, was from anywhere but the Southwest.

"Pull up a chair," Madame May gestured at the chairs around her table. "Want coffee or a drink?"

They arranged themselves around the table so that Mabel and Agent Dan sat on either side of the Madame.

"Oh, I remember you. You came with a young gentleman one morning." Madame May touched the edge of Mabel's scarf. "Nice scarf."

"Thank you. You're right, I did visit earlier." Mabel's smile was genuine and expressed her surprise at being recognized.

"You were looking for *retablos*. Find any?"

"Not here. But you knew that."

Madame May laughed at her own joke, and while everyone was smiling, she let her eyes linger on each of her new guests. "You ladies job hunting or did you just drop by to see the sights?" She laughed again, louder this time.

"Actually, we are sight-seeing," Agent Dan grinned back, "and I for one would like a cup of coffee."

"Of course," Madame May signaled to a man behind the bar. "And the rest of you?"

"Water," Mabel responded. Willa and Edith nodded yes to water.

"Three waters and a coffee," Madame May called out and turned back to Agent Dan. "What sights are you interested in? Maybe I can point you in the right direction."

"I expect you can." He interrupted himself with a slight cough before waving in the direction of Willa and Edith. "These ladies have never been in a saloon before or met women of the sort who work here. Mabel thought you might oblige them with an introduction."

Madame May's eyebrows rose just a little. It was her only sign of surprise. Then she smiled. Edith felt her own face coloring and dropped her eyes.

"I hope you don't mind," Mabel interjected.

"Yes," Willa said, her voice firm. "I am a writer. I am working on a new novel, and Mabel thought we should meet as many different kinds of people as there are in New Mexico. You and the people who work for you will be different from anyone else we have met or are likely to meet."

Edith coughed hard before raising her eyes to see Madame May's smile break into surprised delight. Edith couldn't believe her ears, Willa declaring herself to be a writer! She was stunned. Ever since Willa won the Pulitzer that is exactly what Edith had been appointed to help Willa hide. For the last four years, Edith was the one who made arrangements, signed hotel registers, and made phone calls. She was the one who introduced herself to strangers and neglected to introduce Willa. She, the shy one. And she did it because Willa didn't want to be recognized, lionized, fawned over. Willa wanted to observe, not engage with strangers. But here Willa was, smiling at Madame May. And Madame May was positively radiant in return.

"Of course! Why not?" Madame May responded. "Anyone in particular?"

"Not really," Agent Dan stepped in. "Perhaps someone who has been here for a while? Someone from New Mexico? And maybe someone from elsewhere. Anyone here from Mexico, for instance?"

"Yes, I'll get them. Florence and Angelica." Madame May rose from the table repeating, "Of course, Florence and Angelica," and strode toward the back of the room where several people were gathered at scattered tables apparently playing cards. Business wasn't booming at this time of day, but Madame May's was busy.

"Interesting, Florence and Angelica," Willa repeated, watching Madame May cross the room. "A blossom and an angel. I expected to meet neither in a place like this."

—II—

"Water?" Adam offered the canteen to Maria.

Maria stood next to him and took a long drink. Handing the canteen back, she whispered, "*Gracias*."

"*Sí*," Adam nodded and chose a fallen log to sit on, where Smokey could drop his head and nibble on grass. Another trail was about to join theirs and he would have to choose again which way to go. The new trail looked promising and their own trail through the forest had been narrowing and threatening to peter out. A good place to take a well-earned break, he decided. He had hoped by now they would have reached Taos, but the morning and its bright sun had gotten away from him. It must be well past noon, he guessed. The sky above the trees was clouding over.

He handed Smokey's reins to Maria and motioned for her to sit while he tied the mule to a limb farther down on the log and loosened the saddle girth so the mule could relax and graze a bit, too. "Lunch," he declared and handed Maria a burrito from the pack she had strapped to the back of the saddle that morning.

So far, so good, Adam thought, taking a large bite from his own burrito, but how far or how good he had no idea. In fact, Adam had only a hazy notion of where they were and how far they had to go. He had decided to use trails rather than the rarely travelled road that crossed near the ranch because he feared meeting up with the very men they were trying to escape. But he had never been on these trails and had been choosing among them according to which direction they seemed to go.

There had already been several choices, and no trail seemed to be more travelled or more recently travelled than another. He tried to pick whatever went south and downhill. When they got on one that took a surprise turn upward, he stopped and directed them back to where they had been. Lost time and lost, yes, but he hoped not too lost.

He had never been in a place where it was so easy to get confused. Surrounded by tall trees all morning, he hadn't been sure what the sun was telling him about direction or time. But New Mexico was like that. So changeable. Sunny one minute, stormy the next. Turn a corner and find a whole new landscape. See for miles or be so confined by canyon walls only a piece of the sky was visible. Amazing and beautiful, more beautiful than any place he had been before, but that didn't make this trip down the mountain any easier.

What pleased him most so far was that Maria seemed to be taking the ride in stride. So was he. Both horse and mule had behaved exactly as he hoped. So far, he reminded himself. But so far they were going along together like the horse and mule in his painting. Maria was even in blue. His blue, actually. Adam had given her his extra pair of jeans and shirt to wear for the ride down. They were a little large for Maria, and they both laughed when she put them on. But they would make Maria more secure in the saddle and help to fool anyone who saw them. From a distance, Maria could easily be taken for a boy or man. She let him know her legs were tired when she dismounted, but she didn't seem unduly sore and she relaxed when she sat on the log.

Once they finished their burritos, Maria was game to go on. In fact, Maria started tightening her saddle girth before Adam was done with his burrito. But when he reached her side, Maria's hands froze on the girth. She signaled him to silence. Then Adam heard it, too, horse's hooves moving at a fast trot on the trail that would join theirs not thirty feet beyond. In seconds the horse was visible, its rider standing in the stirrups, stiff and awkward, a rifle in the scabbard under his left leg and a dog running alongside.

A German shepherd, Adam noted. Neither dog nor rider seemed aware of their presence. Adam put his hand over the mule's muzzle and hoped Smokey would simply continue to nibble the blades of grass at his feet. Adam had no idea who this man might be, but the gun stopped Adam from hailing him to ask directions. Odd that this man would suddenly appear. They had seen no sign of anyone on these trails all morning, no recent tracks. But this man seemed to know exactly where he was and where he was going.

Adam felt a sinking in his stomach. Should they choose to follow? The new trail went downhill, and the presence of the rider made it clear it was more travelled than any trail they had been on. Maria stared after the rider, then shrugged her shoulders and finished tightening the girth. Adam retied their pack to the back of the saddle. He wanted a moment to think things through, but there was no real choice and one thing in their favor was that the man was moving much faster than they would so it was unlikely they would meet up with him.

After Adam helped Maria remount he stood on their log to slip onto Smokey's back. Smokey was still too busy nibbling grass to argue and full enough to let Adam lift the reins and urge him to walk off. Within minutes they turned onto the same trail as the mysterious rider. None too soon, Adam thought. A surprise cloud darkened their path and Adam could hear distant thunder. Monsoon. Now he was worried about the man ahead of them and the sky above. He fervently hoped that they were headed in the right direction and closer to Taos than he feared.

—II—

"What!" Andrew Dasburg shouted. "What did you let her do?"

Andrew was in such a state of shock his face took on the hue of a very ripe tomato. Spud thought he might have a heart attack.

"I am sure they will be fine." Nicolai Fechin put his hand on Andrew's arm, his accent blurring the meaning of his words but his attempt to comfort was clear.

"I doubt that," Andrew sneered.

"Mabel knows what she's doing," Spud insisted. "And she has Agent Dan along as well as Willa and Edith."

"Agent Dan? I heard he was wounded. Recuperating in bed."

"He was. He got up for dinner last night and seemed strong enough this morning. Amelia said he was just weak from losing so much blood. His wound wasn't as bad as it seemed, and he really doesn't have to do anything physical. Mabel is driving and they're all posing as tourists." Spud felt himself floundering and finished quickly. "No one will try to harm them. Tony thought they'd be safe enough."

"I hope you're right," Andrew conceded after a moment, his face and voice returning to normal. "Mabel does love confrontation and craves danger. This trip should make her happy. If it doesn't finish her off. Finish all of them off. There are real criminals in Red River. Murderers, too." Andrew took a chair at the table near the kitchen.

Amelia came in from the kitchen with a pitcher of water and glasses for the three of them. Spud and Nicolai sat, too.

"Now, let me see your sketch of Willa, please," Andrew turned to Nicolai.

Nicolai laid the sketch on the table. It was clearly unfinished but bold yet delicate in design.

"Yes," Andrew breathed. "Yes."

Nicolai grinned. He said nothing.

"Intense," Andrew continued, "just as intense as the woman herself. Perfect."

"You approve?" Nicolai leaned forward.

"Makes me want to do more portraits. This will be a wonderful painting."

"She plans to sit more for me in New York." Nicolai was smiling again. "Mabel wants me to do a portrait of her, too. Next year. I promised."

"Good. Good. Two strong women. You will have your hands full. Don't you agree, Spud?"

"Absolutely." Spud was delighted to see Nicolai's sketch of Willa, too. Edith had told him about it. Now here it was. And it was an amazing likeness. Strong woman, yes, and Nicolai caught her exactly. Had Spud not heard her rich laughter, he would never guess from this sketch her ability to tease or simply be jolly. This was a commanding figure, a no-nonsense woman whose luminous eyes had seen much of the world, a woman who had read widely, thought deeply, and become a writer at the top of her game. Spud admired both the woman and Nicolai's sketch of her.

Good thing I'm the one looking at this, Spud thought to himself. Witter Bynner would make fun of Willa, joke about how serious she looks in the sketch. She had always been too serious for Bynner, worked too hard, wanted too much to succeed. Bynner had talked little about his days working with Willa at *McClure's* where he was the poetry editor when Willa joined the staff. What he did say, though, made it clear that he thought her too eager, too opinionated, too pushy, too ambitious. Worse, she was a woman.

Willa was ready to do anything S. S. McClure asked of her, and she talked McClure into doing whatever she wanted. That included hiring Edith. Bynner found it all outrageous. But Bynner would. Willa was an experienced journalist, poet, and short story writer who had also been a high school teacher and administrator by the time she reached *McClure's*. Those facts alone would have annoyed Bynner, who was younger, wealthy, and a highly praised poet interested only in poetry and his own grand self. Spud almost snorted out loud. He liked Willa and loved Bynner, always would, but Bynner was a challenge and had his own opinions of all things. What a clash of titans that must have been at *McClure's*, Spud's smile broadened. Good thing Bynner left *McClure's* soon after Willa arrived.

Spud caught himself. He had let his mind wander from the conversation to his own jaded view of Bynner, a view encouraged by Mabel, who remained angry with Bynner for whisking Lawrence off to Mexico. Such feuds, common with Mabel, were hardly worth more than a laugh to Spud. But when he turned his attention back to Andrew and Nicolai, he found them still chatting about drawing. They, too, had wandered from the two strong women and the jeopardy of their trip to Red River.

XIV

FLORENCE AND ANGELICA stood erect and wore enormous smiles, painted bright red. Edith was fascinated by the fact that except for exaggerated make up and tight dresses, they looked like many of the women she knew. Florence's blond hair might be dyed, she decided, but Angelica seemed perfectly natural and authentically Mexican. Her accent, once she began to answer Willa's questions about life in Red River, made it clear that she was a recent arrival.

Angelica came to Red River, as had Florence, as a mail-order bride, Florence from Texas, Angelica from Chihuahua. Both escaped from their husbands as soon as they could. Florence's husband had made her escape easy. When his silver mine played out two years earlier, he sold her to Jake Torrance, owner of the Silver Slipper, a fly-by-night saloon across the river from Madame May's. After several more mines failed that year and the Silver Slipper lost customers, Torrance nailed a board across the door of his saloon and left town. Florence simply moved across the river to Madame May's. Angelica moved with her.

Angelica's arrival in New Mexico and her escape had been considerably more difficult. She never intended to leave Chihuahua. Her family was poor, maybe as hardscrabble poor as Florence's in the arid Texas panhandle, but it never occurred to Angelica that she might become a mail-order bride or leave her mother and seven sisters and brothers. She and one of her sisters were kidnapped one evening walking home from the river where they had been washing the family's laundry. Each carried a heavy load of wet clothes and had been easily subdued, beaten, thrown into the back of a truck, and covered with blankets. They were across the border by morning and sold that afternoon to men who paid no attention to the legality of marriage or nicety of laws.

Angelica's "husband" was a brute named Emil. He spoke no Spanish and didn't care about what she understood. Emil was on his way to New Mexico to work a mine he won in a poker game, she later learned, and had placed an ad in the El Paso newspaper for a mail-order bride. Her kidnapper answered the ad and sold her to Emil.

Three days later Angelica was on a claim in the mountains five miles east of Red River. Their cabin was a dugout with a lean-to where Emil also kept his horse. Their only source of water was a nearby stream. Emil expected Angelica to carry water, cook, work the claim, and be available to him whenever and however he wanted her. He beat her often and eventually knocked out two teeth on the left side of her mouth. It was exhausting and hot on their side of the mountain and Emil found little silver. One day he took her to Red River where he traded her in a poker game to Jake Torrance. She never saw Emil again. Torrance cleaned her up and put her to work at the Silver Slipper.

For Angelica, Madame May's was salvation. For Florence, the work was easy and Madame May took good care of them. She ran a clean place and kept her girls healthy. She was also, Edith realized, proud of her girls. She gave them a small percentage of her profits and some say in what they were expected to do. They were, she explained, experiencing independence for the first time in their lives.

So far Willa was the only one asking questions. Agent Dan listened attentively but did not interrupt or draw attention to himself. Nor did Mabel. Edith guessed that was because Willa was such a skilled interviewer. Her years as a journalist had taught her to observe and listen carefully. And not to judge or, Edith caught herself, not to be overtly judgmental or shocked. The expression on Mabel's face told Edith that Mabel might be shocked by these stories, but Edith wasn't and she was sure Willa wasn't either. They had heard too many sordid tales during their years at *McClure's*, one of the prime muckraking magazines in New York.

Willa had opinions, of course, but she was also one of the most empathetic listeners Edith had ever known. Willa identified so thoroughly with the person she was talking with, that what for others would be a casual conversation could exhaust her. But Willa hadn't asked for help this time, and Edith was happy to stay on the sidelines. After all, they were all four—Mabel, Agent Dan, Willa, and Edith—engaged in learning every detail about these women's lives. Had the three women who turned up in shallow graves also been mail-order brides? Kidnapped, beaten, and then killed? Edith couldn't wait to hear what Agent Dan had to say after they left Madame May's. Much as they had learned from Florence and Angelica, none of this really made sense, especially not the beheading of two corpses.

⊣ı⊢

When they reached the bottom of a long hill, Adam was surprised when Smokey swerved off the trail toward a nearby stream, determined to reach water. After both horse and mule drank their fill, Smokey stepped into the stream and began to fling water onto his belly. The cool water splashing against Adam's legs felt good. He realized how tired he was. They all were. When the mule stepped into the stream and began splashing around, Maria kicked hard and pulled on her rope reins. The mule gave up and Smokey followed her onto the bank where both animals dropped their heads and began to crop grass.

Adam slid off. He helped Maria dismount and tied both animals to low-hanging branches. Distant thunder still threatened and Taos, wherever it was, beckoned, but they all needed a rest. Adam dropped to the ground and leaned his back against a tree trunk. Maria sighed and stretched out next to him on the grass. She closed her eyes. Adam hoped the monsoon would drop its rain elsewhere and then he, too, closed his eyes.

"Shhh." Maria's hand clutched Adam's right arm. Thunder growled overhead. Smokey and the mule stood with their heads raised, ears alert. Then Adam heard it, an occasional clip-clop on rocks. Still behind them on the trail he guessed. One, maybe two horses. He grabbed Smokey's reins and put his hand over Smokey's muzzle. Maria did the same with the mule. Then they waited.

Adam hoped the underbrush and low-hanging branches were enough to hide them from the trail. Had he not known exactly where the trail was, he probably wouldn't have seen who passed. But he did see. A lone rider, slouching low in the saddle, his hat tipped down and his horse moving forward at a slow walk. It was as though horse and rider were in a trance or perhaps the rider had fallen asleep. There was something familiar about him even in profile, but Adam couldn't be sure what he was seeing. When they were still in view, the rider startled and raised his head. He did not see them, Adam was certain of that. But Adam saw him. And the scar that angled down from the right side of his forehead. It was Blade.

Adam gripped Smokey's muzzle so tight, Smokey shook his head. Adam loosened his grip but kept his eyes fixed on Blade and the six-shooter strapped to his leg. Adam almost groaned. All they had gone through and here they were with Blade. No, no, no, he wanted to shout, their journey couldn't end here. Not with Blade. Adam realized that Maria had stopped looking at Blade and was frowning at him. But he hadn't shouted out, had he? He had only wanted to. And Blade hadn't noticed them, had he? Adam was no longer sure of anything except his own fear.

Lightning flashed and the first raindrops hit the leaves above them. Blade's horse leapt into a trot and he was gone. Adam let the air out of his lungs. Maria slumped against him. Smokey reached over to rub his forehead against Adam's shoulder and the mule nipped Smokey on his haunch. They were okay, all of them. Wet but safe. Adam could breathe again.

"Thank you," Adam stroked Smokey's neck. "You took us off the trail. And thank you," he glanced at the sky and gave Maria a hug. "The lightning kept us safe, and you were wonderful. You knew exactly what to do." Maria had no way of understanding what Adam said, but it didn't matter. She was a marvel and what mattered now was finding Taos.

—II—

Tony joined Spud and Andrew, who were still sitting in the dining room. Nicolai had taken his daughter Eya to the plaza to buy ribbons. He wanted her to wear bright colors in her hair for her new portrait.

"Mabel gone?" Tony wanted to know.

"Probably won't be home until dinner. That's a long drive and they talked about checking out several saloons," Spud shook his head. "I don't think they'll be back anytime soon."

"Everything all right at the pueblo?" Andrew asked.

Tony nodded and pulled out a chair. Spud thought Tony looked tired. He had a right to be. From what he told them at breakfast, the posse had ridden hard until their quarry crossed a stream and travelled for more than a mile over gravel and rock. It was slow going after that.

"Found the hunting camp today." Tony accepted a glass of water from Amelia. She offered more to Spud and Andrew, then paused to listen to their conversation.

"The hunting camp? You went there alone?" Spud was incredulous.

"What happened?" Andrew leaned forward. "Anyone there?"

"Posse. Saw no one." Tony spoke between long drinks of water. "But tracks. Same horses. Same shoes. Same prints. And three horses more." He finished his glass and set it on the table for Amelia to refill.

"That's where Agent Dan was just before he got shot." Spud couldn't believe his ears. Tony took his posse there. He must have known how dangerous it would be.

"My God," Andrew exclaimed. "Was it spooky like Edith said? She was really frightened."

"Like she said," Tony nodded. "Ax, blood, tent. Like she said."

"My God," Andrew repeated.

"Most hoof prints were not fresh, except two. Maybe one day old. Two tracks more fresh, maybe last night."

Spud studied Tony's face. Impassive as usual, but his eyes held a kind of determination Spud hadn't seen before.

"My God," Andrew leaned forward again. "Edith and Willa really were in danger." He stared at Tony. "You, too. And Agent Dan shot. These men would frighten anyone."

"Good to be scared sometimes." Tony looked at Spud. "Mabel drive?"

"Yes," Spud assured him. "Agent Dan rode next to her in the front seat."

"Agent Dan armed?" Tony's face remained impassive.

"I don't think so," Spud was quick to reply. "They thought they'd be safe playing tourists."

Tony snorted. "Those men do not play. Nothing funny to them."

"No," Andrew's expression turned bleak.

"I'm sure they'll be fine. Agent Dan will know what to do." Spud made himself sound more certain than he felt. "Nothing bad will happen to them."

Tony snorted again.

—||—

When they left Madame May's, Agent Dan suggested they try one more saloon before starting home. They could hear thunder in the distance, but Mabel thought they had time for one short stop, so they chose The Watering Hole four doors down. Madame May had warned them against that place. "Not for tourists," she cautioned as they left her saloon. So of course that's where they had to go.

Plain black letters on the signboard above the entrance were the only evidence of paint on the building, but business seemed to be thriving. Several cars were parked outside and even more horses lounged at nearby hitching posts.

Inside, the saloon was less well lighted than Madame May's. The bar room was smaller but crowded. A piano player filled the place with ragtime. Smoke drifted above the tables. Several women stood against the back wall. One or two leaned against men at the bar and a few sat on men's laps at the tables. Edith counted twelve women altogether. The dim light made it to hard see details but all of them appeared to be of Mexican origin and all of them wore provocative dresses. None of them smiled or laughed or engaged in conversation. In fact, Edith noted, each of them seemed to be alone, solitary even when partnered. Curious, Edith thought.

A tall, burly man wearing a black tie and vest stopped Agent Dan less than five feet inside the entrance. Agent Dan was even taller than the man, but he stopped.

"No ladies allowed," the man scowled.

Edith was tempted to say "We're not ladies," but she knew that might be dangerous.

"We just want to stop in for a minute to talk to the proprietor," Agent Dan explained.

"No ladies allowed," the man repeated.

"Where is the proprietor?" Agent Dan persisted.

"You can come in alone," the man replied.

"The proprietor?" Agent Dan repeated.

"Not here," the man's scowl deepened. He crossed his arms.

"His name?" Agent Dan ignored the man's scowl.

"Bart. What of it?" The man somehow seemed to grow taller. Edith found herself wanting to walk backward out of the door.

"Oh, no reason. Just wanted to know. Maybe I'll come back later." Agent Dan took a step back.

"Right. I'll tell him," the man appeared to return to his regular size. "What's your name?"

"Oh," Agent Dan smiled, "that's not important."

Nobody talked until they reached the car. Once inside, Mabel turned to Agent Dan, "So, what do you think? Florence and Angelica got here in the worst of all possible ways. The women in there looked like their stories are no better."

"I'd guess worse," Agent Dan nodded. "Florence made bad choices. Angelica had no choice. I'm guessing these women didn't either, and none of them looks like she thinks The Watering Hole is her salvation."

"You think they were forced to be here?" Willa interjected.

"No doubt about it," Agent Dan nodded again.

"But why? And why here?" Edith began to feel dense. Red River didn't seem to be a mecca for bootlegging or prostitution. Sure, Red River had been more populated a year ago, and from what Mabel told them the place had boomed while the mines ran rich. But even then, why would anyone enslave that many women and bring them here? Dallas, Denver, maybe Chicago, but Red River? Here was one more fact that just didn't make sense.

Mabel started the car. Raindrops began to thud on its roof. Edith closed her window. Rain slanted against the sign on the front of The Watering Hole and slid down the saloon's bare front. The dry clapboards seemed to inhale the fresh moisture and slow the rain's progress to the boardwalk. Edith shivered. Such a dreary place.

"Why Red River?" Agent Dan responded. "Because it's nowhere,

nowhere with a whole lot of men." He twisted in his seat to look at Willa and Edith. Mabel turned to listen. The car ran in place, warming. "Red River?" he repeated. "Because no one will see these women arrive and no one will see them leave. And no one will help them while they're here." Agent Dan turned back toward the windshield. Rain ran in rivulets off the roof of The Watering Hole and into the road.

"Gully washer," Willa pronounced. "How depressing."

Mabel laughed. "This is New Mexico. The rain will end and the sun come out before you know it."

—II—

With Blade well ahead of them on the trail and the rain over, Adam realized that he was finally getting the hang of riding bareback. His legs were stiff and sore when he dismounted but he forgot them when they started off again. And when they had to pick their way through scrub and branches to get back on the trail, Smokey actually seemed to make an effort to ensure that Adam didn't fall off.

It had never occurred to Adam that Smokey might like him or that horses would take care of their riders, but this horse was clearly trying to keep Adam safe. When they encountered a low-hanging branch, Smokey stopped on his own so that Adam had time to flatten himself against Smokey's neck before moving on. And when the mule tried to hang back and Adam had to jerk her lead rope, Smokey slowed without stopping, to give Adam a chance to regain his balance. He even sidestepped a little to help Adam straighten himself. The mule, now, seemed also to be trying to be helpful and move forward more willingly. And Maria was easier in the saddle. She actually looked comfortable, though she, too, must be stiff and sore. Stiff or not they were, Adam thought, all four of them, a team. For the first time that day, he began to feel hopeful.

When they reached the end of the trail, they turned onto a

dirt road that was heavily used, though Adam saw no one on it now. Within half an hour they began to pass buildings, small adobe houses and sheds set back from the road. Smokey wanted to trot, but Adam slowed him back to a walk. With Blade ahead of them, Adam didn't want to rush. Besides he felt more comfortable at the walk and he was sure Maria did, too.

At the fourth house, Adam saw a man in a buckboard swinging through the gate. Spanish or Mexican, Adam couldn't tell. The man wore a cowboy hat and a blue shirt. He turned his team toward them and slowed. Adam hoped he spoke English.

"Howdy," Adam ventured.

The man nodded.

"Maybe you can help us." Adam stopped Smokey. The mule stopped, too. Maria dropped her head. Adam felt silly but forced himself to ask, "Am I heading in the right direction for Taos?"

"Arroyo Seco, then Taos," the man said, "maybe twelve, fifteen miles."

A horse walks four miles an hour, Adam remembered. He calculated and checked the sun. There should be enough time to make it to Spud's before dark.

"Where you coming from?"

The question startled Adam. He didn't want to say. "Up the mountain," he finally managed.

"Heard there were some women killed up that way. See anything?" The man's eyes rested on Maria. She did not lift her head.

"No, nothing," Adam lifted Smokey's reins. "Best get going," he offered by way of goodbye and kicked Smokey on both sides. Smokey and the mule moved off in unison.

Women killed? *Dos mujeres asesinadas.* He heard Maria's voice say those words again in his head. Six women. Two killed. It was just as Maria tried to tell him. She had been one of the six. She told him two died. And now others knew. How did they know when he didn't?

The man said some women. Did some mean two? Had there been more? Adam shook his head. He turned to Maria. She lifted her head and smiled at him. Now he felt even more bewildered. Soon, he thought, soon there will be people who can translate. Then he realized he was holding his breath and let it out in an audible puff.

Smokey stretched out his neck, pulling against the reins in Adam's hand. Adam had snugged him up too tight. Nerves. Adam relaxed his grip. Fear is a difficult thing to ignore, but that's exactly what he had been unconsciously trying to do. Terror is more like it, he corrected himself. His terror. Maria may have felt it, but she seemed calm. She always seemed calm. Had she realized the seriousness of their situation? From the beginning, had she? And now? They had just seen Blade. He must have been nearby the whole time. And those men who came to find him. Where had they gone and what were they doing? Adam shook his whole body this time, deliberately and fully, even his fingers. He wanted his fear to leave. He wanted to be calm like Maria.

XV

SPUD HAD NO idea why he felt restless. It seemed to begin when Tony snorted over the attempt to placate him about the danger in Red River. Tony's snort surprised Spud. Tony never showed any reaction to anything. Tony, the stoic, the calm one. But Tony had not been calm. And now Spud wasn't either.

Spud walked partway home with Andrew, then took the long way around to divert his mind from dwelling on what might be happening in Red River. Good things maybe, he tried to tell himself. Maybe they'll come home with everything solved and the murderer under arrest. More likely not, he had to admit. And probably they'll be late. That thought sent him out for a stroll on his way home to get ready for dinner. He needed a change of scene.

Spud picked his way through the cemetery and open field across from *Los Gallos*. He had shorter ways to get to his house but few as peaceful. Kit Carson was buried here next to his wife, Josefa. Not far away was Padre Martinez, the priest who would always be known locally as "*La Honra de Su Pais*," The Honor of his Homeland. Martinez brought the printing press to northern New Mexico and converted even Kit Carson to the church during his forty years as the most powerful Catholic padre in New Mexico. That was before Archbishop Lamy took control and excommunicated him. Northern New Mexicans never forgave Lamy. Many went underground as *Penitentes*, the group Martinez founded.

Kit Carson's reputation fared less well than Martinez's in Taos, at least among the Pueblo Indians. They knew Carson as the United States Army fighter who forced the Navajo to walk their own trail of tears to Bosque Redondo. Hundreds died before the government finally allowed them to return to Canyon de Chelly. Only the Anglos in Taos seemed to revere Carson. The natives didn't.

Funny, Spud thought, looking at the graves of the two men and their family members. Willa was about to get it backwards in her new novel. Wrong, many northern New Mexicans would say. She had asked an amazing number of questions about both men because she said she wanted to be fair and accurate. But her book was about Lamy's struggle to civilize New Mexico. From that point of view Martinez never had a chance. He represented everything Lamy set out to overcome, so even if Willa wants to, she can't say otherwise. Odd, Spud pushed a clod of dirt with the toe of his boot against Carson's headstone, death comes but it doesn't end a man's life. History, they call it. Carson and Martinez were dead and buried within a year of each other over fifty years ago, but they're still very much alive in the minds of northern New Mexicans.

Still, Spud thought, three women died within a year of each other right outside Taos and, except for Willa's and Edith's persistence, their deaths had barely been noticed, much less avenged. Funny how that works. Maybe their deaths were ignored because they were murdered? No, Spud caught himself, that would draw more attention to them. Maybe because they were women? Unknown? Mexican? Well, he thought, however Willa decides to handle Lamy and Martinez, she and Edith are doing everything they can to bring about justice for those women. Spud was pretty sure some people in Taos would think it a waste of time and effort. The sheriff seemed to think that anyway.

The sun in its long descent threw shadows over the cemetery. Spud felt a chill. He rested his hand on Carson's headstone for a minute. The stone was still warm. Well, Spud thought, we will just have to deal with whatever comes in this upside-down world. It was only eight years ago that the madness of "the war to end all wars" ended. The Great War had been absolutely terrifying. People feared the world might end. And in a way it had. Spud patted the gravestone again. Its warmth and the grittiness of its texture pleased him.

The Great War broke the world in two. What had been was gone. But who were they kidding, "the war to end all wars." Wars live on. The feud between Martinez and Lamy still raged even though they were long dead. Taos Indians still peed on Carson's grave when no one was looking. Fear remains. And hate. And violence. And death.

Spud's way of dealing with human turmoil had always been through satire. Others often joined him, contributing their commentary to his *Laughing Horse* magazine. Even Lawrence, who couldn't win his argument with Mabel about the eternal battle of the sexes, turned to fiction to kill her off in "The Woman who Rode Away." End of argument. Through satire, not fisticuffs or murder or war.

But satire, Spud had to admit, would do nothing to help catch the men who killed three women and buried them in shallow graves. At the very least, Spud thought, those women should have gravestones as substantial as Carson's.

—II—

Mabel throttled down to let one of the bigger trucks coming toward them pass on the inside on its way up the mountain. Edith looked at the view below, a long, long way below, where the stream that had been running alongside their gravel road crossed over and dropped into the valley where it stretched out and lazed into ponds and marshlands.

"Beautiful," Willa exclaimed.

"It is, if you're sitting on your side of the car. Looks like a safe distance from there. From here it is simply breathtaking, which means," Edith whispered, "that I'm breathing as little as possible."

"Have to agree," Agent Dan laughed. "One's perspective does affect how you see things."

"Mmmm," Willa nodded. "So tell us more about how you saw things at The Watering Hole. Can you make an arrest?"

"Have to take a closer look," Agent Dan shook his head. "No obvious liquor around and I didn't see any actual evidence of a crime, just had the impression those women were not there willingly."

"How do you think they got there?" Willa followed up.

"That's a good question, and I don't begin to know the answer." Dan's fingers drummed a tattoo on his windowsill. He made no attempt to hide his frustration.

"Do you think we should try to rescue them?" Mabel's hands tightened on the steering wheel. The car jolted forward again. She glanced at Agent Dan.

"How would you suggest we do that?" Agent Dan responded. "We have no army and no real certainty they need rescuing."

"Well, maybe not now," Mabel nodded. "But you can call on other federal agents in New Mexico, can't you? I'm certain they need rescuing, even if you aren't."

Agent Dan did not answer and for the moment ignored the magnificent scenery on both sides of the road. Instead he stared straight ahead, his jaw clenched. Then he placed a hand over the area on his shirt where bandages held him together.

"Pain?" Willa asked.

"Some," he acknowledged after a moment. "It's been a long day."

"And a rough ride," Edith added.

"Bet you're tired," Willa suggested, "and hungry. We'll be home soon enough." Her voice turned cheery, "Amelia's food and a good night's sleep will put you right again."

Mabel geared down as a giant truck approached them on its way up, its motor wailing with the effort. Once it passed, another, smaller vehicle presented itself, its engine laboring, but more quietly. A Cadillac, somewhat larger than Mabel's and just as covered in dust.

"That looks like one of those Harvey cars," Willa noted as it passed them. "Even says Tours on the door.

"But there's no Harvey, no Detours, just Tours," Edith pointed out.

Mabel squinted in the rearview mirror. "Looks older than Harvey's touring cars. Not sure what it is."

"Or what it's doing up here." Edith twisted in her seat to see behind them, but the car had already chugged around a hairpin curve and disappeared.

"Like you said, not many tourists go to Red River," Willa observed. "And that car didn't seem to have any tourists in it."

"You're right," Edith sat up a little straighter. "That car looked empty."

—II—

Adam began to feel more than a little hopeful. They were already through the village of Arroyo Seco, and for some time now they had been passing buildings on their right, not many but enough to suggest they were getting close to Taos. The fields around them looked increasingly familiar, and Adam was certain the open land on their left belonged to the pueblo. This was the road he had taken when he headed for the Lawrence ranch almost a week ago. He was sure of it.

Adam flexed his knees and swung his legs in celebration, something he couldn't have done with his feet in stirrups. Smokey didn't seem to notice, but twenty feet farther on he ambled off the road toward a small stream. Adam let him have his head. The mule followed and both animals took a long drink. Without a word, Maria untied the canteen and passed it over to Adam. He took a swallow then passed it back. They were running low on water. Maria dropped her feet out of the stirrups and swung her legs back and forth, too. She took a swallow, just one.

"Stiff?" Adam asked and demonstrated by sticking his legs out straight on each side of Smokey's flanks and moaning.

Maria laughed and nodded.

Her laugh made Adam laugh. He had been worried that the trip was too much for Maria, but she seemed to be taking it in stride. More worrisome, now that they were getting close to Taos, was his fear that they might run into Blade or that their appearance—horse, mule, young Anglo man, Mexican woman—would draw unwanted attention. So far the only person who noticed them was the man Adam hailed in the buckboard, and he was going in the opposite direction.

Adam gathered up his reins and urged Smokey back to the road. Maria kicked the mule to pull alongside. She could ride next to Adam now that they were done with narrow trails, and the mule seemed interested in keeping up with Smokey. It was almost as though both animals knew they were coming to the end of their long day and were looking forward to food and a good night's rest. Certainly Adam was. "Won't be long now," he smiled at Maria and patted Smokey's neck. "Soon, soon," he repeated. Maria returned his smile.

Taos mountain was dead ahead. Adam had recognized its distinctive curves and watched it grow and change as they drew closer.

Now shadows etched its face. They would still have daylight for a while, but Adam hoped he was right about reaching Spud's soon. Maybe not so soon, he interrupted his thought. A spiral of dust indicated a rider coming their way, coming fast. Adam's first impulse was to head for cover, but there was no cover now that they were out of the mountains. Sage and grama grass but no piñon or juniper trees, no arroyos, nothing taller than Smokey's knees. They would have to meet this rider head-on or hightail it into the sage with no idea how they might hide.

Might be nothing to be alarmed about, but Adam tightened his grip on the reins and clamped his legs against Smokey's ribs. He urged Maria to do the same, pointing to the rising dust and showing her how to shorten the length of her makeshift reins. He also took the precaution of having her tie the extra lead rope below her saddle horn and reminded her to grab the horn and stand in the stirrups should the mule run off. When they first started out he felt a need to lead the mule, but once Maria took charge with her makeshift reins and the mule seemed happy to do whatever she asked, Adam felt no need to control them.

Adam could only hope the mule's compliance would hold under duress. He wanted both animals to be alert and under control when this galloping rider came upon them. Adam took comfort in the fact that the horse and mule were hardly excitable, but if anything could rouse them, it would be a fast-moving stranger. The situation itself could spark a runaway. The pace of the dust spiral told Adam that the rider was still moving fast and coming directly toward them. He would be in full view any minute now. Adam pulled Smokey to the side of the road and headed both animals toward an open field on the right. Then he waited.

The rider who burst into view was exactly the man Adam most feared. Blade saw them and jerked his horse to a sliding stop, shouting, "Come here, you!" But Smokey reared and plunged into the sage-covered field, the mule tight against him, and they took off at a full gallop. Adam grabbed mane and bent low over Smokey's neck. He shouted to Maria but she was already gripping the saddle horn and leaning forward in the stirrups. After that everything was a blur, the sky, the sage, the dirt, which he hit with a resounding thud. He heard rather than felt himself hit the ground. Smokey's hooves thundered in his ears and then Smokey was gone and Maria and the mule with him.

Adam managed to lift his head to see Blade swing off his horse, drop his reins, and pull his pistol out of its holster. Two shots missed Maria, who clung like a burr to the mule. With the second shot, Blade's chestnut took off after Smokey and the mule, leaving Blade in the middle of the road shooting at a rapidly disappearing target in blue. When Adam counted four more shots, he rose to his knees in time to see Blade fling his gun onto the road and throw his arms into the air. Adam rose out of his crouch and took off running in the general direction the horses and mule had gone. They were no longer in sight. When he glanced back, he saw Blade jumping up and down still in the same place, and in a minute Blade's howls reached his ears. Adam laughed and increased his speed. The horses and mule would eventually stop somewhere. He would follow their tracks and hope Maria was still astride. In the meantime, he might not catch up with Maria but he could certainly put distance between himself and that idiot doing a jig in the middle of the road behind him.

—II—

Spud puttered around his courtyard, pulling a few weeds and watering his three tomato plants. He didn't know why he insisted on growing tomatoes. He knew from experience that the growing season was far too short in these mountains to produce a real crop, but he dutifully planted them in the spring and spent the summer months nursing them along. This spring at least he had put them in a sunny location against an adobe wall that would provide shelter from wind and added warmth from the sunbaked adobe bricks. His reward so far had come in blossoms, several of which he thought were really turning into fruit. The thought lifted his spirits.

This was the sort of lift he needed. Worrying about his friends among the criminals he imagined in Red River and dwelling on injustices and the atrocities of war or the unwarranted oppression of the Navajos and other tribes had taken its toll. Fear. Hate. Torture. Murder. Even genocide. All in the name of making the world a better place, a sanctuary of peace and prosperity. How humans could be so cruel, so unfeeling, so unthinking, so merciless. Well, Spud plunged his hands into the loose dirt surrounding his tallest tomato plant. Well, his mind sputtered in futility. But the earth felt real to his fingers, a cool reminder of possibilities and sustenance. Gritty and life-giving, luring him into replanting each spring. Hope. Spud rocked back on his heels and smiled.

Spud loved gardening and so did his cat Barney, a soft-haired calico who presented him with kittens once a year. Spud let her wind about his feet and paw the loose dirt. She never failed to help him in the garden and otherwise perform daily guard duty in the courtyard. No squirrels allowed, no birds to steal seed, no mice to slip into the house. Spud let his fingers trail through her fur. Her purr settled his nerves and hers. She curled into a ball then rolled onto her back and stretched all four legs as far as they would reach. He could stroke her belly without fear, she was telling him. At least for the moment, he grinned and found her soft spot. Her purr swelled in response.

Sunlight dropped low on the adobe wall behind the tomatoes. Spud rose to wash up and change into a clean shirt and trousers. He had only one good dinner jacket, so whatever else he chose had somehow to match. But it didn't matter. He had very few choices.

And tonight, he thought, he would put on a festive shirt and tie and hope for a celebration. Red River couldn't possibly be all that bad and he would be happy if Mabel just brought everyone home safe before dark. He looked forward to a good meal and conversation with all of Mabel's guests, especially Agent Dan. Spud hoped Agent Dan would be able to tell them much, much more about the criminals they were all willing to help him catch. Spud was ready for a roundup.

—ıı—

Mabel hit the brakes so hard Agent Dan flew forward against the dashboard. Willa and Edith managed to brace themselves against the seat backs in front of them or, Edith thought, they might really have been hurt. All this because of some madman hopping around in the road ahead of them. An idiot in a cowboy hat and boots but no horse in the middle of nowhere. He stopped hopping and stared at them. He had a shaggy blond beard and a noticeable scar that ran across his forehead and disappeared behind his right ear.

"Get bucked off?" Mabel tried to be solicitous.

The man bent down to pick something up from the road. Then he stood and put it in the holster strapped loosely around his hips. Edith recoiled. It was a gun.

"Are you injured?" Agent Dan followed Mabel's lead.

"Nah," the man answered, "but my damn horse ran off."

"Perhaps I can ask the sheriff to drive out to help you," Mabel offered.

"Don't want help." He glared at the four of them.

"As you wish," Mabel's voice retained an odd kind of sweetness. She put the car in gear and drove off. No one said a word. Edith turned in her seat and saw the man sit down again in the middle of the road. Dust from their car billowed around him.

"Well," Mabel broke the silence. "What do you think that was about?"

"Probably just what he said," Agent Dan replied. He once again held his hand against his ribs. "But that doesn't explain the gun."

"Maybe he tried to shoot his horse. You know, to make him stop," Mabel suggested with a laugh.

"Didn't work, I'd say," Agent Dan grinned. "Hard to miss a horse, though. Must be a bad shot."

"He certainly was hopping mad," Willa chuckled in agreement.

"Should we have tried to give him a ride?" Edith worried aloud. "It's a bad time of day to be out here alone with no horse."

"He'll be all right," Agent Dan said softly. "It's not too far to walk to town, and he clearly wasn't in a mood to be friendly."

"He didn't seem like the friendly type," Mabel agreed. "More like dumb and dangerous."

"Thank you for not picking him up," Willa said.

"Might be a good idea to send the sheriff out to give him a ride, though," Agent Dan chuckled. "If he's just dumb he won't mind. And if he's dangerous, well, the sheriff should be able to handle that."

"I didn't like the looks of that scar." Willa paused. "Or the gun."

"He's the sort who probably spends a lot of time in Red River, wouldn't you say?" Edith was curious.

"Seems likely," Mabel nodded.

Edith frowned. The truth was they had no way of knowing whether this was the sort of man who frequented Red River. In fact, they still knew very little about Red River and even less about the men and women they saw there. The women, Edith paused to repeat the words to herself, the women. She could see them clearly in her mind. Mexican women, similar in age and costume. It was pretty clear what they were doing in Red River. But how did they get there? Edith couldn't even begin to guess. She closed her eyes and leaned the back of her head against the seat. Too much, she sighed, this is all just too much.

"What's that ahead?" Willa's voice brought Edith back to attention. They could see a young man jogging about a quarter of a mile ahead. When he heard their car, he cut off into the sage and ducked out of sight.

"Good question." Agent Dan rolled down his window.

"What is that man doing?" Mabel slowed the car.

"Another man without a horse or car in the middle of nowhere?" Edith shook her head. "Do you think there's any connection with the scar-faced man?"

"Does this one have a gun?" Willa shaded her eyes as if the young man were still visible.

"I didn't see a gun," Agent Dan shook his head. "Could have one holstered, though. Care to stop for a minute?"

"Are you sure you want to stop?" Mabel asked.

Agent Dan nodded, "Yes. Maybe if we do, he'll come out."

"Depends on why he hid, wouldn't you say?" Willa kept her eyes on the nearby sage.

"Yes." Agent Dan nodded again. "Yes, it does."

XVI

SPUD FIRST CHECKED the dining room. Neither Tony nor the Fechins were there, despite the fact that dinner was long overdue. Amelia could tell him nothing he didn't already know, but she smiled reassuringly and offered to feed him right away if he was hungry. He wasn't. He was still far too worried about everyone in Red River to pay attention to his own stomach.

Not knowing quite what to do, he walked out toward the barn. Perhaps Tony was there since Mabel had taken his car. Passing the pink adobe, Spud paused to reflect on how quickly everything changed once Willa and Edith arrived. It seemed as though nothing would ever be done about any of those murders, but within a week of their arrival, Willa and Edith had turned everything upside-down.

And Agent Dan. He arrived just six days ago. No telling what he might have turned up left to his own devices, but getting wounded near the hunting camp Willa and Edith discovered had spurred everyone into action. Well, not quite everyone, not the sheriff. Nothing seemed to spur him into action. Still, Spud thought, perhaps his own fears were premature. Red River had been fairly quiet lately and most murders probably took more than seven days to solve. A lot more.

Tony was nowhere to be found at the barn, but old José was happy to have someone to talk to. Spud leaned against the corral fence while José carried hay from the barn and placed it in small piles for the two horses to munch on. "Many little piles keep them from fighting over one large one," he nodded to Spud, who smiled in reply. "Just like children, they are, or very bad men," José grinned. "They are the same."

"Greedy guts," Spud laughed.

Spud hadn't talked with José since he asked him to pick out a horse and mule for Adam to take to the Lawrence ranch. José had been happy to oblige and even took time to coach Adam about how to handle Smokey and use a packsaddle. Adam knew a fair amount about riding already. José said he picked Smokey and the mule because they were best friends, so Adam should have no trouble keeping the two of them together. Spud hoped that was the way it had worked out.

Spud had been to the ranch a few times and called it "a rustic's rustic," a place that he told Mabel would probably go on forever but seemed always on the edge of falling apart. She had laughed and said that's why it suited Lawrence. With tuberculosis, he too was on the edge of falling apart. But she hoped the mountain air would help his lungs and the amount of physical exertion the ranch required could help him rebuild his strength. Spud remembered the ranch as needing more work than any one man, especially one weakened by tuberculosis, could handle. Even Adam, strong young man that he was, might have trouble. But Adam needed a place to live and the ranch needed someone to keep it going. Spud was pleased that he thought of matching the two together.

"You hear from your friend? Did he make the trip okay?" José carried a bucket of corn from the barn to scatter for the chickens outside the corral. They followed close on his heels, and while the hens ran from one kernel to the next, clucking and chasing after each other, José slipped into their coop to search for eggs. Spud followed and José began handing him eggs.

"I haven't heard a word, but I think no news is good news, don't you?" The eggs were so plentiful Spud began to slip some into his pockets just to have a place to hold them.

"Good news is better when you hear it," José handed Spud a bucket.

"Well," Spud emptied his pockets, "you haven't seen Smokey or the mule heading home, have you? That must mean Adam made it okay," he teased. "Of course, given the state of the fencing up there, those two might just decide to bring themselves back at any time."

"No, no!" José laughed. "*La mula* stays where there is grass. Smokey, too. The ranch has lots of grass."

Spud's mind went to the lush meadow spilling through the clearing below the ranch house. It was a beautiful field and gave way to views of more mountains in the distance. Higher than Taos, the ranch provided cool shade among ponderosas and, where there were no trees, held amazing vistas. Adam must be loving it. The perfect place for an artist and the animals that took him there.

Spud was about to answer José when his train of thought was interrupted by the sound of hooves behind him. More than one horse, he counted hoof beats, though whoever it was wasn't yet visible and was coming at a much faster clip than anyone should on this lane.

"Runaway?" José spun around and stepped out of the chicken coop.

"Whoa!" Spud followed and found himself pinned against the corral fence holding his bucket of eggs, with *la mula* on one side of him and Smokey on the other. Smokey reared once but neither animal offered to move away once they reached the fence. José appeared on the other side of Smokey, grabbing for the reins of yet another horse, a horse Spud had never seen, who was plunging and rearing against Smokey's hindquarters. José jumped up and down in rhythm with the plunging horse and finally caught the reins.

But Spud hardly noticed. With so much excitement, all he could think of was how to get out of the way and keep his eggs unbroken. He ducked under the mule's neck and climbed the corral fence until he reached the top, where he could step over to the other side. A mistake, he quickly realized. The horses inside were suddenly on him, milling about and pushing against him to greet the newcomers. It was all Spud could do to hang on to the top rail and edge away from the crowd one foot at a time.

—II—

Adam planted his face hard against the sandy soil. His right hand buried itself in dirt against a tall cholla cactus. His left remained under the sage he hoped would keep him hidden. He couldn't see the car, but he heard it stop and he heard a door open. Someone, a man, called "hello" as if it were a question. Then another door opened and a woman called out, "Do you need help?"

Adam wished the voices would go away. Maybe if he didn't move they would. But then, he reasoned, maybe they wouldn't. Maybe they would think he was hurt and really did need help. Maybe then they would walk out to find him.

"Hello?" the man called again.

Adam pulled his hand away from the spines of the cholla and propped himself on his elbow. He still could see nothing, but the voice seemed closer. It was not a voice he recognized. Blade's voice he knew. And he would never forget the sound of the men who called out Blade's name in the middle of the night.

"Do you need help?" The woman tried a second time.

Adam dropped down. The woman's voice also seemed closer. No, no, he didn't need help. He just needed to find Maria, whose blue-shirted figure racing away on the mule still filled his mind. He had run maybe three miles before slowing to a jog. He found it hard breathing at this altitude, but the road had given him better traction. He wasn't sure how far he had jogged, but he guessed that Maria was not far ahead. It couldn't be long before the mule and Smokey—and now Blade's horse with them—would tucker out and stop. He was sure of that. He was also fairly certain that Maria was still astride the mule. He had seen no sign of her, either lying on the ground or walking, and she had not answered when he shouted her name.

"Hello," the man's voice said again. This time it was directly overhead.

"You do need help," the woman declared.

Adam groaned. He rolled away from the cholla and onto his back. Two people stood above him, a tall man wearing a suit and tie and a well-dressed woman with intense blue eyes. She was staring at him with alarm.

"Can you sit up?" the woman asked.

Adam groaned again. The man reached down and grasped his arm.

Once on his feet, Adam realized how he must appear. He knew he had a large bruise on his right shoulder, but they probably couldn't see that. His shirt was still intact. He was aware that his pants were ripped at the knees and, now that he was taking inventory, he guessed he must have a black eye. When he touched his fingers to the right side of his face, it felt raw and swollen all the way to his hairline. Wow, he thought, that nasty slide after he hit the ground had done some real damage after all. Until this moment, he had felt no pain. Now he winced.

"What happened, son?" the man asked, his voice soft.

"My horse dumped me and ran off," Adam confessed.

"Come," the woman said. "Let us give you a ride. Maybe we can find him."

"Which way did he go?" the man asked.

"You're headed in the right direction," Adam leaned on the man's arm. He could see the car waiting for them on the road. "That's the way to Taos, isn't it?"

"It is," the woman assured him. "We'll see about catching your horse and drop you off at Doc Martin's."

"Oh no, I'm fine," Adam insisted. "Just a little winded. I'll find him. I can keep walking."

"No," she said, "you're coming with us. I insist."

—II—

Once Spud inched along the fence to a place of safety he jumped down and grabbed what was left of Smokey's reins. Smokey must have stepped on them and broken one in half, Spud guessed before realizing how odd all this was. Smokey wore only a bridle, while the mule wore Smokey's saddle with a halter and lead rope. The strange horse with them had both saddle and bridle but no rider. And Adam was nowhere to be seen. "What on earth?" Spud finally said out loud. "Where did these animals come from? And where's Adam?"

"Something is wrong." José tied the new horse to a nearby hitching post and loosened its girth. "Very wrong," he repeated and came back to get the mule and Smokey. He unsaddled the mule and took her with Smokey to the corral where he turned them loose. The excitement over, the mule and horse immediately dropped their heads and began to munch on hay. "Very wrong," José repeated again, shaking his head. He made a little pile of hay next to the hitching post where the new horse could reach it, and what had been chaos settled into a comfortable munching sound.

"What do you think we should do?" Spud felt completely flummoxed. He had no idea how to respond to this crisis and now it seemed to be over. But it wasn't. At the very least, they needed to find out what happened to Adam.

"Look," José held up a skirt and blouse. He had undone the bundle tied behind Smokey's saddle.

"What on earth?" Spud stared.

"We backtrack." José draped the clothes over the hitching post where the new horse couldn't reach them and started walking down the lane.

"You think we can find Adam?" Spud hurried to catch up.

"Don't know." José picked up his pace. "May need to saddle a horse. Don't know how far."

Spud shaded his eyes to look down the lane. He saw nothing unusual, but a short distance ahead the lane took a sharp turn around a building, so the two kept moving at a fast walk.

"Look." José saw the body first. It was sprawled in the lane face down not more than ten feet beyond where the lane turned. One arm was flung out at an odd angle, the other was folded under the body.

For a minute Spud thought it was Adam. Adam had been wearing a blue shirt and jeans when he left for the ranch. But as they drew closer, Spud could see dark hair flowing over the blue collar. It wasn't Adam.

"Horse must have spooked." José got the words out despite his lack of breath. They were both running now.

The body lay still, but as they drew closer Spud heard moaning. A woman's moans, though how could that be? No woman he knew would wear a blue shirt and jeans.

When Spud reached the woman, he did not touch her but instead knelt next to her and asked in English whether she could turn herself over. Her moans increased in volume and she opened her eyes but did not move. José asked the same question in Spanish and this time she raised her head. But still she did not move. What they could see of her face was badly bruised, and blood trickled from the edge of her mouth.

"*Me lesioné el hombro,*" she whispered between moans.

"Injured her shoulder," José told Spud. "Help me turn her to free her arm, then we'll see if she can sit."

"Let us help you," he touched her shoulder. She flinched.

"Déjanos ayudarte," José repeated the offer of help in Spanish. She nodded and made an effort to help, tensing her muscles and holding her breath.

Once they turned her over, they could see how her shoulder and arm were twisted and contorted. José wiped blood from the edge of her mouth. She continued to moan but did not cry out when they raised her to a sitting position and she shed no tears. Strong woman. Spud shook his head in admiration.

"Maria," she whispered when José asked her name, and *"me caí de la mula"* When he asked her what happened.

"She was riding the mule!" José's face registered shock. "Nobody has ever ridden that mule."

—||—

Edith slid over as far as she could to make room for the young man. From where she sat it did not look like he had a gun, and unlike the man with the scar, he seemed to have been injured. She could see even from this distance that he had a nasty black eye and once he started to walk toward the car between Willa and Agent Dan, she saw that he also had a pronounced limp.

"What's happening there?" Mabel bent down so she could see the young man through the open car door.

"I can't tell exactly," Edith said, "but this fellow seems as reluctant as the last one to accept a ride to town."

"Well," Mabel shaded her eyes, "at least this one seems unarmed and sane."

"Also injured," Edith nodded. "I think we really should take this one with us."

By the time they reached the car, the young man was leaning on Agent Dan, but Edith could hear him insist that he needed to walk to town on his own.

"I have to find Maria. I have to make sure she is all right," he pleaded.

"We're going to help you look, that's all," Willa patted his arm. "I'm sure she is fine. Now, please, get in the back seat. You can sit between Edith and me."

Edith smiled to let him know they meant him no harm and patted the seat next to her. Once he was in the car, and Willa and Agent Dan were getting settled, Mabel introduced herself and asked the young man where he was going.

"Mrs. Luhan!" he exclaimed. "Why, as soon as I found Maria I was heading for your house."

"Maria?" Four voices asked in unison.

"My house?" Mabel added.

"Yes," the young man's words tumbled out. "I'm Adam Newman. Spud Johnson sent me to San Cristobal to take care of the ranch. Blade was holding Maria prisoner there. We came down the mountain to find help, but I fell off my horse and the mule ran away with Maria."

Once again, everyone spoke at once and their voices rolled over each other's. "Spud?" "Ranch?" "Prisoner?" "Maria?" "Mule?"

Finally Mabel's voice rose above the rest. "What mule? And who is Maria?" She paused to look at him more closely. "I do remember Spud saying something about sending someone to the ranch. A painter, right?"

"Yes, ma'am." Adam brushed at his pant legs. He was covered with dirt and sprinkles of sage. "But ma'am, I really do need to find Maria." This time his words came out like a plea.

"Of course. We'll help you." Mabel put the car in gear and they lurched forward.

"Here," Edith began to help Adam brush some of the dirt off his shirt. "You can relax now. We will be home soon and that man in the front seat is BOI Special Agent Samuel Dan. He'll help you, too."

"BOI? I don't think I know . . . what's BOI?" Adam blurted.

Agent Dan glanced back at Adam. "Bureau of Investigation, son. We're a fairly new federal law enforcement agency. Really new in the west." Agent Dan turned his eyes to the road again. "Now, tell us more about what happened. And this Blade. Is he the blond man with the scarred face we saw a little farther back on the road?"

"Probably," Adam nodded.

"Was he chasing you?" Willa demanded.

"He never got the chance," Adam gritted his teeth and grinned. "His horse ran away with mine and the mule. But he did shoot at Maria. And at his horse," Adam actually laughed at his mental image of Blade throwing his gun on the ground.

"He seemed a bit crazy," Edith suggested.

"Crazy mad." Agent Dan nodded. "But who is this Maria we need to help you find and why was Blade keeping her prisoner?"

—||—

Spud and José clasped their hands around each other's wrists and picked Maria up as if she were sitting in a chair. Light as she was, Spud grunted and braced himself. He wasn't accustomed to physical exertion and they would have to carry her for at least half a mile to the house. He took a deep breath and told himself the house was closer than Doc Martin's and they would call Doc from there. Amelia could help but Doc Martin would know exactly what to do.

The moment they lifted her, Maria went limp, and her head fell against Spud's shoulder. She had fainted, probably from pain, Spud guessed. He gripped José's wrists as tightly as he could. Maria moaned.

Who on earth is this woman, Spud wondered again, and what is she doing in men's clothes riding a mule that no one had ever ridden? And, he pushed his thoughts a little farther, where is Adam?

How did she come by this horse and mule? The last Spud had seen of Adam, he was wearing a blue shirt and jeans and trotting off on Smokey with the mule in tow. The same mule that dumped Maria. Was this woman a rustler? Had she stolen the mule and Smokey and an unknown horse? That seemed unlikely, but he could think of no other explanation. But why would anyone ride a stolen mule that had never been ridden and not Smokey or the saddled horse?

"Your friend who took Smokey and the mule to San Cristobal, where is he?" José's brow was furrowed. He stared at Spud.

"I have no idea."

"Where did she get these animals?"

"No idea," Spud repeated. His lungs began to feel odd, as if they were tired of hauling in air and wanted a rest. The muscles in his shoulders and arms told him they, too, wanted to go on strike. But Spud couldn't stop. They couldn't just put Maria down. Her moans had become louder and her body, pressed against his, felt even more limp. Spud wondered how that was possible and then began to fear that she might slip from their makeshift chair. He felt a bit chagrinned. José didn't seem to be having the same difficulty. Not calling him *old* José anymore, Spud made a silent vow. Up close, José didn't look all that old and he certainly didn't seem old now. "Need to catch my breath," Spud finally whispered.

"*Sí*," José paused and nodded toward the big house. "Not far now. We find a bedroom?"

"The one next to Agent Dan's," Spud nodded. "I think it's not being used. I'll show you."

When they reached the bedroom, the third one down the long *portal* off the living room, Spud placed Maria on the bed while José went to fetch Amelia and call Doc Martin. As soon as Amelia began to clean Maria's wounds, Maria's eyes fluttered open, but she seemed to see nothing before she lost consciousness again.

Spud realized it would be some time before she could tell them what had happened.

—||—

"So what did you do then?"

Adam cleared his throat. Edith thought about intervening. Agent Dan didn't really need to push him so hard. Adam seemed about to pass out as it was. She could feel him wilting against her shoulder. As soon as they reached Mabel's, she would see to it that he was put in bed and his wounds treated.

When Adam didn't answer, Agent Dan turned back to staring out the window. Mabel was driving much faster now, and all of them watched for two loose horses and a mule with a rider in blue.

"This young man needs to rest, not talk just now." Willa spoke with authority and patted Adam's hand.

"I suppose," Agent Dan nodded.

"Won't be long now," Mabel interjected. "We'll put him right to bed and call Doc Martin."

"No," Adam struggled to sit up. "Maria."

"Of course," Willa patted Adam's hand again. "We'll find her."

Adam slumped and this time Edith found herself pressed against her car door until they turned a corner and Adam's limp body shifted toward Willa. Once around the corner, Mabel pressed the accelerator and the car leapt forward. *Los Gallos* loomed ahead. Once they passed the barn and the pink adobe, they would climb the sharp rise toward the house and pull into the courtyard where they could help Adam into one of the available bedrooms. But just as they leapt forward, Mabel hit the brakes and they stopped.

"Smokey and the mule!" Mabel exclaimed. "They're right there," she pointed to the corral.

"Thank heavens." Adam's body jerked upright. "And Blade's

horse, too!" he pointed to the chestnut munching hay by the hitching post. Edith could feel Adam's excitement even when he went limp again. "But I don't see Maria," he sighed.

"Let's find José," Mabel shouted José's name out the window. When no one appeared, she started the car again. "Let's get to the house. Someone there must know what's happening."

They saw Doc Martin's car already in the courtyard and Tony and Nicolai Fechin standing by the door to one of the bedrooms, the one Mabel had suggested they use for Adam.

"A woman named Maria," Was all Tony had a chance to say before the car doors flew open and everyone spilled out, except Adam, whose limp body slipped sideways on the seat.

"Huh, fainted," Agent Dan frowned.

"There's an extra bed, just carry him in there," Mabel directed. "Doc Martin's already there. It'll be our infirmary."

Tony and Nicolai Fechin each took one side and half-lifted, half-carried Adam through the door.

"This is Doc Martin's lucky day," Agent Dan chuckled. "Two at once."

"And what a day this has been," Willa nodded. "For all of us."

Edith took hold of Willa's hand and squeezed it.

XVII

USING THE TELEPHONE in his office, Spud called the sheriff for Agent Dan. The operator, who knew Spud well, understood immediately that his call required emergency attention. She rang the sheriff's home number, and Agent Dan told the sheriff to drive out to arrest Blade and hold him overnight.

Blade, Spud guessed, must be the man who caused the mule to run off with Maria, but Spud's jaw dropped when he heard Agent Dan say that Blade had actually been shooting at her. Poor woman.

But Spud could tell the sheriff wasn't listening to Agent Dan anyway. Even from the doorway Spud could hear the sheriff hemming and hawing—he was at home having dinner, he had no deputy available, the suspect probably had disappeared. Agent Dan finally got him to agree to pick up Blade and told him he would stop by the jail to question Blade after breakfast. As Agent Dan hung up, Spud could hear the sheriff still sputtering.

José had returned to the barn and Amelia to the kitchen when Spud and Agent Dan joined the others, who continued to mill about on the *portal* outside the bedroom now shared by Adam and Maria. Doc Martin was doing what he could to make his patients comfortable so they could sleep through the night. No questions until morning, the doctor ordered. When Agent Dan tried to barge in, Doc Martin stepped outside and closed the door.

"You hang around," Doc Martin told Agent Dan. "You look pale. I'll take another look at you as soon as I'm done here. But no questions tonight." He told everyone else to leave including Spud, who volunteered to return after dinner to sit with the patients through the night, just as he had with Agent Dan.

No one could quite comprehend what had happened, not even those who had been involved. Mabel did her best to describe how they found Adam and how Maria was connected to him, but Tony's brow furrowed halfway through, Spud resorted to squinting, and Nicolai Fechin finally said out loud that he did not understand.

Edith started to help with the explanation until Willa touched her arm, "It's complicated," she turned to the others. "It's late. Let's talk more over dinner. This will take some time."

—||—

"So, what do you think really happened at the Lawrence ranch?" Willa held her hairbrush in her hand and stared at Edith.

"I haven't a clue." In the mirror, Edith's reflection matched Willa's. We're beginning to look alike, Edith realized with a start. Something about the laugh lines around our lips and eyes. I guess that's what happens when you live together as long as we have. Almost twenty years. She let the thought linger. Twenty-three if you count from when we first met. We looked nothing alike then. I was prim and shy, properly dressed in high-necked white shirtwaists. Willa was self-confident and bold even then, professionally dressed in starched shirts and ties. Partly the difference between growing up in Lincoln instead of Red Cloud, between Smith College and the fashionable McClungs, between . . . Edith caught herself. Willa was, after all, nine years older and fairly worldly when they met. Edith was just starting out. She had found a job and an apartment in New York City before Willa moved there, but she hadn't yet landed a job in journalism. Willa took care of that, bringing Edith onto the staff as her assistant at *McClure's.*

"Clues." Willa returned to brushing her hair. "We need more clues."

"We really have very few," Edith agreed, leaning forward to examine the lines around her eyes and mouth. Smile lines, she decided, somewhat exaggerated by the dry climate of New Mexico. Willa's face had similar lines. She studied their reflected faces. And Willa has a few gray hairs. Not me, not yet. Edith rubbed Woodberry face cream into the lines around her eyes and lips, then used Jergens lotion on her neck and arms for *The Skin You Love to Touch* effect. It was, after all, one of J. Walter Thompson's better advertising slogans. She was proud of it.

"Well, maybe we know more than we think," Willa paused her brush again, then used it like a conductor's baton to emphasize each point as she made it. "We discovered the first body. We've seen where the other bodies were dumped. We found the hunting camp. We know there are at least three criminals. We've been to Red River and talked with some of the women. And we've been to Lawrence's ranch. We know what all those things look like and we know that they are somehow connected. So the question is how. And why? And who? How hard can the answers be?"

"Pretty hard so far, but tomorrow we should have a chance to talk with young Adam and Maria. And Agent Dan will question that silly Blade. I'll bet we have things pretty well figured out by this time tomorrow night."

"By bedtime tomorrow we should have it all figured out," Willa nodded.

—||—

The day began with clouds hovering over the mountain and darkening the sky. Spud thought it was early but without the sun he couldn't be certain, and the air felt oddly chilly for this time of year. There were no lights showing in the pink adobe across the field and none in any of the other little houses Tony had built for Mabel. Spud yawned and stretched his arms above his head as far as he could reach. Anything to ease the stiffness in his back and legs. Carrying Maria had tightened his muscles more than he realized, and spending the night in a chair, while Adam snored and Maria moaned, finished the job. Spud's body felt like one long, taut rubber band.

"How are the patients?" José surprised Spud with a cup of coffee.

"Still asleep. I don't know what Doc Martin gave them, but it had to be powerful and they must have been exhausted. That was a long ride they took yesterday, even without all the excitement."

"We need to wake them," José nodded. "Amelia is coming with breakfast."

"What time is it?" Spud sipped his coffee. "I didn't expect to see you here. Everything all right in the barn?"

"Yes, yes. It's very early and I don't usually come to the big house, but I wanted to see about Maria and the young man. She was in such bad pain yesterday."

"She was. So was he." Spud knocked softly on the door and then led the way into the bedroom. Adam was still stretched out on his back in his narrow bed, snoring, but Maria was apparently in the bathroom. They could hear water running.

"That should help her feel better." Spud knew the ranch had no indoor plumbing, no bathroom and no hot water from a faucet. He wondered whether she had ever had such luxury. He guessed not. Mabel had put bathrooms in everywhere, and since she insisted on as much light and air as possible, her own bathroom had windows covering two walls, windows that Lawrence decorated with abstract paintings. To preserve her privacy, he said at the time, but Spud thought Lawrence's paintings were as much to hide the sight of Mabel's body from Lawrence's own rather prudish eyes. The irony, Spud smiled, the man whose art and fiction were internationally banned as pornography was a bit of a prig.

José arranged a chair next to the little desk in the room so Maria would have a place to sit and eat her breakfast. Then he waited while Spud roused Adam to tell him breakfast was on the way. Finally, Amelia and a young helper arrived with two trays heaped with scrambled eggs and bacon and bread and coffee. José had already eaten so Spud contented himself with fixing three plates while Amelia went to help Maria. Spud was sure Maria needed help since she could use only one arm, but Amelia would know what to do. When Maria sat down at the desk, her hair glistened from Amelia's brisk brushing and her injured arm was in a fresh white sling.

"All of you eat a good breakfast now," Amelia patted Adam, propped against the pillows on his bed, and glanced at Spud, who had returned to the chair where he spent the night. "You know Spud and José?" she asked Maria in Spanish. "They carried you in from where you fell?"

Maria looked at each of them for a long minute. "*Gracias,*" she whispered and smiled. José smiled back.

"No matter." Spud bit into a piece of bacon. "Glad you're both okay. Happy to help."

—||—

"Poor Amelia," Willa exclaimed. "Will she ever be able to stop cooking breakfast this morning? Nine-thirty already and people keep showing up. Hungry for information," she gestured toward Andrew Dasburg and John Collier, "and for these wonderful eggs," she grinned at the Fechins. "I don't usually like my eggs scrambled," she added, "but green chile makes them special."

Edith laughed and passed the raspberry jam to Andrew Dasburg, who was sitting next to Tony. Mabel had chosen as usual to have breakfast in bed.

"Amelia's eggs are always special," John Collier took another spoonful from the serving bowl and turned to Agent Dan, "but tell us more about what happened to those women who died and how they may be connected to what is going on in Red River."

"Well," Agent Dan paused to wipe his mouth with his napkin, "no way to be sure at this point, but I think the women might have tried to escape from the men who abducted and enslaved them."

"And Maria?" Willa asked.

"Enslaved them?" Nicolai Fechin put his fork down. "Strong language. I think I do not want to hear more just now."

"Of course," Agent Dan coughed. "Later. We'll talk more after I've had a chance to question that crazy Blade. Adam told Spud he actually bought Maria from Blade. That should say something about connections."

"So, what happens now?" Willa wanted to know.

"Now," Nicolai Fechin smiled at Willa, "maybe you will come with me and I will work a little more on my sketch of you."

"Ida and I will be going back to the pueblo for an hour or two this morning to do some sketching." Andrew Dasburg turned to Edith. "Join us if you like."

"I would like that. There's not much we can do here and with those awful men still on the loose, horseback riding is out of the question, even on pueblo land."

"Good thinking," Agent Dan nodded approval.

"Will you get the sheriff to go with you to look for those men at the hunting camp? We don't want you to get shot again." Willa's voice was edged with worry.

Agent Dan stared for a moment at the coffee in his cup. No tea leaves to read in there, Edith thought, but she imagined his reluctance to answer might have something to do with his memory of the ambush or the difficulties he expected in dealing with the sheriff.

"My posse can help," Tony offered.

"The camp is out of your jurisdiction." Agent Dan shook his head. "And I don't want you to put yourself or your men in danger again."

"No danger," Tony assured him.

"Oh, but there is danger," Agent Dan insisted. "And when we find those men, I want the authority to arrest them. I need the sheriff and other federal agents to do what needs to be done."

Tony lowered his eyes and straightened his braids. "You tell me what to do."

"That's true for all of us," Willa said.

"Yes, of course. Tell us what we can do," Andrew Dasburg pushed his chair back from the table.

"And what we should not do," Edith ended their conversation.

—ıı—

"The swelling is down and nothing is broken." Doc Martin explored Adam's cheek with his fingertips. "Just a few bruises." He turned to Maria, who remained sitting in the chair where she had eaten breakfast. "And you, my dear," he touched her shoulder. She winced. "Your shoulder is back in its proper place. Don't worry about the pain. That will pass. Just keep your arm in the sling for now."

"She doesn't speak English," Adam said to explain her worried eyes and unchanged expression.

"Of course," Doc Martin nodded. "Have Amelia tell her what she needs to know. I have to go. It seems that idiot the sheriff brought in last night shot himself in the foot. Just grazed his heel, the sheriff said, but they didn't know until they took his boot off this morning. Asked me to take a look."

Adam began to laugh. Maria's expression changed to surprise.

"It's okay, Maria," Adam patted her uninjured arm. "Everything is okay. We're safe now." Maria smiled at him for the second time that morning. The earlier smile happened when she took her first bite of scrambled eggs. Now she leaned back in the chair and let her whole body relax.

"Perfect," Doc Martin grinned, opening the door. "Keep her that way."

"Keep her what way?" Spud came through the open door carrying a fresh pitcher of water.

"Relaxed," Adam smiled. "I will, Doc. Thanks."

"Geez, I don't know how either of you could relax after what you've been through." Spud filled water glasses and handed one to Maria.

"With Blade in jail and the two of us getting such good care," Adam nodded goodbye as Doc Martin closed the door, "I'm more than relaxed. I'm thrilled."

"Sure you are. We are, too, at least I am. I had no idea I was sending you into such danger. A bear or a mountain lion, maybe, but not a crazy man with a gun." Spud returned to the chair where he spent the night. "But tell me more. What's her story, for instance?" he indicated Maria.

"Truth is, I don't know," Adam shrugged. "If she said, I didn't understand. We haven't known each other long, but she seems fearless and gentle and loyal and strong. She saved my life and I hers. It's been quite a week."

—ı|—

Agent Dan used the phone in Spud's office to arrange for the Bureau of Investigation to send agents from Albuquerque to raid The Watering Hole in Red River. After that he wanted some of the agents to come with him to check out the hunting camp in the woods. The Bureau was fine with his plans, but the sheriff, who wouldn't even bother to talk to Agent Dan, wasn't. Emilio told Agent Dan that the sheriff questioned the Bureau's authority and had decided not to help them. In fact, Emilio told him, the sheriff was planning to release Blade.

Agent Dan quietly returned the receiver to its cradle. His anger was obvious, but Spud was pleased to see that he chose not to take it out on the phone. Spud had been encouraging Mabel to buy one of the new desk phones, but his was still the old candlestick model where the receiver literally dangled from its holder when not in use. It could take some abuse, but not as much as Agent Dan might have given it under the circumstances.

"You know this sheriff?" Agent Dan sputtered. "Why is he making things so difficult? It almost seems like he's working with Blade and the others."

"Could be, I suppose," Spud responded. "I don't know this sheriff, but I am learning more every day about the people and pace of things in northern New Mexico. I love living here, but I can tell you this sheriff may just be doing what's usual. I mean, nothing gets done early or fast in Taos. And descendants of the original Spanish settlers have little to do with Indians, Anglos, and especially Mexicans. Except for the Indians we're all interlopers, you know? You and I are Anglos and here we are trying to help Mexican women, three of whom are dead."

"They don't regard women highly?"

"On the contrary. They hold their own women in the highest esteem. They place them on pedestals, like Our Lady of Guadalupe. They value other women less and Mexican women not at all."

"That's unfortunate."

"Of course," Spud chuckled, "all women are supposed to behave with decorum. Those who don't are considered contemptible. Mabel is one of those, along with the women artists and writers who visit her. And Mexican women like the ones you saw in Red River, well, you can guess how they fare."

"Yes, but," Agent Dan began.

Spud raised his hand. He was not finished. "No buts, and if you still wonder why the sheriff is resisting you, think for a minute about who you are—an Anglo federal agent, a white law man from the big city who mostly wears suits and ties and tries to tell this local elected official who only wears boots and a big hat what to do. Of course, the local elected official says *No* in whatever way he can."

"Well, that does sound about right."

"Doesn't mean he's being paid off or is part of the gang he's supposed to arrest. He could be, but that's not the only way to understand his behavior."

"Yes, okay, I get it."

Spud felt suddenly exhausted and flushed with embarrassment. He never talked like that with anyone, certainly not with someone he didn't know. He prided himself on observing, not on telling others how to see or think except through satire in his magazine, the *Laughing Horse*. But with Agent Dan he felt somehow comfortable. He trusted him. And Agent Dan needed to know what he was up against. He also needed to know that he shouldn't waste energy on someone like the sheriff. As far as Spud could tell, the sheriff was just being himself.

—II—

When she came back from sketching with Ida and Andrew at the pueblo, Edith found Willa talking with Spud and Agent Dan in the hall outside Spud's office. The three of them looked so serious, Edith chose not to interfere. Instead she nodded her greetings and leaned against the wall to listen.

"Let me see if I understand," Willa paused, so intent on her thoughts she didn't even take note of Edith's arrival.

"I'm in a bit of a hurry, but how can I help you?" Agent Dan's response sounded professionally polite.

"Actually, I don't understand."

Edith noticed that Willa's stare was intense, her eyes a steel blue. She felt a little apprehensive for Agent Dan. Willa could be difficult at times. This looked like one of those times.

"Let me get this right," Willa began again. "You made arrangements to raid Red River and the hunting camp, but you have not really questioned Adam about his experience at the Lawrence ranch?"

"That's right."

"And you haven't even talked with Maria?"

"Yes. Well, you know they were both injured," Agent Dan placed his hand over his own wound. "I didn't want to bother them and, well, Maria may not know anything important. She's just a woman and doesn't speak English. And I'm not really that fluent in Spanish. I want someone to translate, one of the other agents, perhaps."

"Those agents won't be here until tomorrow morning at the earliest, right?"

"Tomorrow, yes. I do plan to talk more with Adam before then, but Spud said even Adam doesn't know much. In fact, he knows very little about what happened to Maria before he got to the ranch."

"So she is the one who should be able to tell you what you most need to know. Right? And what do you mean, Maria is 'just a woman.' She should know more than anyone about all this because she IS a woman."

"Willa's right, you know." Edith could hold her tongue no longer. Her face felt as flushed as Willa's and she could feel blood pounding through her temples.

"Ladies, ladies," Spud interrupted. "Agent Dan didn't mean to be rude. I'm sure he was just trying to be considerate of Maria's situation." Spud's expression turned hopeful.

"Yes," Agent Dan repeated, "considerate."

"That's nonsense," Willa sputtered. "There's still time before lunch. I propose we ask Amelia to come with us to translate so we can talk with Maria and Adam right now."

—||—

Adam walked around the room for the third time in ten minutes. Even the walls seemed closer than they had last night. He almost asked Maria what she thought about the walls. Did it seem to her that they had closed in? But of course she wouldn't understand his question. He contented himself with a fourth stroll between the beds and into and out of the bathroom. Finally, he gave up and sat in the chair Spud used through the night. It felt firm, too firm. How could Spud have managed to spend a whole night there?

Maria sighed and tried a bright smile. Adam smiled back. She was propped up on the pillows on her bed. She looked comfortable and sleepy. Adam was neither. He felt he would burst if he didn't do something soon, something to help catch those monsters. They were still out there somewhere. Blade was behind bars. That much was done. But Adam knew there were at least two more, the two who came for Blade at the ranch. And he was certain they planned to come back to the ranch. And. He paused. And what? Without knowing why they were there in the first place, or, for that matter, why Blade was shooting at Maria yesterday, he really had no idea what was happening. If only Maria could tell him what she knew.

Adam tried smiling at Maria. She smiled back. He looked down at his hands. Artist's hands. Well-shaped fingers, a little blue paint under the nails. Otherwise clean, his nails trim. If only he had a canvas and brush now, he knew how to relieve the agitation that was about to make his head explode. He placed the tips of his fingers against his temples and tried to focus, to clear his mind. It didn't work.

"Hello."

Adam reached the door in less than a second. Spud entered first, followed by Amelia, the federal agent, and the two ladies Adam remembered sitting between in the car. Once they introduced themselves to Maria, the two ladies and Amelia sat on the edge of his bed, while Spud and the agent took the two chairs. Adam perched on Maria's bed and patted her hand. He wanted her to feel safe, though with Amelia and the other ladies in the room he thought Maria would be all right. Amelia had helped the doctor tend to Maria's wounds, assisted her in getting dressed, and fed them. Twice. And Amelia spoke fluent Spanish. Maria would be fine. And she could tell them what she knew. Adam felt his smile widen.

XVIII

"YOU WILL *NOT* leave us behind. So figure out how to include us." Willa stood tall, her voice forceful.

"It could be dangerous, too dangerous for the two of you. We don't know what to expect." Agent Dan shrugged his shoulders and held his hands palm up.

Edith thought Agent Dan was trying to be conciliatory. That would make Willa become even more forceful, Edith almost laughed, though she knew in fact the ranch could extremely dangerous, dangerous for all of them. The men they were looking for were barbaric. According to Maria, they not only cut the heads off two women who tried to escape, they used those bloody heads to frighten the women who were still alive. No wonder Maria and the others were compliant. They were terrified.

"We need to take Adam with us, and we'll need as many men as the car will hold." Agent Dan waved his hands. "There may be a fight."

"Nonsense. We're not afraid. We can handle ourselves," Willa made it clear the "we" included Edith. "And, I dare say, we can deal with whatever happens. After all, *we* are the ones pushing you to do this now, before anyone can escape. And *we* are the ones who found the first body, discovered the hunting camp, and went with you to Red River. We'll be fine."

Her mind racing, Edith put her hand on Willa's arm. "What if they're not at the ranch?"

"Adam thought by now they would be," Willa reminded her. "And that idiot Blade told Agent Dan they were planning to go back to get Maria. They were furious with Blade for selling her. No surprise there. She knows too much to have her on the loose."

"At the very least," Agent Dan agreed, "Maria knows what those men look like. If she felt a little stronger, I'd say we should take her with us to identify them. But that can wait. We'll at least have Adam with us. He knows what their voices sound like."

"Willa's right, you know," Mabel interrupted. "You don't need to leave any of us behind, except for Maria. What you need is a second car. If those men are there, they don't have to know we're women. We can stay in the car and wear men's hats so we'll appear intimidating just by our presence. They'll think you have that many more men with you. Tony can drive us in our car, and if John Dunn is free, he can take you with Spud and Adam."

"Long John Dunn? Brilliant idea." Willa nodded vigorously. "And from what you've said about him, he can easily handle men like those."

"But we don't have time to organize a raid," Agent Dan objected. "We barely have enough time to get to the ranch and back before dark. And as I said, we're talking about something extremely dangerous here. Not something for ladies to be part of."

"Ah, but we're not your usual ladies." Mabel's voice was edged with excitement. "I'll call John Dunn. The rest of you get ready."

—||—

Adam could only stare at this tall, skinny man with the droopy mustache and well-chewed cigar. Long John Dunn, Spud mentioned his name. Long John Dunn, who was in the midst of saying he would be happy to introduce them to his friends at the ranch. His friends at the ranch! Adam almost choked. Then he realized the man meant to be funny, funny with the sort of tongue-in-cheek humor Spud printed in the *Laughing Horse*. Still, John Dunn was making it clear he knew first-hand these terrifying outlaws, these horrible men who cared so little about human life they beheaded two women and shook those heads in front of the other women to frighten them into doing whatever the men wanted.

The women *had* been frightened, too, Adam was well aware of that. All of the women, including Maria. They had been at the ranch for at least a week, according to the scratches Maria showed Adam behind the door in the little cabin. Seven scratches, one of the women made with the little silver cross she wore around her neck. One scratch each day. On the seventh day the woman with the cross escaped with one of the other women. Managed to run only a hundred yards or so through the woods before two of the men caught them, bound their hands behind them, and carried them off on horseback.

The men locked the rest of the women in the barn and left Blade to guard them. The next day the men returned and showed the rest of the women the two severed heads. Then they put all of the women, except Maria, in a car and took them away. Only Maria remained. They told her she must do whatever Blade told her to do, but of course Adam stopped that. Adam patted his empty pocket. Thank goodness he had shown up with ten dollars in his jeans the same day.

"Good idea," Agent Dan interrupted Adam's train of thought. "Good idea," he said again to John Dunn. "You drive us in your car. They'll recognize your car, won't they?"

John Dunn grinned and nodded.

"Tony can drive the women. You take me and the boys with you."

The boys. Adam swallowed hard to keep from objecting. If he objected, what would he say? That he hadn't been afraid? But he had. And now he supposed he would seem like a boy to this federal agent and the weathered, older man about to drive them back up the mountain. But Agent Dan was wrong. After all Adam had been through in the last few days, he was no longer a boy.

Neither was Spud, who was definitely older than Adam in years and experience. Though Adam had to admit, neither he nor Spud exhibited the rough-and-tumble kind of manliness Agent Dan would find helpful under the circumstances. Spud was a poet, Adam a painter. What did they know about guns or justice? They preferred being with gentle men and women.

Adam glanced at Spud, who was admittedly balding but otherwise slim and fit. Good looking, too, especially compared to the cigar-chomping, mustachioed Long John Dunn. Or, for that matter, Agent Dan, whose height and muscular build suggested the kind of male beauty Adam would normally consider attractive, but whose businesslike manner struck Adam as both cold and calculating. Spud on the other hand was always thoughtful and warm. Adam loved it when Spud tilted back his chair, lit his pipe, and quoted from whatever he had been reading. Or writing. Spud's poems and essays were nothing a boy might write, Adam smiled to himself. And Spud's *Laughing Horse* was one of the boldest, most experimental magazines in this country. Had Agent Dan read it, he would never call Spud a boy.

⊣II⊢

Spud took the back seat next to Adam. Once John Dunn put the car in gear, they lurched forward and slipped into a brisk pace. Tony's car backfired behind them in its attempt to keep up. Sounded exactly like a gunshot. Spud and Adam jumped in unison. Calm down, Spud told himself. No need to be afraid now. Later, yes, but not now. He glanced at Adam, who seemed to be telling himself the same thing, settling his back deeper into his seat.

Spud had never held a gun and was shocked when Tony handed

them rifles. "Load them later," Tony said. Load them later? Neither Spud nor Adam knew how to load a gun, let alone shoot one. Agent Dan assured them there was nothing difficult about it and he would show them how when they got closer to the ranch.

Not a good idea to ride in the car with a loaded gun. Spud agreed. And he hoped Agent Dan was right when he guessed they wouldn't actually have to use them. They just needed to look like they could. It was all a charade, really. The three women in the car behind them had no guns and wouldn't even get out of the car, though each of them had a man's hat to don once they got close and had been instructed to look fierce. "No problem there," Willa laughed at her own joke.

When they reached the turn-off toward the ranch, Spud spotted Old Man Manby standing in his stirrups, his horse in a fast trot toward Taos. People said Manby was crazy and joked about the way he sat a horse. Spud thought Manby's style of riding had more to do with the fact that he was British than with his mental faculties. Crazy like a fox was more like it. Spud had heard a lot of rumors about Manby, including some about how he murdered his partners at the Mystic Mine. Killed and beheaded them, that's what people said. But after thirty years, no one had been able to prove that Manby had committed even one crime. Maybe just a matter of a little more time, Spud grinned. Manby might even have had something to do with the murders at the ranch.

The sound of Mabel's voice shouting "Wahoo" floated out from Tony's car as they turned a corner. The cold steel of the rifle barrel against Spud's leg quelled his own excitement. He no longer felt fear, but what they were planning to do was no game. He preferred to sit still, very still, and think about all things other than what they might encounter.

"You okay?" Adam's brow was furrowed.

"I think so." Spud tried a smile that felt more like a grimace. "This is not my idea of a pleasant outing."

"No," Adam chuckled, "but we should be all right. If those men are back at the ranch, we'll have the element of surprise on our side, to say nothing of numbers and guns."

"If only we knew how to use the guns."

"Well, yes," Adam nodded. "I'm just hoping we don't actually have to use them."

"Probably won't," Agent Dan assured them from the front seat. "Just follow my lead. From what Mabel said, Long John Dunn here has had plenty of experience with guns and thugs. The rest of you will just be window dressing. But I'm guessing Mabel's right. Our numbers alone should scare these guys into submission."

—||—

Edith remembered the drive to the Lawrence ranch last year as being much shorter. They were travelling at the highest speed Tony could coax from his Cadillac, fast enough to stay in the midst of the large cloud of dust John Dunn's Ford raised. But until they began to climb the narrow, rutted mountain road to the ranch, Edith felt as though time spread out around them like sand, their wheels slipping and spinning deep without propelling them forward. An illusion, of course. Just an illusion, though the dust was quite real. And once they began the climb, the ruts were real, too. Willa's grasp on her arm felt reassuring, a solid presence securing her in place.

"How long now?" Willa sounded anxious.

"Not frightened, are you?" Mabel turned to address them directly.

"No more than we were when John Dunn treated us to the vision of a scarecrow hanging from a dead tree. His idea of a joke." Edith smiled.

"What scarecrow?" Mabel frowned.

"Oh, just an effigy he said some boys dangled from a dead cottonwood near the gorge to scare the tourists coming in from Taos Junction." Willa waved her hand in the air as if to dismiss the image.

"Some joke," Mabel shrugged. "Those boys have too much time on their hands, I'd say."

"Well, we're not frightened, and this is no joke." Edith's voice was firm.

"No joke and this time real danger." Tony removed one hand from the steering wheel long enough to smooth his braids against his chest. Edith thought the gesture was meant to be calming.

Tony glanced at Edith and Willa in the back seat before turning to Mabel, who sat with her hands folded in her lap with such ladylike composure, Tony paused to regard her. "I have been doing other things and do not know all that has happened."

"We're still trying to put all the pieces together," Mabel assured him. "What we know for sure is that the man Blade is in jail now, telling what he knows. Trouble is, he knows the two thugs but doesn't seem to know much about what they're actually doing."

"He did know their names," Willa interrupted, "or maybe just their nicknames. Nick and . . . ," she paused.

"Nick and Dick," Edith filled in the missing name.

"Yes, that's right!" Mabel almost shouted, throwing her hands in the air. "Sounds like some kind of silly practical joke their parents played with names. But they're no joke. We think they are the two who shot Agent Dan."

"The men I tracked toward Red River?"

"The very ones," Mabel nodded. "When I talked John Dunn into coming with us today, he told me he had seen them a time or two at The Hole in Red River."

"The Watering Hole?" Willa exclaimed.

"We were just there," Edith couldn't contain her excitement. "They might have been there, too, but we had no idea what they looked like."

"Nothing much to look at, according to John Dunn. Mean, too, he said."

"Certainly are mean," Edith found herself thinking out loud. "If they beheaded those women and shot Agent Dan."

"Yes." Mabel turned to look at Edith. "And according to John Dunn they are hardscrabble brothers from the Texas Panhandle just like he is, except he never turned mean. Claimed he shot a man once but left his head on."

"Agent Dan needs to hear what John Dunn knows about them," Willa leaned forward to emphasize the urgency of her message.

"They're probably talking about that right now. But Agent Dan said the plan is to stop when we're about a mile below the ranch. We can be sure he knows all about this then."

"Good," Willa settled back with a chuckle. "And then we can talk about how we'll make our approach look more like a social call than a raid."

"When I told John Dunn this was to look like a social call," Mabel said, "he shook with laughter and his voice climbed a whole octave. 'A social call to Nick and Dick,' he shouted. 'Now that's rich!'"

—ıı—

Adam found it difficult to get comfortable. His shoulder ached and he had forgotten to unclench his jaw during their slow, bumpy progress up the mountain. Maybe he had even been grinding his teeth. It felt like he might have a toothache.

When John Dunn pulled off on the side of the road to let Tony ease alongside so they could finalize their plans, Adam breathed a sigh of relief.

"Should work okay, this social visit thing," John Dunn grinned. He looked past Agent Dan to include Tony and Mabel, who were sitting quietly in their own front seat. "They won't expect us, and we'll be armed."

"Right," Agent Dan agreed. "Tony and the ladies need to hang back out of sight, and we need you guys," he glanced at Adam and Spud in the back seat, "we need you to stay in the car. But everyone needs to come running if you hear gunshots."

Gunshots. Adam flinched.

"Wait a minute," Willa interrupted, leaning forward from the back seat of Tony's car to single out Agent Dan. "They've seen you, remember?"

Agent Dan's eyes widened. Mabel gasped, "Of course they have."

"When they shot you. You didn't see them, but they saw you, maybe even close up."

"True." Mabel was nodding now.

"Take me instead of Agent Dan," Tony offered.

"No," Spud leaned forward. "Take me or Adam. Leave Tony behind. He can drive John Dunn's car if something bad happens. Never know what we may need."

Adam wanted to say he would go instead, but his throat felt tight and his mouth refused to form the words. He had been brave enough in the ranch house at night, but he didn't want to die and he had never fired a gun.

"Let me borrow your hat," Agent Dan eyed Spud's wide-brimmed straw hat. "We'll trade. They won't recognize me in that, and my face will be in shade. They probably won't see the two of you in the back seat anyway."

"True," John Dunn agreed. "I think that might work."

"It has to work," Mabel declared with emphatic certainty.

As soon as Agent Dan hid his face under Spud's straw brim, Long John Dunn drove on until Adam could no longer see or hear Tony's car behind them. Tony had remained where they stopped but kept his engine running. They didn't want the sound of his car to reach the ranch, but they did want him to be ready to drive on once he heard gunfire, either a single signal shot or many shots, which would mean serious trouble.

"Are you all right? You look pale."

Adam could feel Spud's concern and took a few seconds to do a mental inventory of his physical well being in order to report back.

"I'm fine. Just scared."

—II—

Edith pulled the brim of her Stetson snug against her ears. It made her feel somehow safe. Of course nothing was safe now. She strained to hear a gunshot above the quiet sound of Tony's engine, but only silence and the steady trickle of a nearby stream greeted her ears. She could feel Willa breathing next to her. Tony and Mabel seemed to have stopped breathing altogether. The wind picked up. She could hear it moving through the top of the pines around them. Aspen shimmered near the stream. Nothing else moved.

"Hear that?" Willa whispered.

Edith didn't answer. She could see Tony's fingers tighten on the steering wheel in front, but she heard nothing unusual.

"What?" Mabel turned to look at them.

"Thought I heard someone yell."

"Maybe a raven cawing," Mabel suggested.

"Maybe," Edith whispered.

Tony drummed his fingers on the steering wheel. If Edith hadn't noticed, she'd have thought she was hearing a herd of buffalo on the run. She squeezed her eyelids together.

"You two all right?" Mabel's voice startled them. It was coming from outside the car. Edith stared. How had Mabel managed to slip out of her door and appear next to Willa's window without their noticing? And she was practically shouting her question.

"Shhhh." Edith leaned over and looked though the window on the passenger's side.

Mabel stood next to Willa's open window, arms akimbo. Edith had closed her eyes again. Can't stand not being in charge, Spud had told them, that's Mabel for you. Love her or hate her, see her or not, she always has to be in control. But, of course, he conceded, that was one of her strengths. Edith guessed he was right on both counts.

"We're fine," Willa whispered. "You need to get back in the front seat. No way to tell when we'll need to move up."

"I can't stand this not knowing."

"None of us can," Willa agreed.

—ıı—

Spud squeezed his hand around the door handle but didn't push his door open. John Dunn and Agent Dan were just then stepping away from the car as if they hadn't a care in the world. *Nonchalant*, the word came and went. That's what they looked like. *Nonchalant*. Long John Dunn even paused to relight his cigar. Agent Dan paused with him, his straw hat shading his face. Then they moved toward the ranch house with a steady pace. *Inexorable*, the word slipped though Spud's mind. *Nonchalant* and *inexorable*. Spud tightened his grip on the door handle but forced himself not to move.

Spud noticed that Adam's grip on the other door handle was so taut that his knuckles turned white. Spud tried to think what to whisper to ease Adam's tension until he realized that their tension served a purpose. They needed to be ready to spring out of the car at a moment's notice and hold their rifles as if they intended to shoot.

Spud thought they could handle that part all right. Actual shooting would be considerably more difficult. And iffy.

John Dunn reached the ranch house first and banged on the door. He called out Nick's name, and the door cracked open. When John Dunn's "Howdy" floated back toward the car, Spud began to relax. Then Nick's "Howdy" turned into "What the Hell," and both Spud and Adam bolted from the car, but before Spud could clear the running board, Agent Dan had snapped a pair of handcuffs on

Nick. And within seconds he was snapping a second pair of handcuffs on Dick.

It was over. Just like that. John Dunn had grabbed Dick and knocked a rifle out of his hands the second he came tumbling out of the door behind Nick.

It really was over. Spud released breath he hadn't realized he was holding. Adam pounded on the side of the car and shouted in Spud's ear. "They got them! They got them. And not a shot fired!"

—II—

Edith changed her position for the fourth time. Would this vigil never end? No gunshots, but no one to tell them it was over. It felt like they had been sitting on their hands for so long, waiting had become almost boring.

Edith drummed her fingers on the windowsill. She had rolled the window down, then up, and then down again. She was agitated, but she realized with a jolt that Willa was not. In fact, Willa was so quiet and her breathing so measured, Edith decided she must have slipped into silent meditation, something they had both learned from Achsah Brewster, Edith's college roommate, and her husband Earl, whose *Life of Gotama the Buddha* was about to be published. No thinking when meditating, no anxiety, no fear, just stillness. The perfect way to be in moments like these, Edith thought.

Edith wished she could find that still point for herself, but her mind wouldn't stop. Instead she began thinking about how Willa had given the experience of meditation to the archbishop in her new novel, placing him in an ancient Navajo *hogan* for an elemental transcendence, not as a single act but as a merging, fusing, embracing of all that is foreign, unknown, outside of the self he had been and become. No longer the French priest who civilized the American Southwest, he, his history, his culture, his beliefs all became fused in that moment with everything outside himself. And once that happened, the cathedral he built would represent a similar kind of transcendence and acceptance, a merging of beliefs, peoples, customs and even, as Willa described it, a fusing of earth and air.

Gerunds. That was Willa's secret. The *-ing* ending that makes a verb into a permanent event with no beginning and no ending, a present forever becoming was Willa's message of hope to a world torn asunder and fragmented by war. Edith sighed and shifted her position once more. As much as she wished she could meditate too, she knew meditation was an inside job and right now her own insides were in total turmoil.

Edith saw Mabel stumble on her way back to the car. Mabel hadn't gone back to her seat as Willa had suggested but slipped into the woods and moved closer to the ranch house. Now she kicked a rock that pinged against the car's fender. Edith hoped the sound would not carry. She also hoped Mabel's return meant she would tell them they could move on toward the ranch house. More than anything, she hoped that those two evil men were there and that Agent Dan had arrested them and would see to it that they were incarcerated for the rest of their lives. Men without empathy or understanding, Edith began an internal rant. Men of evil who killed those women as if they were not also human, who wreaked havoc not as soldiers trying to hold a broken world together, as Willa's cousin and so many others had done on the battlefields in France, but as unfeeling monsters who cared nothing about the world or the lives of others in it. Nothing.

When Mabel reached the car, Edith stopped her rant without having said a word.

"What on earth is taking so long?" Willa opened her eyes.

Mabel slipped into the car, saying only that she never got close enough to the house to see anything.

"What shall we do? It feels like we must do something." Willa sounded full of renewed energy.

"Wait." Mabel shook her head. "That's really all we can do."

—||—

Adam paused briefly to catch his breath. He had run the full mile as fast as he could to reach Tony's car. He had been sent alone to let the others know Agent Dan had the men in handcuffs.

"Adam, what is it?" Mabel cried out.

At the sound of Mabel's voice, Adam shifted to a slower pace long enough to shout back, "It's okay. You can come now."

"Where are the others? Did they catch those men?"

"It's okay," Adam repeated. "They have them handcuffed. You can come."

"Oh, thank heavens." Mabel clapped her hands.

Thank heavens echoed though the car amid cheers and shouts. Tony pounded the steering wheel and Willa shouted, "Wow! Wow! Wow!"

Mabel grabbed Tony and held on like a fierce momma bear. "What a relief," she sighed. Relief, yes, Adam sighed with Mabel. It was over. The men were captured. They could all drive on to the ranch house. Agent Dan said so.

But once Adam began to catch his breath, Agent Dan said something else altogether. "It's not over yet."

Agent Dan and John Dunn had in fact caught the men and locked them in Maria's tiny cabin, but when Adam and Spud ran toward the ranch house to help they had caught a glimpse of an old touring car pulling out from the trees above the house. Adam kept going toward the ranch, but Spud veered off to take a better look. When he joined the others outside Maria's cabin, he told them the word *Tours* was barely decipherable on the passenger's side door and there seemed to be several passengers inside.

While Adam's chest continued to heave, everyone spoke at once. What? What on earth? Passengers? How could that be? Where were they going? Where had they been? That can't be.

But it was.

Adam slumped against the car. Spud was standing guard. John Dunn and Agent Dan had already driven off in pursuit of the touring car. Tony could drive the women on to the ranch house. But it wasn't over. Not with this touring car on the loose.

Not yet. Not at all.

XIX

SPRAWLED OUTSIDE THE door of the tiny cabin, Spud stretched his legs until his heels pressed deep into the dirt of the path to the nearby ranch house. A respite. The two thugs had been captured, yes, but they were still not delivered to Taos. They were in fact inside the tiny cabin behind him.

He could hear grunts coming through the locked door from the men trussed up inside like calves at the rodeo, hands cuffed behind and ropes looped around their ankles. They could grunt all they liked. They weren't going anywhere. And even if there was more trouble to come, John Dunn and Agent Dan could take care of it. Spud leaned back against the solid door, happy.

Adam was celebrating the capture of the two men by dancing. Wearing dirt-stained trousers and a silly grin, Adam looked very much like Charlie Chaplin doing the Charleston but without music. Spud laughed. Adam ended by throwing himself on the ground next to Spud. They both laughed.

"Be careful of your shoulder." Spud couldn't help himself. He felt responsible for Adam.

"Who cares?" Adam giggled. "I don't. Not a care in the world right now."

It was good to laugh. The anxieties of the drive from Taos had simply fallen away. Spud felt washed clean and sparkling. The tight, claustrophobic darkness that had filled his mind and constricted his muscles during their suspenseful wait had turned to light and ease, his fear released to air. It's amazing what dread can do. He spread his fingers just to feel that he could. They no longer knotted involuntarily in tight, unaccustomed fists. No fists needed. He laughed again.

"Oh, lord, it feels good to be here again. Here without fear!" Adam crowed and sat up.

"Here with hope," Spud whispered. "Yes, I feel it, too. But let's also hope the sheriff arrives soon to take these buffoons off our hands."

Once Agent Dan had secured their prisoners, he and John Dunn told Spud to stand guard while they went after the touring car. Tony and the three women joined Spud and Adam in scouring the grounds and buildings. It was clear that several people had been there since Adam and Maria had gone, had probably even spent the night.

Half-eaten plates of food littered the table in the main house, a woman's bracelet had rolled under the narrow bed in the cabin, and a few articles of clothing—a brightly colored woman's shawl, a torn white blouse, and a stained skirt—had been tossed aside and left in the barn. Eight distinct footprints, at least five of which belonged to women, appeared on the paths, tire tracks left grooves behind the house, and three horses stood munching hay in the corral, their bridles and saddles still stowed in the barn. The general disarray suggested that several scuffles had taken place and that all but the two men had left in great haste.

Mabel immediately took charge of the search for evidence and once they locked the two men in the cabin, she decided that Tony would drive her with Willa and Edith back to Taos. Once he dropped the women off at home, he would notify the sheriff to collect these new prisoners. He would then follow the sheriff to bring Spud and Adam back to Taos.

All of that was fine with Spud. John Dunn and Agent Dan were not likely to return any time soon. The start of their pursuit may have been delayed, but how fast could that touring car go on these narrow dirt roads? And where? There was nothing in San Cristobal, the closest village, and nothing of interest to tourists except in Taos and maybe Red River.

Spud caught himself in mid-thought. Mountain passes would make it difficult, but it was still quite possible to reach Raton from Red River. And cross-continental trains stopped in Raton just as often as they did in Albuquerque. From Taos, it was also possible to cross the Rio Grande and catch the narrow-gauge railroad from Taos Junction or Tres Piedras south to Santa Fe or north as far as Denver. John Dunn collected mail and passengers from those places several times a week. So the passengers in that touring car could go just about anywhere.

Spud wriggled his boots deeper in dirt. The sunlight filtering through the pines had dimmed and his stomach told him they were missing dinner. With the sun going down, Spud still had too many unanswered questions. In fact, Spud poked at a small rock with his toe, he seemed to be the only one who hadn't seen a touring car like that outside of Santa Fe. And the passengers. Agent Dan said they probably weren't tourists, but what else could they be?

—II—

Edith was delighted that Amelia and Maria had dinner waiting when Tony delivered them from the ranch. Everyone else had already eaten, so Amelia wrapped Tony's meal in a tortilla to take with him to the sheriff's office and sat Mabel, Willa, and Edith at the large table in the kitchen.

With only women around the table, Mabel invited Amelia and Maria to join them for dessert. Maria was hesitant at first, but Amelia assured her these women could be trusted.

Edith ran her thumb back and forth over the silver bracelet she had found in a crevice under the bed in the tiny cabin. Too small to fit her wrist but large enough to belong to an adult woman, a woman with Maria's build. Its textured center rose above a black background bordered by smooth silver. The center band felt pleasantly rough under her thumb.

A rustic bracelet, easy to dislodge but pleasing to touch. Edith guessed its owner had no more intention of leaving it behind than had the woman with the silver cross. Edith could only wonder as she set the bracelet on the table next to her plate, what must be happening to its owner now. Things hadn't turned out so well for the woman with the cross.

"More coffee?"

"Oh no, thank you. It's much too late for me even to think of drinking more coffee. I shouldn't have had the first cup." Edith smiled up at Amelia, who stood between Willa and Maria. She offered coffee next to Maria.

"*No, no. De nada. Gracias.*" Maria smiled and shook her head at Amelia.

"Would you ask Maria whether she remembers seeing this bracelet at the cabin?"

"*Pulsera de mi amiga,*" Maria answered Edith before Amelia could ask.

"It belonged to her friend?" Edith gasped. "One of the women with her there?"

"*Sí.*" Maria dropped her eyes. "*Y mi amiga es muerta.*"

"Oh, how sad." Edith handed the bracelet to Maria. "You should have this."

So began a long and sympathetic conversation. Willa and Mabel asked most of the questions, Amelia translated, and Edith jotted down a few notes.

Maria told them everything she knew about what she and the other women had experienced, how they had been kidnapped from their homes and families—Maria was snatched while hanging laundry—how they had been drugged and blindfolded and thrown together into the back of a truck and hidden under heavy tarpaulins for passage into the United States, how they had then been transferred to a long car and driven blindfolded for long hours through flat country until the car climbed into the mountains and finally arrived at the ranch house where Adam eventually appeared.

"No, no, no," Mabel interrupted. "None of this makes sense. Why? Why would anyone do all this? Did they beat you? Did they want sex from you? Why kidnap you and bring you here?"

Maria shrugged. She didn't know. Mostly they left her alone. They beat some of the women. Maria heard their screams. And she saw a man drag a woman into the ranch house by her hair. Maria did not know what happened to that woman. She never saw her again. Several women she saw only briefly.

They kept Maria locked in the little cabin with two other women. One of them wore the cross she used to mark days on the wall behind the door. The other owned the bracelet Edith found. When those two women tried to escape, the men caught them and took them away. The next day, the men returned with their severed heads.

Edith found it impossible to print *severed*. Her pen scratched the page but would not form the word. She dipped the tip of her pen in the ink well, but still nothing appeared on the page. Finally she set her pen down and simply stared at Maria, who continued to recount her story with a steady voice, though Edith thought her eyes looked blank.

"What happened then?" Willa whispered.

"Were you frightened?" Mabel asked.

"*Estaba aterrorizada*," Maria flinched and looked down.

"Of course you were!" Willa patted Maria's arm.

Maria told them the rest of the women had been locked in a fence-like structure attached to the barn. She didn't know how many there were, how long they were there, or exactly what was happening to them. She continued to be locked in the little cabin alone. She thought she heard the car return several times. They may have brought in more women or taken some away. She lost track of time and had no idea how long it had been since she was kidnapped from her home in Mexico.

What surprised Edith the most was that Maria had never seen any of the women before. She got to know only the two they kept in the little cabin with her. Those two had come from different places in Mexico and, like Maria, had been grabbed from behind while they were doing things outside. None of them actually saw their kidnappers, and none of them knew where their captors had taken them. New Mexico? Maria had never heard of New Mexico. Or lived in the mountains. Now here she was.

—||—

Adam could hardly believe his luck. The sheriff carted off the two thugs he and Spud guarded at the ranch. And Tony drove them back to Taos in record time. Better yet, when Adam and Spud joined the ladies in the kitchen for a quick, celebratory dinner of chicken enchiladas, Mabel invited Maria to stay on at *Los Gallos* and help Amelia in the kitchen. Mabel explained that Maria would certainly have to remain available to testify against Blade and the others, and Maria assured Mabel that she had nowhere else to go. She had no family looking for her in Mexico.

In the meantime, Amelia had already taken Maria under her wing and José had come by at least three times while they were gone to see how Maria was doing. It was clear to Adam that Maria was doing just fine and no longer needed him to feel safe. He might miss her at the ranch, but with José taking time from his work to visit three times in one afternoon, Adam thought perhaps Maria's transition to *Los Gallos* would become permanent. Spud had suggested as much, telling Adam he hadn't seen José so happy since his wife died. Adam could see for himself how pleased Maria was whenever José was around. Of course, José spoke Spanish, as did Amelia. That alone could explain Maria's delight in his presence, but Adam thought he detected something more, however subtle and sudden.

Spud and Adam joined the ladies and Tony in Mabel's Rainbow Room. Tony made himself comfortable in his favorite chair to pass the time drumming. Mabel invited everyone to share after-dinner *digestifs* and Lucky Strikes. Adam felt silly refusing such pleasures. He felt his cheeks turn pink.

"You've been through so much this week, Adam, I'm glad to see you're still young and not jaded like the rest of us." Spud laughed and patted Adam on the back.

"Speak for yourself, young man. What are you, not quite thirty?" Willa looked at Spud from his feet to his forehead and down again. "We may be older, but we're not jaded. This is just very good liqueur and we have much to celebrate." She raised her glass of cognac high enough so lamplight shone through. "This is superb, Mabel. How do you manage to get such liqueur during Prohibition?"

"We have our ways," Mabel laughed and raised her own glass in salute. "As you may have observed, nobody pays much attention to the law around here. Unless you kill someone and then it takes a year or two before the sheriff takes note. But we got our quarry and we put them in jail." She saluted the others with her glass. "Agent Dan can take care of the rest."

"We have noticed your sheriff's diligence, yes." Willa took her own celebratory sip, then placed her glass on the table next to her chair before turning to Adam, "So, young man, you are a real hero now. What will you do next?"

Adam's eyes widened, but Spud answered before Adam could say anything.

"With Maria newly situated, I thought Adam might use my spare room until we can be sure the ranch is safe. Then he can return to caretaking and painting. No more heroics necessary."

"Tell us about your painting, Adam. Watercolors? Oils? You could hardly be in a better place to paint." Willa lit a Lucky Strike and settled deeper into her chair. "Waiting for our lawman to return doesn't mean we can't talk about things other than murders and kidnapped women. I, for one, enjoy hearing about what young artists are up to."

"Don't we all." Spud's grin widened. "Adam, the floor is yours. Tell us what you're up to, my friend."

Adam felt the pink on his cheeks turn to flame, but he gripped the arms of his chair and found talking about his painting to be only a little more difficult than riding Smokey down the mountain bareback.

It was past ten when the sputter of John Dunn's car caught their attention. For Adam the news was bittersweet. John Dunn and Agent Dan had not caught up with the touring car and were not even sure which direction it went.

Spud shrugged, but Adam cried, "Will this adventure never end? Enough with suspense." All he wanted was to get back to the ranch and his easel.

—||—

Morning comes too early. Edith smiled at the absurdity of her own thought and watched the early morning sunlight slip around the edges of their window shade. Willa was snoring gently next to her.

Let her sleep. Edith yawned. It had been quite warm when they finally got to bed, but mountain air always turned cool at night, making sleep especially delicious. Edith wished she could just roll over and go back to her dreams. But the rumble of cars arriving at the big house, along with a confusion of men's voices, brought her to her feet. Edith dressed quickly and hurried over to see what was happening.

Strangers milled about the courtyard with Agent Dan. So many people made Agent Dan too busy to interrupt, but Amelia would know what was going on. Maria met Edith at the door. *"¡Mira!"* Maria pointed at the men crowding closer to Agent Dan, who stood tall among them and seemed to be giving directions. Edith was not surprised. Agent Dan had told them the night before to expect his fellow federal agents, who were to go with him to Red River to raid The Watering Hole.

"The women may already be gone," she heard Agent Dan shout above the din. "They seem to be moving them about in old touring cars."

"Old touring cars? Odd," One man's voice carried over the others. "Not with Harvey, then?"

Edith moved away from the courtyard and farther into the kitchen. Maria remained by the door, clearly excited by all the activity.

"Do we know what's happening?"

"Not really," Amelia poured a cup of coffee and handed it to Edith.

"They're getting ready to go to Red River? There must be at least three cars' worth. Maybe more?" Edith blew on the hot liquid.

"Yes. Probably three," Amelia nodded. "They hope to rescue the women at The Watering Hole."

"I wish them luck." Edith took a sip. The coffee was as good as it smelled. "Anyone else up yet?"

"Just Spud and Maria. Spud came in about half an hour ago. He's already in his office." Amelia tipped her head in the direction of Spud's office. "Oh, and José. He came to see if he could help Agent Dan in any way." Amelia's smile turned sly.

"But Agent Dan needs no help from José, am I right?" Edith pursed her lips and cocked an eyebrow.

Amelia laughed and dropped a pat of butter in the frying pan. "How would you like your eggs this morning?"

"Morning, everyone!" Spud let the kitchen door slap behind him. He handed Amelia his empty cup and said, "Over easy, please."

Amelia laughed again and glanced at Edith.

"Straight up, I guess." Edith laughed, too.

XX

SPUD WAITED IN his office for Mabel to come down after breakfast. She loved eating breakfast in bed, and this morning Maria had the honor of taking up her tray. But Maria was already back in the kitchen with Amelia, and Spud could hear from their voices that the dishes were done and the breakfast things put away.

For the moment Spud felt that he and Amelia were in charge of *Los Gallos*. It had already been an hour since the cars filled with federal agents pulled out of the courtyard and he returned to his office. Edith had carried a pot of coffee back to the pink adobe for Willa, and Tony had said good morning before driving himself to his cornfields near the pueblo.

Spud decided he would check on Adam later. For now, he just wanted Adam to sleep as long as he liked. Poor kid was still worn out from his trip down the mountain and the drive back up to apprehend their prisoners. Prisoners, all of them. Two toughs in their thirties and one still in his teens, Spud scoffed. How could they have frightened everyone the way they had. Kidnappers. Murderers. Terrorists, though Spud guessed they wouldn't realize how beheading their victims would place them in that category, one that began with the French Revolution and its Reign of Terror.

In fact, Spud thought, the three of them probably didn't know much about anything. They were just punishing the women who ran away and scaring the others into compliance. Unwitting cogs in a very large machine, ignorant players in an international white slave trade they most likely knew nothing about. That was Spud's guess.

Agent Dan's, too. For a moment Spud almost felt sorry for them, but the memory of Agent Dan's pain, the women they killed, and the hurt and fear they caused Adam and Maria made that impulse pass quickly. Ignorant, yes. And dangerous. Extremely dangerous.

"Daydreaming?"

Spud jumped at the sound of Mabel's voice.

"Whoa, I didn't hear you coming. You're down early." Spud sat up straight and put his hands on the desk as though he needed a solid surface to hang on to. "No, just thinking about how stupid those brutes are. And dangerous."

"Right on both counts." Mabel sat down. "Amelia said you had some phone calls?"

"Two," Spud nodded. "Hal called from Santa Fe. Said he was hearing rumors there that someone was pressuring the governor to stop the raid this morning. He wasn't sure who was doing it. The rumors didn't say. But you know Hal. He hears everything. Everything important, anyway."

"Everything unimportant, too. Hal Bynner doesn't discriminate between the two. News runs straight into his ears and out through his mouth." Mabel laughed. "And the other call?"

"Another friend in Albuquerque. Said he heard the Bureau is getting pressured there and in Washington, DC to call off its troops on this case. Odd, don't you think?"

"Depends on who's doing the pressuring." Mabel leaned forward. "More interesting than odd. Your caller didn't say?"

"Thought it might be coming from our state representative's office."

"Cutlass! Steven P. Cutlass!" Mabel expelled a burst of air. "Odious man. Of course, it could be Cutlass! He's behind every evil in this state. Corruption, fraud, graft. Jovial meanness, that's how John Collier described Cutlass. Opened mining up to huge corporations to strip this land, like the moly mine in Questa, and refuses to do anything to help the pueblos. He's single handedly blocking John and Tony from regaining Blue Lake for the pueblo. Indians, women, Mexicans, they're all dispensable. Only money has meaning for him. Only money flowing into his pockets, I should say."

"Cutlass? You really think so?" Spud pushed back from his desk. "I was thinking Manby. I've heard so many rumors about Manby. He's a madman and some say he beheads his enemies."

"I've heard that, too," Mabel acknowledged. "Some of the people he's dealt with have disappeared. No question he's land-crazy and a cheat. He wants to own all of Taos valley, thousands of acres." Mabel's expression turned grim. "He's after power and money as much as Cutlass is, but I don't think he'd traffic in women and he wouldn't have much sway with the governor. Cutlass would. Cutlass is more powerful than Manby. And less crazy."

"Maybe they're in it together?" Spud speculated.

"Possible. If Agent Dan is right, what has been happening with these women in Red River is extremely lucrative." Mabel rearranged the papers on Spud's blotter without looking at them. "I don't know about Manby," she declared after a moment, "but I'm willing to bet Cutlass is involved." She paused. "And right this minute I'll bet he's in a panic."

—II—

Adam woke slowly. A glance around the small room reminded him that he was at Spud's, in the same room where he spent the night before setting out for the ranch. He was the same person in the same room, but how much was not the same. He held up his hands and inspected them, first one, then the other. He no longer felt pain in his shoulder and he could easily hold a brush and apply paint just as he had, but he wondered now what he would choose to paint and how he would approach his subjects.

Only a week had passed, but Adam felt twenty years older,

heartened by knowing Maria and saddened by the men who had imprisoned her. Such fear and violence those ignorant brutes created. But Adam also felt blessed. He was the one who first interfered with their plans and gained Maria's freedom. Amazing. All his life he had been the lightweight, the laughing-stock, the one not chosen to play baseball, not included for afternoons at the movies, not invited to have a beer with buddies. In fact, except for fellows like Spud, he had no buddies.

Wonderful Spud. Adam rolled over and closed his eyes. Spud must have gone to Mabel's already, he decided. He visualized Mabel's face, her intelligent eyes and knowing smile framed by short dark hair. He had heard a great deal about Mabel before he accepted Spud's invitation. Most of what he had heard—that she was cantankerous, loved to start rumors and create havoc, and, of course, that she was rich—most of it was true. But now that he was here, he saw another side, the side that kept Spud working for her. Warm, generous, thoughtful, kind. And odd, Adam grinned. Odd enough to be interesting, just like Spud and everyone else there. Odd almost seemed to be a requirement at *Los Gallos*.

Adam had heard a great deal about Spud, too. That Spud had grown up in Greeley, just as Adam had. That he left Colorado for Berkeley, where he met Hal Bynner, a wealthy poet, and then moved with Hal to Santa Fe, the same Hal Mabel claimed had single handedly "homosexualized" Santa Fe. And presumably Spud, too. The same Hal who introduced Spud to every literary person in New Mexico, including D.H. Lawrence, and took Spud with him and the Lawrences to Mexico. And finally, when Hal and Spud broke up, Spud left a very angry Hal and moved to Taos to work for Mabel.

And now, because Adam had heard all these things, here he was, too. No longer a lightweight in this crowd but a hero. Adam laughed out loud. The future was bright. Maria would marry José, and Adam would return to the ranch to paint glorious things. Just the idea made him happy. A very happy, very odd hero. Adam closed his eyes again and, almost immediately, fell back asleep.

—ıı—

Edith found Willa already dressed and reading the loose pages of her manuscript in one of the rocking chairs on their *portal.*

"You said you weren't going to start working on the novel again until after I left for New York."

"Just having a look. Calms my mind when it reads well, you know. And it does now."

"Here," Edith held out the tray she had carried from the main house. "I brought you hot coffee and cold toast."

"You must have gotten up at first light." Willa accepted the tray with a smile. "How did you do that? It was such a late night."

"It was." Edith nodded and took the other rocking chair. "And I'm sleepy again. Agent Dan got up before dawn and with the whole lot of federal agents is on his way to Red River. Exhausting just seeing them off."

"Do you think they will find the women there?" Willa sipped her coffee.

"I doubt it."

"I do, too, but they should be able to gather incriminating evidence at The Watering Hole. There and at that hole of a hunting camp. I hope they go there soon."

"We never really had a chance to look around at the hunting camp, and from what Agent Dan said, he had planned to return for a closer look when he was shot."

"Miserable place." Willa paused. "I'd suggest taking the horses out again later this morning, but I don't ever want to go back there."

"Nor do we have to."

Edith studied the face of Taos Mountain, rising high above the cottonwoods that flanked the *acequia.* Mabel had covered a huge area between those cottonwoods and the main house with flagstones and edged them with a series of large pigeon-houses, almost Victorian in their ornateness. Homing pigeons, Edith guessed. Interesting birds, whose cooing added comfort to the medley of other animal noises at *Los Gallos*. So lovely, the big pueblo-like house that reached high above the cottonwoods. And so restful, the sound of the pigeons after the cacophony and chaos of federal agents milling about there at dawn. Whatever they found in Red River, Agent Dan and at least some of his fellows would return to investigate the repulsive hunting camp and to transport their prisoners to Albuquerque for trial at the federal courthouse.

"Nor do we have to," Willa repeated Edith's phrase, rocking back in her chair. "Agent Dan and the Bureau can handle whatever comes next. The murderers are in jail, the ranch is secure, young Adam and Maria have their futures before them, and justice will be served."

"Justice, yes. Not something I was certain about when we first arrived," Edith nodded. "And not as simple as hanging someone in effigy."

"A good deal more satisfying, I'd say," Willa chuckled. "I'm glad we had a hand in it."

"Maybe now the sheriff won't be so complacent about a woman's death."

"A Mexican woman's death," Willa specified. "And then two more Mexican women. All violent deaths."

"Was it because they were women, do you think, or because they happened to be Mexican that caused the sheriff to be so casual?"

"Could be either. Could be both." Willa's expression turned thoughtful. "Maybe now at least men like the sheriff will take a woman's death seriously, and men like Agent Dan will realize the importance of gathering information directly from women. And in circumstances like these, from women like Maria."

"You'd think by now men would understand that. We finally do have the vote, after all." Willa shook her head and patted the manuscript on her lap. "It will be a relief to get back to the intrigues of seventy years ago, you know?"

"Mmmm," Edith smiled, "your archbishop listens to women like Maria."

"Yes. Some worldly women he doesn't. But my archbishop is guided by the Feminine Principle. If he doesn't listen so well at first, he learns to listen, especially to women like Maria and the natives who befriend him, his Sada, the poor Mexican woman he rescues, and his guides Eusabio and Jacinto."

—||—

Sheriff Santistivan came out of his office and glared toward the door to the jail cells. He had heard about enough out of that boy they called Blade.

"What on earth is that idiot whining about now?"

"Says he wants something better than beans and rice," Emilio looked up. "Been shouting like that for the last half hour."

Blade was so dumb, Emilio explained, he had shot himself in the foot and couldn't put his boot back on. He had been banging on the cell door with that empty boot and shouting nonsense ever since the sheriff brought him in.

"Who does he think he is, Billy the Kid?"

The sheriff retreated to his office.

"Put a call in to Albuquerque. Tell the feds I want them to take these crazy criminals off our hands right now."

Emilio covered his ears with his hands. The other two prisoners the sheriff brought in from the ranch near San Cristobal looked a lot tougher, but at least they were quiet.

They were too quiet when Agent Dan had come in to question them, the sheriff said. Agent Dan left knowing little more than when he arrived. The sheriff said that was because these men didn't know anything more than what they were told to do. They didn't even know who their real boss was. But, the sheriff told Emilio, there was a boss. Someone had to be smarter than they were to run an operation as big as Agent Dan said this one was.

When the shouting finally stopped, Emilio reached for the phone.

"No one's here to come after your prisoners," the voice on the other end of the line said. "All our men are up there. We even brought in extra agents by train, just so Special Agent Dan would have enough men for his raid. What's happening with that? We need to know. There's a lot of people around here who don't want this raid to succeed."

Emilio didn't know how to answer. He had no idea what was happening. And he didn't know what the man meant about this raid not succeeding.

"Well," the voice finally said, "you'll just have to wait until Agent Dan comes down off that mountain. He's running this operation, and he has all our available men with him."

Emilio hung up the phone and opened the drawer to his desk. He took out the little silver cross Agent Dan had told him to hold in their evidence room, the evidence room that turned out to be Emilio's desk drawer. Emilio ran his finger over the cross, feeling for the edge that had been rubbed until it was shorter than the rest. He wondered about that, as he had since Agent Dan handed him the cross, but he had no answers. He guessed he wouldn't have any until Agent Dan came back to collect his evidence.

Emilio put the cross back in his drawer and folded his hands on the top of his desk. The sheriff would not like what he had to tell him.

—||—

Adam stopped for a few minutes on his way to the main house

to check on Smokey, whose ears pricked forward at the sound of Adam's voice.

"Smokey is good as ever," José assured Adam. "The mule, too. They will be ready to go to the ranch when you are."

"Glad to hear it. I did give them quite a workout."

"*Sí*. You and Maria, too. Lucky you were not hurt worse."

Smokey came over to the corral fence to nuzzle Adam. Blade's horse joined Smokey, but the mule hung back until she saw the carrots in Adam's hand. Then she nipped Blade's horse in the haunch and pushed her way to the fence.

"They will stay here for now. *Señor* Dan said he would bring the other men's horses down from the ranch later. And all their tack and whatever they find at the hunting camp where *Señor* Dan was shot."

"This is all so complicated." Adam scratched behind Smokey's ears. The horse responded by rubbing his head against Adam's good shoulder. "We have no idea how many men are involved or how far their scheme reaches. Agent Dan seems to think they might be shipping these women as far as Denver. Or Chicago. Or even New York!"

"I heard him tell his men California, too."

"They treat those women like cattle, just ship them to the highest bidder." Adam shook his head.

"Maria is lucky you saved her."

"We're all lucky. The timing was lucky, too. If Spud hadn't sent me to the ranch and Maria and I hadn't come down the mountain just when we did, Agent Dan might not have realized that the ranch was involved. And if Willa and Edith hadn't found that hunting camp, well that, too, seems to be important. Otherwise, Agent Dan would be looking at Red River only, and Spud is guessing they will find nothing there but an empty saloon."

—||—

Spud saw Adam pause to pet Jamie on his way across the courtyard.

As usual the cat was hanging around the pigeon houses, an endless source of fascination. Adam straightened up and started to walk around toward the kitchen. Spud decided to join him.

"Glad to see you slept in."

"Slept like the dead." Adam grinned.

"Glad you aren't among them, though." Spud clapped Adam on the shoulder. Adam didn't flinch. "Much better, are you?"

"Almost no pain left. Sleep heals, I guess."

"Maria is mending, too. She was busy helping Amelia in the kitchen this morning when Agent Dan was getting ready to head out to Red River. Seemed very excited by all the goings-on."

"Agent Dan gathered his posse?"

"Sure did. Federal agents from all over. If anyone is still at The Watering Hole, they'll bring them in."

"You still think they might be gone?"

"I think we saw the last of them taking off in that touring car."

"But that wasn't in Red River."

"No, but that car was in such a hurry, my guess is they were pretty sure we were coming. And if they knew, whoever was in Red River would, too. Agent Dan said the two guys who were still at the ranch when we got there were preparing to make a run for it. They just hadn't had a chance to make their get-away."

"Wow, you mean we were almost too late to catch them? What luck."

"I'm not sure luck had much to do with it. If Willa and Edith hadn't pushed Agent Dan into going when he did, we wouldn't have found anyone there to catch. But they did and we did. And then you and I saw that car slipping away through the trees."

"What luck," Adam insisted.

"Well, yes," Spud nodded with a smile. "I guess that part was luck."

—||—

Mabel Dodge Luhan's Los Gallos

Dinner that evening was the most festive Edith could remember at *Los Gallos.* Mabel and Tony were in their matched finery. The royal blue and lavender that twined through Tony's braids reflected the vivid colors in Mabel's dress and shawl. Their guests were equally colorful in "dress-up" clothes, though as Spud once teased, dressing up in New Mexico usually meant putting a belt on your jeans.

The dining room was filled with guests, children as well as adults. There would have been another dozen, all men, Mabel laughed, had she been able to invite all of the agents who participated in the raid on Red River, but all but three were on their way to Albuquerque, taking the prisoners from the Taos jail with them. A fact that greatly pleased Sheriff Santistivan, Agent Dan added. What pleased the sheriff even more was that Agent Dan and the remaining agents planned to return to the ranch and the hunting camp to retrieve horses and evidence. The sheriff had to do nothing more about the murders of the three women.

When all the guests were seated, Edith realized that Mabel had invited everybody she and Willa had seen during their visit. Andrew

Dasburg and Ida Rauh and their sons sat at one long table with the Fechins. John Collier's family filled another. Willa, Edith, Spud, and Adam were interspersed with Agent Dan and Long John Dunn at the main table between Mabel and Tony. It was, Mabel declared, an evening to celebrate.

Mabel even rose to give a little speech. She wanted to thank each of their heroes—Willa, Edith, Spud, Adam, John Dunn and, of course, Tony—for their courage and determination. It was they, Mabel declared, who proved most helpful to Agent Dan in apprehending the murderers in their midst. And it was Agent Dan who set in motion the forces that would finally bring to justice all those involved in an international conspiracy to kidnap, transport, and enslave the women from Mexico.

Edith thought Mabel's words a little formal for what her heroes had managed to accomplish, but she ducked her head and felt her cheeks redden only a little. Willa murmured *thank you*. Spud made a little wave with his right hand. Adam flushed a deep red. John Dunn grinned until his teeth were actually visible beneath his mustache. And Tony remained his usual stoic self.

Mabel also introduced Maria, who was helping Amelia and several women from the pueblo do the serving. Maria was a special hero, Mabel explained, the most important of all for helping Agent Dan understand what had actually happened at the Lawrence ranch. Maria would now be living at *Los Gallos* and deserved their special thanks. Maria understood nothing Mabel was saying, but she colored deeply and appeared to study her toes when everyone applauded.

Finally, Agent Dan rose to bring everybody up to date on what had transpired during the day. He chose to start with the bad news first: they found no one at The Watering Hole in Red River, and no one could tell them where the women had gone. But not everything in Red River was bad news.

Once Agent Dan had assured Madame May that he had no interest in arresting her, she remembered seeing a touring car pull away from the back of The Watering Hole. She couldn't say how many people were inside, but she had noticed the touring car before. Several times. Always at the back of the saloon, never in front. She never inquired because she didn't want to know about anyone else's business. Didn't want anyone to know hers, either, though she did enjoy talking to that novelist person who visited with Agent Dan. Agent Dan paused to grin at Willa before adding that of course Madame May didn't know then that he was *Agent* Dan.

When they broke into The Watering Hole, Agent Dan said, they found it in total disarray. Tables were overturned, beds upended, and clothes strewn about. The only area not affected was the back of the bar, where glasses and liquor bottles were still neatly lined up on the highly polished shelf that ran the full length of the mirror. It was as silent as if only ghosts had occupied the place, but lingering odors of spent tobacco and spilled liquor made it obvious that these ghosts had just recently departed.

And these ghosts, Agent Dan continued, had been extremely careless. On the floor of what had been a small office, he found letters strewn about and a worn ledger. The letters revealed that The Watering Hole was but a tiny outpost in an elaborate, well-established and widespread white-slavery operation. Women from all over Mexico had been kidnapped, drugged, brought across the border, and transported to places as far away as Washington, DC and Los Angeles. Only a handful ended up in New Mexico. Many more passed through the state on their way north or west. The Lawrence ranch and The Watering Hole were just two of several distribution centers or "holding pens" north of the Mexican border.

The operation itself was huge and, according to the ledger, which recorded transactions in New Mexico, extremely lucrative. So lucrative, Agent Dan said, that some very wealthy and powerful men were involved, some of whom were well-known to the residents of Taos, though he would share no names until the men had been arrested and prosecuted. Agent Dan sat down, and everyone began talking at once. When the talk landed on those slimy bastards who made money off of women's lives and deaths, the adults kept the word *bastards* to a whisper. But all agreed, this was the most sensational thing to happen in northern New Mexico in a very long time. Well, Mabel said, one of the most sensational.

—II—

After the guests left, Mabel invited Spud and Adam, along with Willa and Edith, to join her and Tony in the Rainbow Room for an after-dinner indulgence of cognac and conversation. There with the door closed, Mabel confided that despite Spud's insistence on Manby's guilt, Agent Dan had told her in utmost secrecy that no, Manby's name was not among those in the letters or ledger. Spud half rose to protest, but Mabel put her hand up to silence him.

"Wait until you hear the rest," Mabel's voice rose. "The name of the greatest villain in New Mexico history is there!"

"Who's that?" Spud dropped back in his chair.

"Drumroll, please, Tony." Mabel waved her hand toward Tony, who had been quietly drumming and singing in the background. He responded with a flourish of quick, loud and deep drumbeats. Mabel rose from her chair and raised her glass of cognac in jubilation.

"The current New Mexico Representative to Congress, the foe of all that is good and decent in northern New Mexico, Steven P. Cutlass!"

"Oh, my God," Spud couldn't help himself. "Your nemesis!"

"And Tony's, yes. And everyone's at the pueblo and the artistic community here and in Santa Fe." Mabel sounded out of breath.

"Oh, God," Spud sputtered, "I can't wait to tell Hal."

"Don't you dare," Mabel glared. "Hal Bynner would have it all over Santa Fe in seconds. This needs to be kept secret until after the Bureau arrests Cutlass."

"Yes, of course," Spud conceded. "But how exciting for you and Tony. Cutlass has been the major force blocking the pueblo from getting Blue Lake back. John Collier will be ecstatic."

"John Collier and a lot of women who might now be able to find their way back to their previous lives in Mexico," Edith broke in.

"Absolutely," Spud agreed.

"Let me propose a toast to all of us," Willa lifted her cognac. "We did it. We put an end to Cutlass and his cronies. An end to the fear their reckless greed, misogyny, and murderous carelessness about women and Mexicans generated here and, from what Agent Dan suggested, all over this country."

"You did," Mabel took a sip of her cognac. "You and Edith. If you hadn't pushed this investigation along and found the hunting camp, we might never have succeeded."

"We did," Edith smiled. "But young Adam here, without knowing what he was doing, had an even more important and heroic role."

"A drink to Adam's health," Spud offered.

"Hear, hear," Willa cheered, and Tony struck his drum with several loud beats.

"Last words," Tony raised his voice. "No more fear. Justice, goodness, peace return."

Afterword

Willa Cather and Edith Lewis in Context

WHEN I FIRST visited Taos in the mid-1960s, I knew nothing about New Mexico, had never heard of Mabel Dodge Luhan, and paused only briefly at the Kiowa Ranch because D.H. Lawrence was buried there. For a graduate student in English literature, reverence to D.H. Lawrence was a given. I had read one novel by Willa Cather, *The Lost Lady*, and no professor in any class had mentioned her. Not one. Today I live in New Mexico, Mabel Dodge Luhan is widely recognized as a writer of memoirs and the wealthy art patron who single-handedly brought writers and artists to Taos, and D.H. Lawrence is still a writer of stature. So is Willa Cather whose *Death Comes for the Archbishop* is set in New Mexico.

What I began with *On the Rocks*, my first Willa Cather and Edith Lewis mystery, I continue in *Death Comes*: a fictional account of Willa Cather and her partner Edith Lewis, set among people they actually knew and situated in a time and place they actually lived. Cather and Lewis visited Taos, New Mexico at least four times: in 1913, 1915, 1925, and 1926, the year *Death Comes* takes place. They stayed in Mabel Dodge Luhan's pink adobe casita for the first time in 1925, and Edith Lewis wrote a line-a-day in her Blue Jay notebook describing their two-week stay. Cather asked to return in 1926, though it is not clear they actually did. Mabel Dodge Luhan wrote Cather that Tony was in the hospital in Albuquerque, so they would not be there to receive them. Most likely Cather and Lewis remained at La Fonda Hotel in Santa Fe. It is partly for that reason that I chose to set *Death Comes* in 1926. I would be free of the line-a-day schedule in Edith's 1925 account and could set my own fictional agenda.

Characters directly involved in the mystery, including the federal agent Samuel Dan and Adam and Maria, are fictional. Other major characters are drawn from real people, all of whom were actually in Taos in 1926: Mabel Dodge Luhan, Tony Luhan, Andrew Dasburg, Ida Rauh, Nicholai Fechin, Long John Dunn, Arthur Manby, Doc Martin, Walter Willard "Spud" Johnson, and John Collier. In *Edge of Taos Desert* (1937) and *Winter in Taos* (1935), Luhan gives a detailed account of her life in Taos and refers to many of the people featured in *Death Comes.*

Mabel Dodge Luhan first arrived in Taos in 1917, rented living quarters from Arthur Manby, divorced Maurice Sterne, hired Tony Luhan from the Taos Pueblo to build her new home, and in 1923 married Tony, her fourth and final husband. Long John Dunn, Doc Martin, and Arthur Manby were already well known in Taos when Luhan arrived. Ernst Bluemenshein and five other artists had founded the Society of Taos Artists in 1915, but Luhan wasted no time transforming Taos into a nationally recognized art colony. Writers and artists from all over the world accepted Mabel's invitation to Taos, including Marsden Hartley, Georgia O'Keeffe, Ansel Adams, Leopold Stokowski, Martha Graham, Thornton Wilder, and Willa Cather.

One of Luhan's first guests was the Cubist painter Andrew Dasburg, whom she had known in Greenwich Village and who later returned with his partner, Ida Rauh, recognized in New York as a lawyer, activist, actress, and sculptor. D.H. and Frieda Lawrence arrived in 1922, and the British painter Dorothy Brett joined them in 1924. As Luhan recorded in *Lorenzo in Taos* (1932), her friendship with Lawrence was turbulent. Mabel's offer of the Kiowa Ranch twenty miles from Taos allowed Lawrence enough breathing room to stay in New Mexico and plan to return. In the spring of 1923, Lawrence and Frieda travelled to Mexico with the poets Witter (Hal) Bynner and Spud Johnson. From there Lawrence went to England and then to Italy where he and Frieda stayed with Cather and Lewis' good friends, Earl and Achsah Brewster.

Spud Johnson, Witter Bynner's secretary and partner during their 1923 trip to Mexico with the Lawrences, worked for Luhan occasionally until she hired him as her fulltime secretary in 1927. Johnson brought with him his iconoclastic literary magazine, *The Laughing Horse*, which featured his own poetry and essays, but friends like D.H. Lawrence and Mabel Dodge Luhan frequently contributed to its pages.

Emigrating from Russia in 1923, Nicolai Fechin first settled in New York City, where his reputation as a portrait painter was well established. Diagnosed with tuberculosis, Fechin first visited Luhan in Taos with his wife and daughter in 1926. In 1927, they returned and joined the growing community of Taos artists. In addition to artists and writers, Luhan also invited people like John Collier and his young family, expecting to engage Collier in the campaign she and Tony Luhan were waging to save Taos Pueblo lands and their sacred Blue Lake high up on Taos Mountain. That campaign became Collier's life work. In 1933 he became US Commissioner of Indian Affairs.

Over the years, Luhan's generous and numerous invitations changed the lives of countless artists and writers and helped to shape the future of Taos. For Willa Cather and Edith Lewis, Luhan's 1925 invitation was a warm welcome to visit old friends in comfortable circumstances. Cather and Lewis were at first wary of staying at *Los Gallos*. Luhan was said to be jealous and quarrelsome, a troublemaker mischievously gleeful about breaking up established relationships. Focused on doing research for Cather's novel, Cather and Lewis wanted no drama or disagreeable interruptions. They were relieved to find Luhan a charming hostess who wanted editorial help with her memoir. Far from jealous or cantankerous, Luhan encouraged Tony to be their tour guide and made an effort to see that they fully grasped the details of Archbishop Lamy's life and the culture of Northern New Mexico. She also encouraged them to move to Taos, at least during the summers when Lewis could take time away from her job at J. Walter Thompson. But they chose instead to build a cottage on the Canadian island of Grand Manan, a location at once as remote as Taos and more familiar. Cather and Lewis had already spent several summers there as part a women's summer colony at Whale Cove, the setting of my first Cather-Lewis novel, *On the Rocks*.

Why Grand Manan and not Taos? Or Santa Fe, where they spent still longer periods doing research for *Death Comes for the Archbishop*? All three locations are far removed from New York City, and when Cather was writing, that's exactly what she wanted—quiet and distance from the distractions of the city. Taos was less hectic than Santa Fe and the home of the Society of Artists, most of whose members Lewis knew from New York. But Cather and Lewis chose Grand Manan because people there proved even less intrusive for a writer at work. For Cather and Lewis, the drawback with Santa Fe and Taos was exactly what enticed other writers and artists to live there: they were lively arts communities. But with so many artists and writers living there and so many of them old friends, Cather and Lewis chose instead to spend their summers on a quiet island in the Bay of Fundy.

Old friends in Santa Fe and Taos included Witter Bynner, whom they knew from their early days at *McClure's Magazine*; another old friend from that period, Elizabeth (Elsie) Shepley Sergeant, was building her own adobe home just north of Santa Fe in Tesuque and publishing accounts of its progress in *Harper's Magazine*.

(Cather's friendship with Sergeant had already cooled. In 1953 Sergeant published *Willa Cather: A Memoir* that rivaled Edith Lewis' 1953 *Willa Cather Living: A Personal Record.*)

Just a few miles northeast of Sergeant's adobe, the serenity of the Española Valley and the village of Alcalde drew Cather and Lewis to the San Gabriel Ranch. Run by the wealthy New England renegade from high society, Carol Stanley Pfäffle, the Ranch was but one of several ranches around Alcalde owned and run by wealthy female movers and shakers like the anthropologist Mary Cabot Wheelwright (who, along with Hosteen Klah, established the Wheelwright Museum of the American Indian in 1937). These "New Women" worked closely with women in Santa Fe, including wealthy party-givers Martha and Amelia Elizabeth White and the novelist Mary Austin, to support and sustain Indian arts and culture. The anthropologist and feminist Elsie Clews Parson and Alice Corbin Henderson, co-editor of *Poetry* whose daughter married Mabel Dodge Luhan's son John Evans, also helped apply political pressure to preserve Indian lands and lives.

Alcalde, Santa Fe, Taos, these and the other places Cather and Lewis stayed in New Mexico—including Lamy, Albuquerque, Laguna Pueblo, and Gallup—were important for developing Cather's knowledge of the land and people she portrayed in *Death Comes for the Archbishop.* Mabel Dodge Luhan always hoped she could entice someone to extoll the virtues of New Mexico and Taos Pueblo's way of life. Luhan expected D.H. Lawrence to do that. He never did. Instead, Willa Cather's classic *Death Comes for the Archbishop* so illuminates Northern New Mexico and its culture that even today tourists read it as a much-loved travel guide.

Cather and Lewis chose never to engage directly in political causes, but Cather's fiction reveals her own love of New Mexico and her attention to the political issues of her day. Learning about the details of their stay with Mabel Dodge and Tony Luhan in Taos adds to our understanding of Cather's fiction, places Cather and Lewis in their historical context, and provides a compelling backdrop for *Death Comes*.

—ıı—

A Final Note about the FBI*

On July 26, 1908, Charles J. Bonaparte, the United States Attorney General appointed by President Theodore Roosevelt, created the federal Bureau of Investigation (BOI) after a political showdown with Congress, which had banned the loan of Secret Service agents to the Department of Justice. One of the bureau's first official tasks was visiting and making surveys of houses of prostitution across the country in preparation for enforcing the "White Slave Traffic Act," the Mann Act, passed on June 25, 1910. In 1932, the bureau was renamed the United States Bureau of Investigation. The following year, the BOI was linked to the Bureau of Prohibition and renamed the Division of Investigation (DOI) before finally becoming an independent service within the Department of Justice in 1935, when it was renamed the Federal Bureau of Investigation, or FBI.

Although the FBI's Albuquerque Field Office didn't officially open until 1949, the federal agency's presence in the area went back many years earlier. Since the Bureau's beginnings in 1908, its agents investigated federal crimes in Albuquerque and the rest of New Mexico. Through the 1920s and 1930s, the El Paso, Texas office handled the territory now covered by the Albuquerque Division. Bureau agents in New Mexico pursued car thieves and interstate traffickers in women.

---

* Wikipedia.org and FBI.gov

Acknowledgements

MY VIEWS OF Willa Cather and Edith Lewis come from reading their unpublished letters; the 2015 *Selected Letters of Willa Cather,* edited by Andrew Jewell and Janis Stout; and Edith Lewis' 1953 memoir, *Willa Cather Living.* My greatest debt is to them and to the many archives across this continent that hold Cather's and Lewis' correspondence—from the Huntington Library in California to the Houghton Library at Harvard, from the University of New Brunswick-Fredericton to the Grand Manan Museum in New Brunswick, Canada.

—||—

My knowledge of Taos, the artists and writers associated with *Los Gallos,* Mabel Dodge and Tony Luhan, Spud Johnson, and D.H. Lawrence's Kiowa Ranch come primarily from reading their memoirs and fiction, my research on location and at the New Mexico History Museum, and from interviews with Claudia (Taudy) Smith Miller (Mabel Dodge Luhan's great-granddaughter), Kevin Cannon (current owner of the pink adobe), and Sharon Oard Warner and others familiar with the Mabel Dodge Luhan estate and D.H. Lawrence's Kiowa Ranch.

—||—

Thanks to the American Council of Learned Societies, Rutgers University, and Princeton University for giving me opportunities to pursue my research. I am also grateful for the advice, encouragement, and generosity of the Arbor Farm Press Editorial Board: Lynn Miller, Hilda Raz, Ruth Rudner, and the late Lisa Lenard-Cook; The Willa Cather Foundation and its Executive Director Ashley Olson; The Willa Cather Archive and archivist Joshua Caster; and Cather scholars John J. Murphy, Janis Stout, Andrew Jewell, and Melissa Homestead. Special thanks to those who helped with the production of this book—Ann Weinstock, Sara DeHaan, Mary Bisbee-Beek, and Charlie Capek.

A final thanks to my wife and long-time partner Mary Ellen Capek: without her, this book simply would not be.

About the Author

SUE HALLGARTH is a former English professor. She has written scholarly articles on Willa Cather and Edith Lewis, and this is her second book of fiction featuring the two of them. Her first book in the series is *On the Rocks,* set in 1929 on the island of Grand Manan in New Brunwick, Canada. She lives in Corrales, NM.

Follow Sue on Facebook at suehallgarthauthor, *on Twitter* @suehallgarth, *and on Goodreads.com. And follow Sue's blog, reviews, and other news about her books and writing at* suehallgarth.com.